SPECTRE OF

The eldritch glare from the jewel fell upon the figure of a tall, dark-haired man garbed in pale robes of a curiously antiquated style. Before I could properly focus upon him, the jewel flared with such unbearable brightness that I almost dropped it. To my intense dismay, I felt the chain press against my flesh as the pendant slowly but firmly loosed itself from my grasp. I could not completely stifle a cry of disbelief as the blazing stone floated through the empty air toward the robed figure, which had raised a hand in obvious summons.

I was further appalled to realize that I could discern the far wall's masonry lines *through* the very substance of the figure. My opponent was horribly transparent, as if drawn upon a vertical sheet of river ice. I gazed upon the figure's ghastly face and saw that his eyes lacked whites, but were solidly dark orbs whose regard held me as a serpent's stare overawes its prey.

Suddenly, I thought I heard him speak——the result of some hideous magic causing sounds to form within my mind!

ALSO IN THE SECRETS OF THE WITCHWORLD SERIES:

The Key of the Keplian
by Andre Norton and Lyn McConchie

PUBLISHED BY
WARNER BOOKS

THE MAGESTONE

ANDRE NORTON
& MARY H. SCHAUB

ASPECT®

WARNER BOOKS

A Time Warner Company

WARNER BOOKS EDITION

Copyright © 1996 by Andre Norton and Mary H. Schaub
All rights reserved.

Aspect ® is a registered rademark of Warner Books, Inc.

Cover design by Don Puckey
Cover illustration by Kevin Johnson

Warner Books, Inc.
1271 Avenue of the Americas
New York, NY 10020

W A Time Warner Company

Printed in the United States of America

First Printing: May, 1996

10 9 8 7 6 5 4 3 2 1

To the loving memory of my mother,
Deane R. Schaub,
who encouraged the writing, listened
to each chapter as it emerged, and
sometimes said, "That middle part could
be somewhat clearer."

—Mary H. Schaub

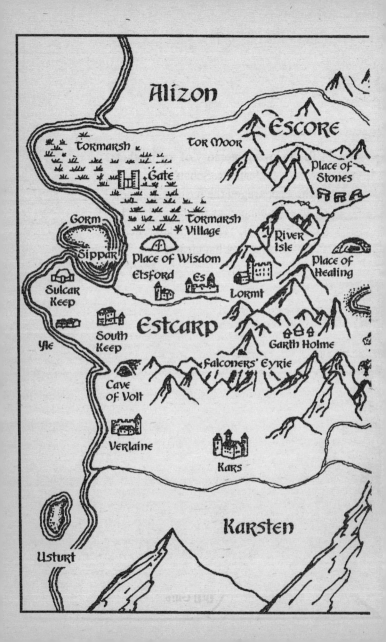

THE MAGESTONE

CHAPTER I _____

Mereth of Ferndale—her private journal
during the voyage to Estcarp
(Dales calendar: Month of the
Fire Thorn, Year of the Horned Hunter)

My valiant Doubt—if you could see me writing this journal, you would smile. No, not merely smile; I am certain that you would laugh to behold this aged Daleswoman wedged below decks at the height of a winter storm, striving to impose some order upon what the Sulcar fondly term their cargo accounts.

I should have been reduced to fingering my tally sticks in the dark had I not recalled the clever bracket you crafted to steady a lamp no matter how violent the motion of a ship. Persuaded of its virtue by my sketches, Captain Halbec ordered his carpenter to construct several brackets for our cabins. Expecting the winter drafts that surge through every passageway, he had prudently stocked ample numbers of horn-shielded lamps.

While my lamp light is thus fairly assured, my perch on this writing bench is erratically precarious. I must wield my quill most deliberately to avoid frantic blots and smears. I vow the effort is more frustrating than writing on horseback; at least while riding, I was always able to curb my horse. Would that this heaving ship were governable by bit and bridle! The Dames who taught me in childhood would be sorely disappointed by the appearance of this page. It is fortunate that the secret trade script you and I devised so long ago requires no fine sweeps or flourishes. If I am jarred much more often, not even I shall be able to make sense of these marks.

Oh, Doubt, I *miss* you. I cannot number the times I have thought and written those words these twenty years past. With every new dawning, I long for the sound of your voice, the touch of your sleeve against mine at the work table, the glint of sunlight on your hair.

The way of life we once shared together has been ripped away. What now prevails is beyond any of my earlier imaginings. So much has changed . . . but not the ache of parting from you. That pain gnaws as if it were only hours ago, not years, that you kissed my hand in farewell. Just as my Clan duty forced me to preserve what I could of our family trading business, so yours drew you to defend your home Dale against Alizon's ravening Hounds. Unlike all of our previous partings, from that final one there was to be no joyful return.

When that unspeakable year broke upon us, we might as well have been stricken by the very scourge of its Year Name: the Fire Troll. Our Dales were seared in spirit as well as flesh when the invading Hounds boiled ashore. I heard accounts of the metal-sheathed man-carriers supplied by their Kolder allies, creeping monsters that spouted liquid fire and battered through gates and walls along our coast. I thank the Amber Lady that your death was clean, by swordblade. Even now, when my dreams are troubled by fragments of remembered battles, I burn with regret that I was not at your side, to live or die together with you.

But I was away, traveling far inland when Vennesport was attacked and our trading storehouses were plundered. Those were times of waking nightmares. As I fled toward the western mountains, a fellow refugee passed me word of your fate. I think if I had been alone, I would have turned back then, to seek my death in the fighting—but I could not ignore my Robnore clan obligations. Uncle Parand was among those killed in the sacking of Vennesport. All of Mother's remaining brothers and most of our coastal trading colleagues were suddenly gone. The surviving remnants of the Clan turned to me for leadership. Grieving and distressed, I felt they were making a hopeless choice, but I could not deny their pleas for direction.

For weeks of torment that stretched into months, I scarcely ate or slept or paused to think. Always, *always* I longed for you. I stumbled onward, forcing myself to envisage what you would have done to meet each new crisis. Memories of you served as my anchor; without them, I would have been overwhelmed by despair.

Constantly, I reminded myself that we had been separated more often than we had been together. You said once that our letters linking us while apart could comprise an ample chronicle—except no scribe could read our secret script. Despite the turmoil of the war and my travels since, I have preserved some few of your letters, together with the little sketch of you that Halbec made during your long-ago trading voyage aboard his ship. These documents are my most treasured possessions— your lasting legacy to me.

Another very different legacy has driven me to endure this unseasonable voyage. I suspect that you would shake your head ruefully at the surface appearance of my recent behavior. You would ask how, after more than sixty years as a trader, I could turn my back on all that I knew to pursue the flimsiest of hopes? I can hear you say it—chasing moonbeams or catching snowflakes would be more profitable than this journey promises to be. Yet if only I could lay my reasoning before you—of all the people I have ever known, you would be the most likely to understand why I must dare this quest. I believe you would urge me to seize this chance, however slight or foolish it seems.

Dear Doubt . . . you were always an eminently cautious, deliberate man. Uncle Parand once said you were the most prudent risk-taker he knew, for you constantly weighed every possible gain against any potential loss before you committed yourself. No matter what later obstacles arose, you would press on until you accomplished your task.

I had observed a similar strain of persistence in my mother. It was her force of will that converted Father's improved breed of sheep into the foundation of our trading success. I have been told that I am as obstinate as she was, so the three of us shared the trait, for I recall times when each of us accused the others of excessive willfulness.

Habits honed in one's work, especially when rewarded, often spill over into other aspects of life. I think of the hours you and I spent together compiling kinship lists. How excited you were to discover that one of your forebears claimed blood-ties to our Robnore Clan. You rode leagues to search for verifying documents, and brought half the dust from an abbey's archives back with you. We pored over lists for so many families. I shall never forget those parchments stored in the wax-lined sea chest from Wark. You said there could be no doubt of that clan's devotion to their trade, since every bundle of records for generations reeked of fish!

Here am I, all these years later, still asking questions about kinship. But these particular questions do not concern missing names from the kin lists of other folk; these questions concern my own kin, and the farther I pursue them, the more my disquiet grows. I cannot rest until I find answers. For years, I did not know where to search. I had only guesses, suspicions, fragments that made scant sense by themselves. It was as if I sought to plan a trading journey without knowing where I was to ride, or what goods I should take.

Then, nearly two months ago, in the Month of the Shredbark Tree, Dame Gwersa's letter reached me at Vennesport. I am certain she did not intend it so, but her news was the firebrand that ignited my accumulated store of worries. From your visits to Rishdale Abbey, you would recall the Dame's special devotion to the preservation of old records. Since the war, she has endeavored to restore the archives at her own abbey as well as several others tragically damaged in the fighting. Dame Gwersa is now very old and blind, but she dictates occasional letters to me, her student from almost seventy years ago.

A visitor to Rishdale Abbey this past summer had brought her word of an amazing discovery across the sea in Estcarp. Two years before, in the Year of the Kobold, an unprecedented quaking of the earth was wrought by Estcarp's Witches to halt an invasion across their southern border from Karsten. One of the subsidiary results was the destruction of parts of the walls and towers at Lormt, the ancient citadel famed for its archives. Previously unknown storage rooms and cellars were exposed beneath the rubble, adding an untold wealth of documents to those already prized by kinship scholars.

The moment I read Dame Gwersa's account, I knew that I must journey to Lormt. Until then, I had felt like a jeweler attempting to assemble a chaplet of Ithdale pearls, but lacking most of the significant gems needed to complete my pattern. My missing pearls were of two sorts: kin-facts, and knowledge about a very different kind of jewel. What better place could I seek both than Lormt?

Two primary questions had been—and still are—hammering in my mind: who was my true father, and whence came my mother's chief legacy to me, that curious jewel she termed my betrothal gift?

From childhood, I had always assumed that I knew who I was. On the day I first met you, I identified myself on my writing slate—Mereth of far Ferndale, speechless since my birth in the Year of the Blue-horned Ram. You said that was an appropriate Year Name for one engaged in the wool trade, and a script as clear as mine should be as useful to a trader as a voice, yet far less likely to be misunderstood. I was seventeen then, and grateful for your kindness. Not many busy traders would pause to read my slate, or have the time or patience to answer my questions.

From that initial meeting, you were distinctively different from all the other traders, and not just because of your singular courtesy. I was bemused when you confided that you had two names: Lundor, given you by your parents, and Doubt, bestowed on you by the trading community. I recall thinking what a strange name Doubt was, so I wrote on my slate, "Why 'Doubt'?"

You smiled, and replied that it was due to your deplorable habit of foreseeing all the possible objections to proposals—all the reasons why suggested plans might not work.

That night, I wrote queries to Mother about you. She laughed aloud, and said you also peppered your speech with frequent doubts. Assuming a severe expression, she imitated your deep voice, "Oh, I doubt we shall acquire any usable wool from that Dale this season—excessive rains spoiled their grazing land. Besides, I doubt they've yet repaired the only bridge allowing access by our wagons. This venture you propose will go ill, I've no doubt." For all your gloom, she added, you were a very keen trader, and the Clan was fortunate to secure your service.

By the time two years later when Mother's own trading wagon was swept away in the mountain landslide, my acquaintance with you had expanded from chance encounters to joint ventures. When I discovered that you shared my interest in kinship tracing, it was a pleasure to pass on to you some of the requests for kin lists from the merchants and landholders we met in the course of our regular trading work. Soon we were helping each other trace our own family histories. Your folk had clustered for generations in the coastal Dales near Seakeep, while Mother's Robnore Clan had traveled from town to market to trading fair.

Mother first met Father at Twyford, whence both were drawn by the great annual wool fair. From her few remarks years later, I judged that she had been immediately impressed by his knowledge of the finest wool bearers. He confided to her his desire to locate the fabled blue-horned sheep of the western crags, for he was convinced that he could use them to improve the quality of the Dales' wool. Knowing Mother, I expect she gave deep thought to his likelihood for success before she consented to wed him and accompany him on his search inland well past Uppdale and Paltendale.

Mother said to me once, with a fond but exasperated sigh, "Your father was a good man, but too enwrapped by his dreams of breeding the perfect sheep. To be fair to him, I must say I never met his equal for tracking and caring for sheep. Still, he needed to attend more to the trading side of the matter. Not my Dwyn—always off over the next ridge to snare yet one more wildling to add to his flock. Would that he had possessed more of the trading blood of his forebear Rodwyn of Ekkor! Yet each man must weigh what wool he can shear, and tally his own accounts."

Father (as I then believed him to be) was a third son and distant lord-kin to the House of Ekkor. I remember him only dimly, since I was scarcely four when he set out during a storm to search for a lamb and never returned.

After his death, Mother placed me with the Dames of Rishdale Abbey to see if they might cure my muteness. They could not, but Dame Gwersa taught me diligently for six years. Mother came for me when I was twelve. Although the Dames offered to accept me for training as a religious scribe, Mother said that my writing skill would be of more use to her in trade. When the Dames objected that my muteness would be a disadvantage beyond the shelter of their cloisters, Mother asserted that on the contrary, it would be a positive trading advantage, since I could neither tattle secrets nor offend customers with unwise chatter.

I soon found that in Mother's trading business, I had a talent for handling accounts, determining values, and locating goods. A far rarer talent—uncommon among Dalesfolk—was my ability to find lost articles, especially if I could touch some other object belonging to the owner.

In those days, too, I experienced occasional vivid dreams. All I could recall upon waking were flashes of bright colors and snatches of strange music. When I was about fifteen, I wrote haltingly about my dreams one day when I was alone with Mother. She was always occupied; her hands were never idle longer than it took for her to snatch up a new hank of wool or the next bundle of tally sticks. That day, when she read my slate, she actually dropped her knitting in her lap and sat rigidly still. I vow her face paled beneath its ruddy sun-warmed hue.

In a manner quite unlike her usually brisk speech, she said slowly, "I once had peculiar dreams for a time . . . before you were born. After your birth, they stopped. I had not thought of them for years." She shook her head, and resumed her knitting. "Such things are mere night vapors, banished by the light of day. Put them from your mind."

It wasn't long after that incident that Mother first mentioned my betrothal gift. I had found for her a missing bracelet, one of a pair she prized, for she loved fine jewelry. In her pleasure at the recovery, she told me that there was one very special piece—a gift—put away for my betrothal.

Excited, I wrote on my slate, "Whose gift? See it now?" but she only paused at the door on her way out. "No," she said firmly, "you may not see it until you are promised to be wed. It is an old and valuable gift from a . . . secret source that I cannot name." I was disappointed at the time, but in the subsequent press of work, I gradually forgot about the gift until the accident in the mountains reft Mother from me.

You were assisting Uncle Herwik then at our base in

Ulmsport, while I was in Vennesport, a week's travel to the south. Mother had argued for a second trading base there, and had only just shifted her chief residence to the port—if she could be persuaded to halt in any one place long enough to be said to reside there. I was almost twenty when she died. You and Uncle Herwik's party had been delayed by storms, so I employed the time of waiting by sorting through Mother's possessions, setting aside those items she would have wanted to be given to various relatives and friends.

In the course of my sorting, I chanced upon a parcel tightly wrapped in dark blue leather. The instant I touched it, I *knew* that my betrothal gift lay within. It had never been listed among the family treasures, and no other person in the family had ever mentioned it. I assumed that Mother must have acquired it in her trading, instead of inheriting it.

Curious to view Mother's secret gift, I pried loose the lacings and uncovered a pendant jewel set in silver. The stone was an unusual blue-gray color, the size of a hen's small egg, cunningly polished to sparkle and flash as the light fell upon it. When I reached to pluck it out of its soft leather nest, my fingers were jolted as if I had plunged them into snow melt. Had I possessed a voice, I am sure I would have cried out. As it was, I snatched back my hand without picking up the stone. After a breathless moment, I folded the leather around the necklace and retied the lacings.

On previous occasions, I had welcomed opportunities to handle fine brooches or belt buckles because I could somehow sense, often in later dreams, images associated with the objects' former owners. On this day, however, I wanted no more contact with Mother's pendant. I remember thinking that if I should hold the jewel in my hand, I would be unbearably reminded of our separation. I did not want to be any more forcefully linked to nightly visions of her than I already was in unguarded waking moments. In haste, I packed the leather roll away with other precious items to be stored in our protected treasure room, and fled outside as if pursued by demons.

I never had the opportunity to show you that jewel. You were busily traveling between Ulmsport and Vennesport, and I was frequently away from our main Vennesport storehouse. It never occurred to me to retrieve that particular locked casket until nearly twenty years later when you raised the subject of marriage. You were so deferential, so shy about asserting yourself, that I wonder you managed to utter the word "wedding." Had we been left in peace, I would surely and gladly have shown you the pendant. Any bride would have been proud to bring such a jewel to her lord-to-be. Yet those days were fated to be far from peaceful.

You had been concerned for some time by rumors of trouble stirring across the sea, and tried to convince Mother's brothers that our trade links were being affected. You expressed alarm when strangers from far Alizon arrived at several Dales' ports in the guise of traders, skulking about, asking too many questions. I listened to you, and shared your disquiet. I wrote Uncle Parand several times, warning him of the danger, but in those days of willful blindness, seemingly no words could be found to rouse the Dales.

We suffered sorely from our lack of leadership—the separate Clan lords refused to recognize the threat to all, and would not cooperate or plan together until it was too late. When Alizon's invasion broke upon us from the sea, just as you had warned it would, all that we had built in Vennesport was destroyed. When next I saw our storehouse years later, only a burned-out shell remained. Thus Alizon robbed me of both my betrothal and the gift that should have graced me as a bride. You had been killed, and the jewel—there was no way to discover what fate had befallen it.

The more I thought about the jewel, the more convinced I became that it had to be an object of Power. How else could I explain my immediate aversion to its touch? I thought at the time I was distressed because of its association with Mother, but I was even then touching items she had used regularly—her tally sticks, her hair brush, her favorite writing quills. My dreams were undisturbed by any painful intrusions linked to those objects.

I knew little then about Power, except that Dalesfolk have always been deeply uneasy discussing it, and even more averse to experiencing the use of it. Our Wise Women possess knowledge of the uses of Power, but their own exercise of it is of the personal kind, tending ills or sensing would-be outcomes by consulting their rune-boards. We prize our Wise Women's herb lore and healing skills, but any Dalesman recoils from the thought of the raw Power wielded by the Witches of Estcarp across the sea, or the storied mages of ancient Arvon.

When Mother died, I still thought of myself as wholly of the Dales—although I had only to glance at my image reflected from burnished metal or water to observe my marked outward variance from my fellow Dalesmen, including my parents. Not for me their red-brown hair that bleached in the sun, or their green or blue-green eyes. From my youth, my hair was dark gray-brown, like rare lamantine wood, you used to say, and my eyes a very pale clear blue. My skin, too, was pale, and refused to darken during the hot summer months. My appearance, as well as my muteness, set me apart as a child.

Some of the Rishdale Dames muttered about me until Dame Gwersa made plain that I was under her special protection. Only once I heard a kitchen maid hiss at me, "Spawn of Arvon," but I had no idea what she meant. When I wrote the evident insult for Dame Gwersa, she pursed her lips and said that some folk preferred to invent troubles when there were quite enough under foot to deal with day to day. I subsequently searched the abbey archives for lore on Arvon, but could find few references to that daunting land beyond the mountains bordering the northernmost Dales. Dame Gwersa would say only that no Dalesmen traveled there because the Arvon folk were close-knit and preferred their own company. She also conceded that there were Powers and Forces in Arvon that were best avoided by prudent men. Many years later, I attempted to trace vague rumors of rare weddings between folk from Arvon and the Dales. The suspected children of such unions were shunned in the Dales, as if they were somehow different from us. I suspect I began then to wonder whether my own strangeness could be ascribed to a blood-tie to Arvon. I had, after all, been born in a remote Dale near the borders of both Arvon and the shunned Waste.

I made a list of my peculiarities: my muteness from birth, my un-Daleslike appearance, my strange dreams (possibly similar to the odd dreams experienced by my mother), my ability to find lost objects. It occurred to me that Mother's betrothal gift might have originated in Arvon. I could no longer ignore the inference that my real father might not have been Dwyn of the House of Ekkor.

One other piece of evidence had to be included in my

list. When I was sixteen, Uncle Parand borrowed me from Mother to accompany him on coastal trading voyages. He said I should be able to learn much, while keeping his records for him. After those first short trips, he pronounced me useful and trustworthy (and also happily not subject to illness due to the motion of our trading vessels). He then invited me on the much longer voyage across the sea to the eastern lands, whose great ports I had only heard about—Verlaine, Sulcarkeep, and Estcarp's inland river port, Es City.

While I was walking alone near Es Castle, I encountered a solitary Witch of Estcarp. I was eighteen then; Uncle Parand had warned me to defer to any lady of the Old Race garbed in the distinctive gray robes of the Witches. I drew well to one side of the path to allow her ample room to pass by. She seemed not to have noticed me at all initially, but as soon as she passed me, she stopped abruptly, turned, and made a sign in the air with her right hand. To my amazement, the very lines her moving fingers sketched flared with a blue light (I have since been told that this indicated I was not tainted by the Dark). The Witch shook her head dismissively, and walked away without speaking a word to me. She therefore failed to see the delayed secondary glowing of her sign in the air—first red, then orange, then yellow—before it faded away entirely. I did not report this incident to my uncle, nor did I write any account of it for anyone else until now, as I marshal my arguments to persuade . . . I suppose I seek to persuade myself. My stalwart Doubt—if you were here, I believe you would accept my reasoning.

When I arrive at Lormt, I intend to request leave to search their archives for any records concerning jewels of Power. Captain Halbec has described for me the ap-

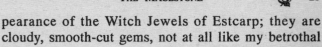

pearance of the Witch Jewels of Estcarp; they are cloudy, smooth-cut gems, not at all like my betrothal gift. Surely, however, Power can reside in different kinds of stones. I shall also search for lore about Arvon and whether any other folk like me have been described in kin lists.

If only the winds would rage this forcefully on a steady tack, we should complete our passage in far less than a month. But I must strive to be patient, and hope that the vessel holds together amid the storm waves. It will be good to see the sun again—and to be able to stand still, and get dry!

CHAPTER 2

Kasarian of Krevonel—his account of
the Baronial Assembly, Alizon City
(Alizonian calendar: 5th Day, Moon of the Knife,
the 1052nd Year Since the Betrayal)

I first saw the magic-cursed jewel when it was placed upon a silver chain around the neck of my sire's murderer. It was the fifth day of the Moon of the Knife, in the One Thousand Fifty-second Year Since the Betrayal. All land barons of Alizon were required to attend the New Year's Assembly for Presentation to the Lord Baron of that year's noble whelps come-of-age.

I was standing not two spear lengths from the throne when Lord Baron Norandor raised his sword to amend the customary order of procedure. Except for his eyes, his face was concealed by the white-furred Lord Hound's mask. He was a thinner man than the previous Lord Baron Mallandor, his dead littermate, so his voice echoed within the mask as he summoned Baron Gurborian to approach the throne.

Any matter concerning the murderer of my sire demanded my most wary attention. Gurborian's schemes had for years permeated all of Alizon. Only the slowest-

witted barons were unaware of his ambition to seize the
Lord Hound's mask for himself. Four moons before, I
had received a private letter from Volorian, my sire's
elder littermate, complaining that Gurborian's hirelings
were prowling near our northeasterly estates. Could yet
more threats against our Line be straining at Gurborian's
leashes?

When Gurborian had knelt before the throne, Norandor arose, sheathing his sword. "Worthy Gurborian of
the Line Sired by Reptur," the Lord Baron proclaimed,
"my unfortunate littermate esteemed your counsel, as do
I. For your able warfare in the Dales across the sea, as
well as for other valued services, he allowed you to bear
this singular token of Alizon's approval."

The torchlight in the Great Hall seemed to ignite a
coal of blue fire in the Lord Baron's outstretched hand. I
edged forward to secure a better view. The light glittered
from a jewel the size of a moor hen's egg, and flared between Norandor's fingers as he stooped to attach the
stone to Gurborian's baronial neck chain. "Now I, Norandor, Lord Baron of Alizon," he continued, "reaffirm
that approval by conferring upon you his notable prize,
to be borne by you during your lifetime."

A muffled snort erupted from the elderly baron standing next to me. "As soon as Gurborian's dead," he muttered, "Reptur's pack had best hasten to return that
bauble before the Lord Baron's guard break in to claim
it."

I was the only one near enough to hear the remark, but
I gave no sign that I had. I was fairly certain that old
Baron Moragian was not a member of Gurborian's current faction, but it was unwise to acknowledge such a
comment where an unfriendly witness might notice. My
outward detachment, I must admit, was also partly due

to my attention's being so closely focused on the jewel; never before had I seen such a stone. It continued to draw my eye even after Gurborian rejoined his coterie.

Our Line had no whelps to be presented that year. When Sherek, the new Master of Hounds, called for our pack's representative, I strode forward to kneel before the throne. "In the stead of Baron Volorian," I asserted, "I, Kasarian, appear for the Line Sired by Krevonel." Norandor acknowledged me with a wave of his hand, and I withdrew to one side.

The Great Hall's air seemed suddenly stifling, the torches far too bright. Within my head, the nagging pain that for some nights had frustrated my efforts to sleep redoubled its thumping. Desiring a temporary refuge away from the noisy throng, I slipped out into the corridor leading to the oldest part of Alizon Castle.

I knew of one particular room where I was unlikely to be disturbed. The ancient mosaic designs on its walls and floor were similar to those in one room in my own castle here in the City. I plucked a torch from a hall sconce to carry with me, but torches within the mosaic room had already been kindled by the servants.

Behind the pierced stone screen along one side of the chamber was a long bench probably used by serving slaves in times past when the room was more frequented. Due to winter drafts, a large tapestry had been hung across the room side of the screen, but it was threadbare in spots. If a person behind the screen chose his vantage point with care, he could see quite well into the main chamber. I had not intended to spy unseen, but I had only just sat down on the bench when I heard the scrape of boots entering the main room.

There were two intruders—one whose voice I did not recognize, but the other voice was Gurborian's. I moved very quietly to obtain a glimpse of them through the tapestry fabric. The second man was Gratch of Gorm, Gurborian's prime henchman. He had been named in Volorian's letter as one of those prying and poking about in the mountains near our estates. From their first words, I could draw two immediate conclusions: they mistakenly assumed that the mosaic chamber was empty, and they plotted treason against Lord Baron Norandor.

Keeping his voice low, as befitted a devoted conspirator, Gratch said, "We are safe here from interference, my lord. No one followed us. I commented openly that we were going to the Kennels to survey the breeding bitches."

Gurborian scowled: "Lord Baron Fool has named Sherek to be Master of Hounds. I had hoped to influence the choice from among our faction, but my bribes were evidently insufficient. That naming is done, and of less import than your news. How stands Bolduk's faction— for us or against us?"

Reluctant to answer, Gratch toyed for a moment with his belt dagger. "I tried both the strategies we had discussed, my lord—hinting at dire costs for rejection, while promising fair rewards for alliance. Despite my best efforts, old Baron Bolduk continues obstinate, clinging to the senseless notion that only the Kolder are strong enough to vanquish Estcarp. I told him that the last Kolder within our borders have been dead for seven moons. The late Hound Master's misguided foray into Estcarp should have convinced the very doorposts that Alizon can no longer expect any aid from the Kolder."

"Bolduk *is* very like a doorpost," mused Gurborian. "Perhaps a brisk fire at his base might melt his stubbornness. His blood feud with Ferlikian could always be revived by a word or two in the proper ears. Still, I would prefer Bolduk's Line to be with us or neutral. Was he not impressed by your mention of our planned Escorian alliance?"

Gratch shook his head. "It is a delicate matter, my lord," he said dourly, "to speak of any magical matter to Bolduk. Even though by our hoped-for alliance we should control the lash of spells, and for a welcome change, Estcarp's crones would suffer the effects, Bolduk persists in abhorring any recourse to the weapons of our sworn enemies."

Gurborian paced back and forth, his impatience evident in every stride. "Why can he not *see*—any weapon that might succeed must be employed? The Witches have thwarted us far too long with their foul containment spells woven from the Forbidden Hills across the Alizon Gap. It would be rare sport for them to be scourged by magic stronger than their own. If only we had an Escorian mage to exhibit . . . even an apt apprentice could persuade the undecided among the barons to join with us."

Eager to placate his master, Gratch leaned toward Gurborian. "My lord, I am certain that I shall be successful in my latest negotiations. Today I received a message from my most reliable source near the Escorian border. If his information is correct, he should soon be able to arrange a meeting for me with a lower level student who has traveled in Escore and—"

Gurborian seized Gratch's neck chain and jerked him so that his teeth rattled. "If—should—lower level student," he scoffed. "I have heard such weasel words too often with nothing tangible to show for them. Norandor is already suspicious of our comings and goings. So far, I have mollified him." He thrust Gratch away, and flourished the jewel on his own neck chain. "He awards me this to assure my loyal allegiance. Fool—it was mine thirteen years ago as Mallandor's reward for my aid in deposing Facellian. Once our new plans are firmly forged my faction will feed Norandor to the hounds just as we earlier served his littermate. But I need more backing! I dare not move too soon without sufficient preparation."

"There is one definite word of cheer, my lord." Gratch had prudently stepped beyond Gurborian's reach. "I was able to hire the poisoner we spoke of. The supply of smother root that you required will be delivered by tonight."

"I shall make good use of it." Gurborian smiled. "Bolduk's younger whelp—is he not in the Castle with his sire? Should he suddenly fall ill or worse, Ferlikian would be blamed, and my quiet offer of sympathetic alliance could be well received."

"I shall see to it, my lord," said Gratch briskly. "Would it not be wise if we were seen at the Kennels, in case anyone should seek us there?"

Gurborian started for the door, then paused. "Indeed . . . although I do not care to encounter Volorian's fosterling in the Kennels. I hear that he is as tediously keen a houndsman as that troublesome border lord himself."

"While I was in the mountains during the Second Whelping Moon, I saw Baron Volorian from a fair distance," Gratch remarked, as he followed his master out into the corridor. "He was wading through his pack, choosing new breeders. They say he's too old and too involved in the breeding to leave his estates nowadays. As you saw, he did not come for this year's Assembly."

"Volorian may be old," Gurborian replied with a laugh, "but he's wily. He well remembers how I disposed of his younger littermate, so he keeps his distance from me." Their voices receded, trailing off into a murmur, then silence.

I sat half dazed, my thoughts racing. A murder plot against Baron Bolduk's younger whelp—Bolduk's Line currently harbored no active animosity toward the Line Sired by Krevonel, but neither were we obligated to dispatch a warning. I judged that an admonitory word to Ferlikian would be more potentially useful. Such commonplace baronial machinations, however, were thoroughly dwarfed by Gurborian's threat to forge a treasonous alliance with the magic-wielding fiends of Escore. Should Gurborian ever suspect that I had overheard his plotting, he would move swiftly to send me after my murdered sire.

I had been five years old when Gurborian ordered Oralian's death. My sire had led a faction of the older barons who steadfastly resisted any alliance with the foreign Kolder. When the then-reigning Lord Baron Facellian had rammed through the alliance despite all opposition, Gurborian curried his favor by removing Facellian's most prominent baronial opponents. Facellian eagerly acceded to the Kolder's demand for war with the Dales across the sea. The Kolder being few in number, it fell to Alizon to provide the warriors, but the Kolder did supply us with uncommon weapons to advance our invasion.

I remember hearing my elder littermates discuss those early, exciting, and successful years of the war. Our coastal invasion was initially invincible. The moving metal boxes the Kolder supplied to shelter our fighters could scarcely be withstood. Even so, as our sire had warned the Baron's Council before his murder, we were totally dependent upon the Kolder for the supplies required to maintain the boxes and their fire spewers. When those supplies were blocked by the Dales' Sulcar allies, we lost our most powerful advantage. Two of my littermates died in the fighting, and when the third was too severely wounded to ride, his men cut his throat to prevent the Dales hags from loosening his tongue by magic.

I was twelve when it was clear the war was lost. Having nimbly positioned himself with Mallandor's faction, Gurborian wielded an equally strong hand in Facellian's overthrow. Even then, Gurborian's ambition was overly fierce to be safely accommodated too close to the throne. In order to allow time for Mallandor's justified suspicions to cool, Gurborian withdrew for six years to his coastal estates.

I had been quietly fostered with Volorian all those years, well away from the swirl of plotting in Alizon City. Following my unremarked presentation ceremony at age twelve, Volorian agreed that after a prudent time, I might take up residence in our pack's castle in the City. I arrived at the castle when I was fifteen, the same year, I later learned, that Gratch first appeared at Gurborian's side to become a shadowy partner in his scheming. They both returned to Alizon City when I was twenty, but they carefully stayed out of Mallandor's way until two years later, when Estcarp's Witches worked their foulest magic, tearing the very roots of their southern bordering mountains to foil Karsten's impending invasion.

Mallandor yearned to strike while the hags reeled, depleted by their exertions, but their cursed containment spells still held across our mutual border. The pro-Kolder faction of barons then agitated for a concerted effort to open a new magical Gate for the Kolder, so that they might bring us more of their metal boxes as well as more Kolder to reinforce their scant remaining numbers. I was repelled by such plans, but it would have been fatal to say so. Because of my scholarly interests, it was acceptable for me to take part in the search for documents from the ancient days, even as far back as the Betrayal itself, in the hope of finding useful lore on the dreaded mage-work involved in the Gate magic.

During the spring of last year, Mallandor hearkened to more foolish advice—openly endorsed at the time by Gurborian's faction—and sent his Master of Hounds Esguir raiding into Estcarp to seize some Witch pups for the Kolder to use in their Gate magic. The plot failed miserably; all the captive Witchlings escaped back into Estcarp, and the few Kolder left in Alizon Castle were all killed. Gurborian then revealed his true intentions. He rallied Mallandor's enemies to overthrow the Lord Baron. Because his own faction was not strong enough to place him on the throne, however, Gurborian backed Mallandor's ambitious littermate Norandor. Mallandor and Esguir were fed to the hounds, and Norandor assumed the Lord Hound's mask.

From the conversation I overheard between Gurborian and Gratch, it seemed that yet another overthrow was being plotted, and this time I had no doubt that Gurborian sought the mask for himself. But what post could Gratch hope to attain? As a non-Alizonder, he could not be named Master of Hounds. Probably he expected to continue his role of counselor in Gurborian's shadow. He was a dangerous foe, familiar with the rarest of poisons.

I remember wondering as I carefully made my way to my castle, whether my physical discomfort could be due to one of Gratch's potions, but I dismissed the thought. Like all barons resident in the City, I regularly partook of small doses of various poisons to build advance resistance. I had also made a useful study of antidotes, thus I felt reasonably sure I could deal with Gratch's threat. My household servants were all reliable, due to pack loyalty, blood-ties, or fear. To lessen the lure of bribes, I kept my pay levels sufficient.

On my way through secluded alleyways, I had to pause several times to recover from fits of dizziness. As I reflect upon the events of that night, I realize that my weakness was caused by my proximity to Gurborian's accursed jewel.

Arriving at Krevonel Castle, I reeled to my bedchamber and lay down, apprehensive of what dreams might beset me should I fall asleep. All I could think about was that jewel—when I closed my eyes, its image burned in my mind. Somehow, that sparkling crystal seemed to be reaching out to me, drawing me toward its cold blue fire.

CHAPTER 3

Mereth—her journal at Lormt
(4th and 5th Days,
Month of the Ice Dragon,
New Year of the Lamia)

My dear one—what would you say of this curious place, fabled Lormt of the Scholars, isolated amid mountains rendered even less accessible by the Turning, as they term the Witches' spell-shifting of the earth?

I did not think it necessary to dispatch a messenger to herald my coming; that would have been a proper courtesy for a nobleman with a retinue, but scarcely justified for a lone Daleswoman. I recalled Dame Gwersa's assertion that any serious kin-lore seeker who dared the journey to Lormt was certain to be welcomed, but might also risk being misplaced in the countless archive nooks by the resident scholars who were renowned for their complete devotion to their work.

Although our ride had been long and cold, and both of us were politely greeted upon our arrival, the guide I hired at Es City refused to stay at Lormt. Once he had delivered me and my scant baggage at the metal-bound gates, he would have turned to depart if the gatekeeper had not insisted that he allow his horses to be watered and rested for at least a few hours.

You would have exclaimed, I think, at the vast scale of this citadel of ancient learning. I had formerly believed that there could be no larger building stones than those massive gray-green blocks I had seen in Es City's walls and Castle. Upon entering Lormt's great courtyard, however, I concluded that Lormt's builders must have been capable of wrenching and shaping the very roots of the surrounding mountains.

Dame Gwersa's informant had reported significant destruction wrought by the earthquake, but I was appalled to observe the actual extent of the ruin. Of the four round towers anchoring the rectangular courtyard, two appeared untouched, a third had lost half its former height, and the fourth corner's tower had completely collapsed, along with most of its short adjoining wall. The ground beneath that area had dropped away more than a trade wagon's length, bringing down one entire long outer wall.

Obvious efforts had been made since to deal with the damage and repair what could be salvaged. As we rode in, I noticed newer metal fittings and bindings where the gates had been rehinged and patched. What at first glance appeared to be huge, shapeless heaps of rubble, upon closer viewing showed signs of organized excavation and timber shoring. Several sheds of rough-hewn wood were spaced along the lines of the fallen walls, and sturdy fences of brush and woven withes extended between them to hold back the mountain snowdrifts from overwhelming the courtyard expanse. I judged from the sharp-peaked tower roofs and the steep-pitched roofs along the remaining walls and buildings that the winter snows at these heights must be far heavier than those I remembered from my childhood near the Dales' western peaks.

Dark slates sheathed all the roofs here, including those on the two ancient stone buildings within the courtyard. One tall structure with a strip of high windows running its full length nestled against the intact long wall, while the squatter, smaller building was tucked to the left inside the gates and abutting an undamaged corner tower. Stone watering troughs for the animals were placed near a sheltered well at the right interior corner. Except for the gaps caused by the earth's subsidence, all the remaining stonework was doubly impressive for the sheer size of the blocks and the tightness of the unmortared joints. I know exactly what you would have done, had you been here with me—you would have peered at the walls and said, "I doubt whether a knife blade could be slipped between those blocks."

I was not given much initial opportunity to survey my surroundings, however, for I had no sooner dismounted than I was confronted by a party of four figures well-cloaked against the late afternoon chill. To my surprise, when an icy wind gust blew open the leading figure's cloak, I saw suspended from her belt a wooden rune-board like those used by our Wise Women of the Dales. She raised her hands in ritual greeting, and offered me a traveler's cup. Cold and stiff as I was from my long day's ride, I savored the taste of the steaming herbed broth—a welcome cup, indeed!

I extracted my hand slate to write the proper response: "For the welcome of the gate, gratitude. To the ruler of this house, fair fortune. I am Mereth of Ferndale, come here to seek knowledge concerning my kin."

The Wise Woman accepted my slate and read my message aloud for the others as calmly as if she was frequently accustomed to receiving mute visitors. Her features and coloring were those of Estcarp's Old Race, but it was heartening to me that she seemed at least familiar with some of our Dales customs. "I am Jonja," she responded, with a brisk nod of her head. "I welcome you to Lormt."

"As do I." A tall, gaunt man beside her stepped forward, his gray eyes proclaiming him also of the Old Race, although age had turned his black hair to silver-white. "I am Ouen. Lormt's scholars allow me to represent them to guests. This is Duratan, our resident chronicler and invaluable advisor."

This second tall man had been a soldier at one time, I thought. He was bearing no sword at his belt, but his body seemed still to balance as if compensating for the familiar weight. When he moved toward me, he swung his left leg stiffly, as I had seen many Dales fighters after war injuries. He held out his hand to the fourth figure. "My lady Nolar," he said, "healer and scholar." Both of them were of the Old Race, but her face was marred by a dark stain like a splash of wine.

"Come within, out of the cold," Jonja suggested. "The hour grows late, and you should rest from your journey. We can confer in the morning concerning your request."

The other three withdrew, while Jonja led me to a guest chamber deep inside the remaining long wall. Stone stairs led up and down, linking what seemed to be countless storage rooms and quiet sleeping cells. Occasional torches supplemented the waning daylight that seeped through slits in the courtyard side of the wall. A few of those curious round light globes like the ones I had seen in Es Castle so many years before also provided additional illumination. My designated room had a low wooden bed whose mattress smelled of sun-dried rushes. Several plain but well-sewn quilts were folded atop a carved chest. An earthenware pitcher and basin stood on the stone ledge near the door.

"I have asked the cooks to send your evening meal here," Jonja said as she turned to depart. "Should you care to write any queries for our consideration tomorrow, I will ask a scribe to bring you quills, parchment, and ink. May you find here whatever you came to seek. I wish you fair repose this night."

The meal sent for me was simple, but well prepared and sustaining. I found the white-fleshed steamed roots unfamiliar but tasty, and the rabbit stew was savory. There was sweet butter and fruit conserve to spread on the rounds of barley bread. A flask of hearty ale complemented the food.

Soon after I had set aside my tray, I heard a tap at the door. A man nearly my age bustled in, his arms full of scrolls and quills. He set his bundles on the bed and darted back out into the corridor to fetch in a writing bench and a study lamp. Before I could write my thanks, he had hurried away.

I have been sitting at that bench for some time now, attempting to set my queries in an orderly array. My earlier letter to you composed aboard the ship was most helpful in clarifying my thoughts. I find myself deeply affected by the weight of years pressing upon this place. The kin lists that you and I compiled in the Dales stretched back many generations, but Lormt's stones belong to an age unbelievably remote beyond any we knew, even from the Dales' oldest legends. The keen pursuit of learning here by so many scholars over so long a time makes my total candor not only a courtesy but a necessity. I have written the account of my past, including my odd talents and my one encounter with the

Witch at Es Castle. I suspect that along with the famed
kin lists here, there must also be ancient documents concerning magical matters. Perhaps these folk *can* help me
find some lore related to my betrothal jewel . . . if they
choose to allow me access to their archives. I await the
dawn with a mixture of impatience and trepidation.

My sense of apprehension last night was indeed justified. These Lormt folk were evidently as wary of me as I
was of them! After I had eaten a hasty morning meal,
Jonja herself conducted me to the larger courtyard building, which proved to be the main scholarly repository.
Never before had I seen so many scrolls gathered together in one place. We passed through a warren of
study nooks and cubicles, divided and flanked by
shelves, with countless tables and desks all heaped with
sheafs of writings. Scores of elderly men—and a few
women—moved about slowly carrying documents or
perching on chairs or benches.

Jonja did not speak to any of the scholars, but preceded me up a narrow staircase to the upper level, where
she opened a massive door into a study room well illu-
mined by a segment of the high window strip I had noticed from below. The same three Estcarpians who had
met me at the gate looked up from their seats around a
table littered with documents.

Ouen rose to offer me a high-backed chair. "Come
join us, if you will," he invited. "We have been discussing the significance of your arrival."

I held out to him the pages I had written, then took my
seat, placing my slate on the table before me and propping my staff at my knee. You used to claim to envy my
practice of rapping on the floor with my staff to draw attention to my hand slate. You said it invariably stopped

every contentious meeting, and threatened more than once to try a loud shout of your own to award you equal notice . . . but you never did test that tactic, at least, not in my hearing.

Ouen read my statement aloud, not pausing for any comments. When he finished the last page, he looked at me with a keenly assessing gaze. "You are commendably frank," he remarked. "We shall return that courtesy. You should know that Mistress Jonja had alerted us of your approach some hours before your arrival."

Startled, I turned to face the Wise Woman. She had laid her rune-board before her, and touched it now with her right hand. "I bear a certain measure of the foreseeing gift," she explained. "I sensed yesterday that someone associated with Power was drawing near to Lormt, so I asked these friends to join me at the gate. You will understand that any stirring of Power must be carefully examined. Once you had come under Lormt's roof, I consulted both my herbs and my rune-board to determine your allegiance to either the Light or the Dark."

The soldierly Estcarpian, Duratan, nodded and extended his hand above the table. From a small leather bag, he spilled out a few gemstones of various colors, some clear, some cloudy. "I also consulted these crystals of mine," he said. "I see you are surprised that a male could share those talents thought to belong solely to Witches and Wise Women. Kemoc Tregarth, whose talents descend from his mighty father, gave me these crystals. They fall for me in patterns that can convey warnings in time of need. When I tossed them last night concerning you, I received such a warning. You are at the center of potent violence and conflict. . . ."

Before he could finish speaking, I thumped my staff, snatched up my slate and wrote, "No! Violence wrenched away all dear to me twenty years past, in Alizon's war against our Dales. I have no traffic with any magic, nor do I bring you any danger of conflict!"

Duratan smiled, but there was little warmth in his expression. "I did not mean conflict now," he corrected. "I was about to say that my crystals warn of trouble yet to come."

I wiped away my first remark with my slate cloth and scribbled my rejoinder. "I crave your pardon for interrupting. I am an old woman—how can I be a threat to anyone? I fought in defense of our Dales, that is true, chiefly by using my trading experience to supply our men harrying the invaders. But those awful years are gone by. All I seek now is your help in finding whence came my betrothal jewel, and who was my true father."

Ouen again read my words aloud. The lady Nolar seemed deep in thought, then she observed, "This pendant jewel you describe cannot be a Witch Jewel, for I have seen and handled one of those—it belonged to a Witch I assisted in a quest over a year ago, just after the Turning. I must tell you that I briefly possessed a shard found here at Lormt that proved to have been riven from a stone of great Power far to the south. It was not a clear crystal, however, like your betrothal gem, but a creamy, opaque stone veined with green, and wondrous for its healing gifts when rightly addressed. I shall gladly aid you in searching our archives here for any news regarding your lost jewel."

"And we can inquire whether old Morfew might spare the time to sort through his interminable kin lists," suggested Duratan. This time, his smile was warmed by genuine affection. "He is justly famed for his store of knowledge."

"I thank you all," I wrote on my slate. "My questions

have not allowed me to rest. I undertook this far journey with the mere hope that Lormt might provide answers. I rejoice that you offer me assistance."

Thus as the snows of the Month of the Ice Dragon swirled outside, I began my search of Lormt's documents.

CHAPTER 4

Kasarian—events at Krevonel Castle,
Alizon City (6th Day and early 7th Day,
Moon of the Knife)

I did sleep that night, and I did dream. I awoke before
dawn, my bedclothes in a disordered tangle. Although I
tried, I could not recall the substance of my dreams, only
that there had been vivid colors and strange sounds and
whirling motions. Had there not been some prominent
object . . . some patterned design? No matter how intense my effort, I could not retrieve any details.

Feeling unsettled, I climbed the tower staircase to our
castle's mosaic chamber. Always before when I was
troubled, I had found a certain soothing quietness in that
room, as if the ancient designs ornamenting the walls
and floor diverted both eye and mind. Some of the beasts
and plants portrayed were clearly recognizable—the
split-tusked boar, the shrieker, the hooded crow, the
fever-leaf vine; others were bizarre, with too many legs
or heads or fanciful flowers. As I walked slowly around
the room, tracing the more faded patterns with my fingers, I felt suddenly convinced that some of these very

designs had appeared in my dreams—their colors far brighter, the animal forms moving somehow, as if alive. On the heels of this insight came a second revelation. Before my last littermate had sailed for the Dales, we had talked in this room. He discussed the formalities I should follow if he were killed in the fighting, including the surrender by his mate of what we termed the elder's key. As I recalled that conversation, the key's image filled my mind's eye.

When had I last seen that intricately engraved key? It was thought to be as old as our Line, descending to the mate of the eldest male upon the birth of her first male. Volorian's mate having died young, the key had been presented to my dam, and upon my sire's murder, passed to my eldest littermate's mate. With all three of my elder littermates now dead, I had assumed that my mate would eventually be given the key . . . except I had so far bred no whelps, not yet having an alliance negotiated for me. As the persisting image of Gurborian's jewel had nagged me the previous night, I found my thoughts were now fixated on the elder's key. I had seen it only twice: once when I chanced to discover my dam sorting through our pack's treasures, and once when the key was passed to my last littermate to be given to his mate. When she had delivered a female, the key had been returned to its special casket.

Casket—that should be the place to look. I hurried to the castle's strongroom and shifted chests and boxes until I uncovered that particular silver casket. The lock was stiff from disuse, but I inserted my sire's key from my belt ring and pried back the casket's top. Pushing aside layers of chains and baubles, I caught a glimpse of bronze-silver. When I drew the key out into the light, I was startled to realize that it, too, had been part of my dream. I could close my eyes and picture every detail of engraving along the shaft and the thick carved bits. I could retrieve no association for the key from my dream, but as I held it in my hand, it balanced sweetly, like a favorite dagger.

But what lock did it fit? The question struck me so forcefully that I sank down on a bench to consider it. Had anyone in my hearing ever named the purpose of the elder's key? I knew that the breeding females of our Line prized it, but my dam had certainly never told me what chest or door it was meant to unlock. If a key no longer functioned as such, why should it be handed down through generations? There *had* to be a matching lock . . . but where?

I shook my aching head. Why should the elder's key suddenly be so important to me? Where was its lock? Because the key was likely as old as our castle, I reasoned that it must be associated with an equally old lock. I swiftly surveyed all of our treasure chests, but none of them bore locks of the proper size or metal. Doors— there must be dozens of doors in the oldest parts of the castle. Before I could pursue my thoughts any further, I was called to attend to baronial duties. I tucked the key inside my belt wallet until I could snatch the time to continue my investigations.

No opportunity occurred that day, and I was required to attend more Assembly functions that evening. By the time I retired to bed, I had temporarily forgotten the elder's key, but it was not finished with me.

I awoke as if a sword blade had been pressed against my cheek. I was seized by a conviction: the key did belong to a lock made of the same metal, a lock in a very particular door. My visual impression of the door was so strong that I put out my hand to touch its rough wooden surface, only to clutch empty air. My vision had been another dream. I sat up, frustrated and angry at first, then intrigued. I could not have imagined a door in such detail—I must have seen it at some time, in some place. Here, in this castle—the words echoed in my mind.

I pulled on my boots and lit a small hand lantern. What better time to search unnoticed than in these hours when few eyes were likely to be open? I extracted the key from my wallet, and as I held it in my hand, I vow I sensed a tenuous directional pull leading downward.

With the key in one hand and the lantern in the other, I descended the remoter back staircases. One dusty passageway to the left beckoned, then I sought more stairs, always going down. The cellars deep beneath the castle had once provided dungeons, but nowadays were used for storage or abandoned to the silent darkness. Never before had I ventured so far below. The tugging sensation in my mind seemed to be growing more pronounced. I hurried through another passageway, descended a flight of stairs whose gritty steps had not been disturbed for years. My lantern light awoke an answering flash of bronze-silver across the antechamber. I had found the door of my dream vision.

I raised the elder's key and inserted it in the massive lock. When I turned the key, the door opened soundlessly, as if both lock and hinges had been freshly oiled. The space beyond was dark, but the air wafting out was sweet. I had heard of locked rooms full of poisonous vapors sealed to snare the unwary, so I thrust my lantern inside, pushing it along the paving stones. I watched the flame closely, but it burned bright and unaffected. Extracting the key from the lock, I crossed the threshold.

The stonewalled chamber within was bare—no furnishings, no wall hangings, no rugs. I hesitated, disappointed, then a movement among the shadows caught my eye, and I whirled around. The door was closing behind me. Before I could reach back to halt it, the door closed and I heard the lock engage.

Such untoward actions raised the dreaded possibility of magic. The very Betrayal that founded Alizon a thousand years before had been plotted by mages. Since that time, no Alizonder baron of any wit had trusted any magic-wielder. Alizon had always suffered at the hands of mages and Witches.

Still, I was of the Line Sired by Krevonel. This was Alizon City, not Estcarp, and I was properly armed. How could magic possibly infiltrate into the roots of Krevonel Castle? Besides, I held the elder's key in my hand; it had opened the door to this room once. Why should it not function so again?

As I turned toward the door, I think it was the distinct change in the quality of the light that diverted my attention from the lock. The yellow light cast by my lantern from the floor was fast being overwhelmed by a white glare starkly outlining my shadow against the bare wall fitted with the door.

I spun around immediately, crouching as I drew my belt dagger in my left hand. To my amazement, the white light was emanating from a hand-sized spot glowing in mid air at the center of the room. Even as I watched, transfixed, the spot expanded, stretching into an oval tall and wide enough to encompass a man's body. The area within this peculiar space was opaque, but tremulous, like a bank of curdled clouds suffused by moonlight. Simultaneously repelled and attracted by it, I neared it cautiously, circling all the way around it. It continued to hang motionless, its lower rim a step above the floor level.

I thrust my dagger blade warily into its center. The point penetrated unimpeded, vanishing from sight as if it were plunging into a milky liquid. I snatched back my blade. It appeared unaffected, being neither hotter, colder, nor wetter than before.

I suddenly realized that I was still gripping the elder's key in my right hand. That strange drawing sensation I had felt earlier resumed with even stronger intensity. Whatever lay within or beyond that oval of light was attracting the key toward it. Driven to investigate this potential breach of security that could threaten not only Krevonel Castle but Alizon City itself, I clasped my dagger firmly in my left hand, raised my boot, and stepped into the oval.

Instantly, I was blinded, deafened, and stricken as if by winter's iciest blasts. I was not physically touched, yet my body seemed somehow twisted. Before I could cry out, my foot completed its step back onto a level stone surface, and my other senses returned.

But I was no longer in Krevonel's lower chamber— this space was vast, the walls extending out of sight into dense shadows. To my dismay, there were other people in this chamber. Two of them held lanterns, and by that yellow light and the white glare from the oval portal now behind me, I recognized Alizon's direst enemies: gray robes, gray eyes, black hair—male and female Estcarpians! Numbed and shaken by my passage through the light portal, I was afflicted by a roaring in my ears and dimming sight. I tried to speak, to raise my dagger to defend myself, but smothering darkness enveloped me and I felt myself falling.

CHAPTER 5 ⎯⎯⎯⎯⎯⎯⎯

Mereth—beginning her account
requested for Lormt's archives:
events at Lormt (early 7th Day,
Month of the Ice Dragon)

Morfew himself has asked me to record my experiences, commencing with the extraordinary occurrence in one of Lormt's cellars disclosed by the earthquake. I have thus set aside my private journal to compose this report for the archives. In view of the cascading events that overwhelmed my personal quest, all of our collective energies have become engaged in a more urgent search, upon whose outcome the present fates of whole lands may depend.

But my mind outraces my quill, and fingers stiffened by age require frequent warming at Morfew's brazier. As any good trader strives to preserve his accounts in order, so shall I begin properly at the beginning of this remarkable tale.

It was near the second week of the Month of the Ice Dragon, and I had resided at Lormt for only two days when I was abruptly jarred from sleep as if by a battle shout. I kindled a night lantern, wrapped myself in my warmest robe, and secured the padded felt slippers that Ouen had given me. The corridor outside my guest chamber appeared deserted. I heard no stirrings or sounds of distress . . . yet I felt irresistibly drawn to descend the staircase and continue to seek more stairs leading farther downward. I had no clear notion of the object of this singular late-night excursion, but I pressed forward through the empty passageways until I simultaneously spied the flicker of other lamps down an adjoining corridor, and heard the muffled rasp of leather and fabric against stone.

Jonja emerged ahead of me, closely followed by Duratan, Nolar, and Ouen. They were evidently as surprised to see me as I was to encounter them.

Duratan raised his lamp as I approached them. "Why are you wandering here at this hour?" he demanded.

Fortunately, I always kept a hand slate and chalk in the pockets of all my robes. "I was awakened," I wrote, groping for the words to explain my presence. "I found no one near my guest chamber, but I felt obligated to descend and seek the cause of my disquiet."

Jonja nodded, her face grim-set. "Power is stirring, far beneath the settled levels of Lormt. Each of us was also roused from sleep. We must hurry to determine the source of the disturbance. The Turning exposed many storage areas below this level. I sense a growing pulse of Power thence. Come!"

That earlier distortion of the earth had indeed twisted and tilted the stone paving blocks, as well as cracking some of the walls. We picked our way gingerly around and between the displaced stones as we continued our descent. Suddenly, a great space opened around us. Our small lights were mere sparks within a chamber in which

Captain Halbec could easily have moored his trading vessel, masts and all.

Nolar moved her head like a hound questing for an elusive scent. "Can you not feel it?" she asked. "The very air is tingling. Look! Over there, to the left!"

Before any of us could step forward, a spot of opalescent light shimmered at eye level not ten paces away. I stared at it, not knowing whether to advance or retreat. As I watched, the spot of light expanded into a man-sized oval. Duratan's free hand dropped to his belt. I was heartened to see him draw a substantial, long-bladed forester's knife. Setting my lantern on the floor, I grasped my staff in both hands. If the need arose, I had not forgotten how to wield it as a weapon.

The oval's milky surface roiled as a booted foot emerged through it, followed by the remainder of a tall man's body. Nolar gasped audibly. Had I possessed a voice, I should have joined her. The intruder was obviously an Alizonder soldier.

I had hoped never again to have to look upon those archenemies of our Dales. Their distinguishing features were seared into my memory—feral green eyes, short white-silver hair, hooked noses, teeth sharp as those of their own cursed hounds. From his high-sided boots to his blue-green tunic and tight-fitting breeches, this was a typical Alizonder soldier . . . and yet, on closer examination, perhaps not just a mere soldier. As the oval behind him contracted in size, its light flashed on a decorative gold chain across his chest, and an ornate dagger clutched in his left hand. At the sight of us, his eyes widened with alarm. He swayed unsteadily, gave a sudden strangled cry, and collapsed to the floor, just as the shrinking light spot vanished.

Duratan was the first of us to move, kneeling quickly

to disarm the Alizonder. He snatched away the dagger, tossing it out of reach, then removed several other weapons from the wide leather belt—a dart gun, several throwing knives, and some objects I could not recognize.

Without making a conscious decision, I found myself stooping next to Duratan to grasp the intruder's extended right hand. The Alizonder's fingers were tightly clenched around a cold metal object—a heavy key, I soon realized, when I pried it loose. The instant it touched my flesh, it seemed to cleave to my hand. I was assailed by a burst of images flowing into my mind. In all my years of sensing ownership ties to objects, I had never experienced such an intense flood of concentrated information. I dropped from my crouching position to sit directly on the floor, squeezing shut my eyes to try to control my disorientation. As soon as I could regain my breath, I opened my eyes, and thrust the key into my pocket to halt its mental intrusion. Seizing my slate, I hastened to write what I had learned.

Nolar had observed my preoccupation. Perhaps fearing that I had swooned, she kindly bent down to brace her arm around my shoulders. When she saw that I was urgently writing, however, she retrieved my lantern and voiced my startling revelations. "I sense from the key in his hand that this enemy is Kasarian of the Line of Krevonel," Nolar read from my slate. "By magical means he does not understand, he has come here from the vaults beneath his family's castle in Alizon City!"

The members of the Lormt party exclaimed, all talking at once, but I could not focus on what they were saying. My body was shaking as if with an ague. Violent, conflicting feelings raced through my mind—white-hot hatred for those evil Hounds who had ravaged our Dales, killing my beloved . . . but also equally burning curiosity. What magic could convey a living man so many leagues, and how could I be able to sense identifying facts about my deadliest enemies when I knew only a handful of words in the Alizonian speech?

Ouen's clear voice suddenly claimed my attention. "We must send for Morfew at once. When this Alizonder recovers his senses, we shall likely require the aid of an Alizonian speaker."

Nolar gently touched my shoulder. "If I cannot provide healing assistance for you, I can go rouse Morfew."

"Pray do not be concerned for me," I scribbled on my slate. "I am amazed rather than ailing."

"Then I shall hasten to Morfew's chamber," Nolar said, taking one of the lanterns to light her way.

Jonja had been carefully examining the Alizonder's gear. Turning to me, she asked, "Can your gift of insightful touch extract more information for us about this Kasarian before he awakens? The greater our knowledge of the threat he poses, the better."

Duratan nodded in agreement. "Perhaps his House badge or his baron's chain may speak to you, lady, for if I am not mistaken, this man is a war baron or a land baron. His array of weapons argues the former, while the quality of his gear suggests the latter."

At my age, rising from a stone floor consumes inordinate time and effort, so I simply hitched my skirt and crawled back to the senseless figure. His unlined face, relaxed in unconsciousness, seemed superficially vulnerable. I was struck by his relative youth—he could scarcely be thirty years of age. At least, I thought grudgingly, this particular Alizonder was too young to have taken part in the invasion of the Dales.

I could not wholly disguise my reluctance as I reached out to touch the Alizonder's tunic. I shunned the hateful

Hound's head badge on the right breast, and forced myself to finger his House badge on the left, a finely embroidered patch of three blue darts worked in a triangular array against a white background. The instant resulting pressure of mental images made me recoil, breaking contact. I took a deep breath, braced one hand on a paving stone, and grasped his baronial chain in my other hand.

I shut my eyes, stricken by clamoring images. It was as if I were personally viewing a great torch-lit assembly of Alizonders. I *knew* it was the recent New Year's Presentation of Whelps, and the horrifying figure who seemed to have a hound's head was actually the Lord Baron Norandor, wearing a ceremonial mask. Another richly dressed baron arose from his knees before the Lord Baron's throne . . . his name came to me, Gurborian. When he drew back and turned, I was jolted to behold my betrothal jewel suspended from his neck chain! I must have swooned at that point, for I was next aware of a flask of wine being pressed to my lips, and Jonja's voice calling my name.

I gestured for my hand slate. Jonja read the words aloud as swiftly as I could write them. "I have just seen my betrothal jewel being worn by an Alizonder baron at their New Year's Assembly. He is the Baron Gurborian of the Line Sired by Reptur, murderer of this man's father, and his archenemy."

Duratan's exclamation was lost in the general astonished babble. I remained seated on the stone floor, trembling from its physical chill as well as my sensing experience. Previously, my visions of lost articles or places to search for them had come to me in fragmentary dreams. I could not recall so vivid and coherent an impression as this, and certainly never before while I was awake.

Ouen began to speak, but Jonja interrupted. "Look!" she said sharply. "Our uninvited visitor is stirring."

"And feeling for his weapons," Duratan observed. "He will be disappointed to find them missing."

I reached for my staff, and with Jonja's assistance, rose to my feet. I did not want to be at a disadvantage to any Alizonder, whether he was armed or disarmed.

CHAPTER 6

Kasarian—his account requested for Lormt's archives, following his sudden transport to Lormt (7th Day, Moon of the Knife/Month of the Ice Dragon)

Muffled voices intruded into the darkness enfolding me . . . I could hear people talking, but their words were unintelligible. As I became increasingly aware, I struggled to move my limbs. Hard, cold . . . stone beneath me—why should I be lying on a stone floor? My left hand was empty—where was my dagger? I felt for my throwing knives, but my belt loops were stripped bare of all weapons. Worse still, the elder's key was no longer in my right hand. Had I been robbed as well as disarmed? I strove to deal with a daunting rush to memories. I had stepped through that eldritch oval of light deep beneath Krevonel Castle, and by some foul magic, I had evidently been spirited elsewhere. Estcarpian enemies—just before the darkness had claimed me, I had seen Estcarpians.

I opened my eyes, and sat up cautiously to survey my situation. I was indeed outnumbered by foes, but so far, they had only disarmed me, not actively attacked me— nor had they stolen my baron's chain or belt wallet. As soon as I moved, they had stopped speaking. The five of us sat—or stood—in silence, peering tensely at one another. I wondered if more enemies could be lurking beyond the flickering, limited lantern light. The portal through which I had come had disappeared, depriving us of its additional illumination.

This chamber was vast—distant walls and ceilings receded into impenetrable darkness. Unsettling as my surroundings were, I was more immediately concerned with the presence of my adversaries. The four figures before me were formidable: two males of Estcarp's witchly Old Race, one Old Race female garbed like the spell-casting hags of the Dales, and one other startling female. For a heart-stopping instant, due to her properly white hair, pale eyes, and fair skin, I almost mistook her for an Alizonder, but her obvious comradeship with these Witch folk and her inappropriate stance quickly altered my opinion. She was grasping a sturdy staff as if she knew how to wield it; quite impossible for an Alizonder female. When I stood up to attain a better vantage, she was the closest to me. Her hands betrayed her advanced age. Why should an elderly female, clearly not an Estcarpian, join in company with Old Race fighters and a spell-casting hag?

Although he bore no sword, the old male appeared to be the sire of the group. He gestured toward some wooden benches nearby, and said in slowly, carefully-pronounced Estcarpian, "Let us sit down and talk together peacefully."

It had been some time since I had heard the enemy's speech. A few of my fellow barons with scholarly talents had learned the rudiments of Estcarpian in order to be able to question the rare live prisoners that we seized within our borders, but I had not participated in an interrogation for several years. I judged it prudent at this point to conceal my understanding until I had a better assessment of my position. I therefore feigned ignorance of his words, and countered in Alizonian, "May I be told where I am and who you are?"

The younger male held a serviceable knife in his right hand, but he did not flourish it. His easy familiarity with the weapon and his erect bearing suggested soldierly experience. Furthermore, he limped when he moved, as if maimed from an injury to his left leg. As soon as I spoke, he faced the old male, and said impatiently, "Surely Morfew has been roused by now! As you predicted, we do require his skill with Alizonian speech."

Morfew—the name almost caused me to betray myself, but I disguised my reaction by taking a step to one side. There had once been a certain noble Line in Alizon, before my sire's Presentation. I had seen its breeding lists among the baronial records, and the males' names took that form. I was searching my memory for the name of the Line Sire when a spark of light pricked the distant darkness.

As the light grew closer, I could see two slowly moving figures. An Old Race female led the way, carrying the lantern, which disclosed a garish birth stain across her face. I suppressed a shudder. We of Alizon do not allow deformed whelps to live. Far better for each Line to breed only the strong and the fit. The female stretched back her free hand to steady a thin, elderly man with long white hair. Surely, I thought, he could not be an Alizonder . . . but when he sat down on a bench near to me, he peered at me with pale blue eyes and addressed me in halting Alizonian.

"You have nothing to fear in this place, young man," he said. "We intend you no harm. I am Morfew. . . ."

"Not of the Line Sired by Ternak!" I interrupted him, for the name had come to my mind.

He blinked at me, rather like an owl disturbed from its daytime slumber. "My sire was bred of that Line, yes," he replied, "but it has been sixty years since I have received any word of our pack. You will excuse my rough speech—I am the sole Alizonder resident here, so my tongue's facility has declined from lack of practice."

"I must relate hard news of your Line from a time before my whelping," I said. "The Line Sired by Ternak has been considered dead these many years since the last known males perished in the blood feud."

Morfew grasped the edge of the bench, his face drained of all color. "Blood feud. . . ." he whispered, then shook his head as if to clear it. "Wait. Matters concerning my pack can be discussed later. I must convey your words to my friends. This man knows my family," he told the others in Estcarpian. "He bears ill tidings from long ago; they have been destroyed."

"I sorrow that you must receive such dire word from the past," the Old Race sire responded, "yet we need to know now who this man is and for what purpose he has come here."

Morfew bowed his head for a moment, then stared straight at me. "You wear a baron's chain," he noted. "Who sired your Line? Why have you come to us?"

I thought quickly. All the extensive Ternak lands had been seized by the Lord Baron of that day. Half had been awarded to the survivors of the blood feud, but it could be possible that this old baron might mount a valid claim for his land rights. It was advisable to speak him fair. I saluted him properly, touching first my Hound badge, then my Line badge. "I hail you, Morfew, revealed restored Baron of the Line Sired by Ternak. I am Kasarian, of the Line Sired by Krevonel. I know not how I come to stand before you in this strange place. I stepped through a curious portal in Alizon, and must assume that I have been delivered here by magic. Is this place near to our common border?"

Morfew held up a restraining hand. "You have indeed been transported a great distance, young man. These vaults lie beneath the citadel of Lormt, far to Alizon's south."

I could not believe him. I had of course heard of Lormt. In Alizon, it was dismissed as an isolated Estcarpian castle not worth assaulting, a distant gathering place for useless, doddering scholars who scrabbled among dusty writings. Even Estcarp's Witches scorned the old males who laired at Lormt. I had certainly never expected to travel thither.

The soldierly Estcarpian sheathed his knife and stooped to pick up a lantern. "Can we not find a more comfortable place than this for our conversation?" he asked the old sire.

Morfew rose slowly from his bench. "By all means," he agreed fervently. "My bones do not find these cellars hospitable." Turning to me, he added in Alizonian, "Come along, young man. Let us seek a warmer, *softer* place to sit and talk."

I noticed that they arranged for me to walk in their midst, for the spell-casting hag beckoned for me to follow her, and the soldierly male walked closely behind me.

As we picked our way around and over cracked and displaced stonework, I wondered what catastrophe had befallen this place. The massive blocks and style of the joinery implied an enormous edifice above us, perhaps as old as my own castle. We passed through winding corridors and up many stairs, then suddenly an icy wind gushed through an outer door as we emerged onto the snow-covered stones of a night-shadowed courtyard.

Never had I beheld such a space enclosed by towered walls. Moonlight reflected on the snow revealed severe damage to parts of the rectangular enclosure. Teeth chattering in the chill, I clasped my arms tightly across my chest and glanced upward. I halted so abruptly that the soldier following behind collided with me. "The stars!" I exclaimed, jarred into speech. "Beyond the walls— mountains!"

Morfew touched my arm, evidently for reassurance. "This *is* Lormt," he said. "The skies here are somewhat different from those above Alizon City, and we are truly tucked away among the high peaks. At least we have our cloaks to shield us from the wind. Hurry along—we have not much farther to go to reach a sheltered fire-side."

A tall stone building reared before us, and the spell hag plunged into a recessed doorway at its base. We climbed yet more stairs, then the hag opened a heavy door into a snug study lined with scroll-stacked shelves. Kneeling by the hearth, she coaxed a fire from coals banked for the night.

Morfew settled himself on a cushioned chair at the head of a long table, and offered me the chair to his left. The soldier withdrew briefly, then returned with a tray of pewter goblets and a flask of ale, which he poured into a pannikin to warm over the fire. I let the others sip their brew before I tasted my portion. I had noticed that the goblet I chose was empty before the pouring; it seemed unlikely that they would try to poison me at this juncture. Morfew must have observed my brief hesitation, for he smiled and said, "We keep no poisons here, only old documents."

The soldier drew a leather bag from his belt and spilled from it a scattering of crystals upon the table surface. At the same time, the spell hag placed in front of her a carved wooden board ornamented with red, black, and gold markings.

I felt the hair rise on the back of my neck. Was I to be subjected to Estcarpian magic? "Morfew," I demanded, "What means this display?"

"Do not be disturbed," he replied in a soothing tone. "My friends are merely testing whether any Power of the Dark presently threatens us." Morfew repeated his remark in Estcarpian.

The soldier frowned as he scooped up his crystals and tossed them a second time. "I see no taint of the Dark about him," he said, glancing dubiously at me. "There are, however, strong indications of pending danger."

"My rune-board confirms your crystals," said the spell hag, as she returned the wooden strip to her belt fastening.

Stung by their remarks, I held my tongue until Morfew had repeated their words in Alizonian, then I asserted, "My Line has ever rejected any resort to magework. What taint of the Dark do you have reason to associate with me?"

I paused, struck by a tantalizing thought. Could it be possible that these folk might oppose Gurborian's plotting? If they reviled Dark magic, would they not despise any Escorian alliance proposed by Alizon? I decided to take a calculated risk. "How stand you anent any traffic with the Dark Ones of Escore?" I inquired. "In my studies of ancient lore, I have read that Estcarp once warred mightily with those from the east, but we have heard

naught further in Alizon for many years. Is there still enmity between Estcarp's rulers and Escore's mages?"

Morfew seemed intrigued. "What a curious question,"
he observed. After he had relayed my words to the others, he resumed in Alizonian. "As I try to recall how
matters were viewed in Alizon, my counter question to
you would be, 'Why do you ask that? On which side
does your interest lie?' But pray contain your reply for a
moment, for I perceive an opportunity to explain to you
our somewhat different ways of thinking here at Lormt.
More than fifty years ago, I was prevented from pursuing knowledge in Alizon, so I journeyed here, where all
scholars are welcome to reside.

"You must understand, young man, that Lormt has no
rulers like Alizon's Lord Baron and his Baronial Council. As a community of scholars, our sole purpose is to
seek and organize lost lore from the past. The Council of
Estcarp's Witches scorns us for our predominant maleness, but tends chiefly to ignore us. We thus rarely affect
one another—still, two years ago we suffered from their
great Turning of the land, which caused the damage you
observed to our walls and foundations. For our part, we
prefer to be left undisturbed, each of us working as he
chooses.

"As for Escore," Morfew continued, "we have had
scant word of it until relatively recent years, when some
of the Old Race have ventured there. Puissant powers
still abide in that land, some pledging homage to the
Light, but others serving the Dark. I am certain that I
speak for Ouen, our chief scholar (he gestured at the old
sire), when I say that Lormt stands firmly for the Light."

The others around the table hearkened closely to his
translation, their expressions grave.

"But would you fight against Escore's Dark mages?" I persisted. "Would you defend this place against them?"

Appearing alarmed, Morfew repeated my questions. The soldierly Estcarpian frowned at me, and snapped, "Do you warn us or threaten us?"

A sudden loud thump made us all start in our chairs. The white-haired old female had pounded her staff on the floor. She appeared to be unable to speak—yet another maimed foe!—since she scribbled on a slate and handed it to the old sire so that he could voice her message. "Enough questions," he read aloud. "Answers must now be offered."

CHAPTER 7

Mereth—events at Lormt
(early 7th Day, Month of
the Ice Dragon/
Moon of the Knife)

As we plodded back toward Lormt's upper levels, I labored under a double burden: the physical exertion of retracing our way through all those corridors and staircases, added to the internal exertion of controlling my seething feelings. I could scarcely suppress my sense of dread and revulsion at being within actual touching distance of an Alizonder.

It was true that Morfew was also of that cursed race, but from the moment I had met him, I discerned that his spirit was distinctly different from those of his rapacious countrymen. Like Dame Gwersa, Morfew was a true scholar. In recent years, he had been immersed in kinship studies. A quantity of documents had been sent to Lormt from the collection of Ostbor, an elderly Estcarpian famed for his kinship knowledge, who had died some months before the Turning. The lady Nolar had been Ostbor's student, Morfew told me, and upon her settling at Lormt, she had assisted him greatly in bringing some order to her former master's scrolls. Vast quantities of additional kinship records had been disclosed when Lormt's hidden cellars were revealed by the Turning. I had just begun to work with Morfew and Nolar on that section of Lormt's archives dealing with the Dales when this genuinely threatening Alizonder shattered our peace.

I told myself that this young Alizonder baron could have been no more than a child at the time of the invasion. It was unreasonable of me to hold Kasarian personally responsible for the injuries that I and other Dalesfolk had suffered . . . and yet he was an Alizonder baron, and thus represented our direst foes. Countering my aversion was my burning curiosity. He *had* to know something about my betrothal jewel, for it was by his remembered vision that I had seen it worn by his family's enemy. I realized that I would have to curb my natural loathing and seek to learn more from Kasarian of Krevonel . . . if he, in turn, would deign to talk to me.

We settled ourselves at last in Ouen's study, where Duratan served us a most welcome measure of warmed ale. Kasarian markedly refrained from tasting his share until after we had sampled ours.

Duratan's and Jonja's employment of their magical foreseeing tools evoked a forceful rejection by Kasarian for any form of what he branded "magework." After a pause to deliberate, he pressed us to state whether Lormt would defend itself against the Dark mages, who were rumored to hold parts of Escore, the magic-haunted land beyond the mountains bordering Estcarp to the east.

When Duratan sharply demanded whether the baron was warning us or threatening us, I judged that it was time to interrupt before anger—however well-justified—flared into actual violence. I thumped my staff on the floor, and was gratified when all eyes immediately focused on me. Ouen read aloud my message: "Enough questions. Answers must be offered."

An impish smile brightened Morfew's face. "Dear lady," he began, "how helpful of you to direct us to an essential point. Each side in this discussion possesses information desired by the other. Young man . . ." Morfew peered keenly at the Alizonder and asked in Estcarpian, "Am I not correct in believing that you can understand most of what we say? The time required for our exchanges could be halved if I did not have to repeat every statement in both tongues."

The Alizonder smiled—an unpleasant grimace, disclosing his hound-sharp teeth. "You said your Alizonian was slack from disuse," he responded in halting but intelligible Estcarpian. "I also find my Estcarpian similarly rust-bound. If you would speak slowly and assist me as needed. . . ."

"I thought as much," said Morfew. "Let us try, then, to be as simple and clear as we can, for all our sakes. Since you have given us your name, you should know the names of my colleagues. This is Ouen, our chief scholar, as I just mentioned. Next to him is Duratan, a former Borderer and now our able chronicler; his lady wife Nolar, healer and scholar; Jonja, our resident Wise Woman; and Mereth, who has recently voyaged here from the Dales to pursue kinship queries."

The Alizonder gazed intently at each of us in turn, then made a graceful gesture, touching his House badge. "I am honored to speak in such a company," he said.

"These are troubling questions about Escore," mused Ouen. "Morfew, did you not some time ago examine our archives seeking information concerning Escore?"

"So I did, Master Ouen." The old scholar rubbed his

hands together, a habit he indulged, I had noticed, whenever he saw an opportunity to share the fruits of his inquiries. "Kemoc Tregarth came here five years ago to search for lore about the east. In assisting him, I discovered that a thousand years before, the virulent Dark forces in Escore overpowered those of the Light. As they fled for their lives, the remnant of the Light's forces worked a great magic spell to raise a wall of mountains to impede all further access to Escore. At the same time, they set a block in the minds of the Old Race to prevent any thought of the eastern direction. From those displaced Old Race folk arose the Witches of Estcarp. Only since the recent Turning of the earth—a Second Turning, one might say—has the Old Race again become able to think of or indeed travel to the east."

Morfew paused to reflect, then resumed, "I can recall only one incident regarding encounters with Escorian mages in Estcarp. Immediately after the Turning, when traveling far to the southwest, Nolar was captured by a Dark mage released by those very earthquakes from a binding spell set upon him at the time of the First Turning. Fortunately, that single, dangerous echo from ancient Escore was banished by the assistance of a Witch and certain localized powers. Your questions, however, imply some present threat. Do you bring us warning of evil stirring even now in Escore?"

Kasarian had listened intently, sitting motionless except for the fingers of his right hand, which rhythmically turned his gold signet ring. When Morfew posed his question, Kasarian spread both hands flat on the table. His fingers were long and supple, and I had observed from walking behind him how quickly and surely he moved. I suspected he would be a deadly opponent with sword or knife.

"I can tell you no names of Escore's mages," he admitted frankly, "but I have reason to believe that intense efforts are being made by a certain faction in Alizon to forge an alliance with such Dark forces. The roots of this treason stretch back to the time of the Kolder's initial meddling. The alliance that Lord Baron Facellian formed with the Kolder over twenty years ago was a disaster for Alizon. The Kolder sought dominion over the Dales, but contrived to spend our fighters' blood to obtain their desire. After inciting us to invade the Dales, they then abandoned us, failing to supply the vital aid they had promised. Well before the last of our invading Hounds were stranded across the sea and wiped out, it was apparent that the war was lost. Lords Baron of Alizon do not lose wars and survive. Mallandor took the throne. . . ."

Kasarian broke off to refresh himself with more ale. My thoughts were clamoring—it was as well that I had no voice, or I would have screamed at him. I clutched my staff until my knuckles ached. That he should dismiss so coolly the torment that Alizon had inflicted upon our Dales! And yet . . . I had never before considered how Alizon must have reacted when their Kolder alliance had failed them so miserably. With their fighting ships and trade ships, the blessed Sulcar had harried Alizon's coast, and intercepted the Alizonders' ships, thus contributing to the Kolder's inability to supply the invaders. Suddenly, I could understand why Alizon's version of those frantic years would require excuses as well as revenge for what they had to view as a sure victory snatched away from them. When Kasarian resumed his tale, I forced my fingers to relax their grip on my staff.

"There remained yet a few of the cursed Kolder in Alizon City," Kasarian continued. "They bided their time, strengthening their ties with certain of our barons, and attempting to gain access to Lord Baron Mallandor's ear. Three years ago, the faction favoring the Kolder persuaded Mallandor that an energetic effort must be made to bring new Kolder forces to Alizon by means of a Gate to be opened by magic. It was proposed that unguarded Witch pups could be brought from Estcarp to provide the Power needed for the Kolder's Gate spell."

Jonja seized her goblet so fiercely that I feared she would snap its stem. "We were told of that horrid raid," she said, her voice shaking. "It was an evil affront to all of Estcarp."

Kasarian nodded calmly. "I was opposed to the tactic from its first suggestion," he said. "The ill-advised ploy failed disastrously, as I had suspected it would, leaving all of the Kolder dead. The Witchlings escaped, fleeing back into Estcarp. Another faction, headed by Baron Gurborian, then argued that Alizon should forget the Kolder and employ a bold new strategy. Gurborian's chief henchman, Gratch from blighted Gorm, suggested that we could sweep away our enemies with assistance from other and closer sources. Through inquiries, he had identified certain lower-level mages in the mountains between Alizon and Escore. Gurborian endorsed Gratch's plan to seek a linkage with the Dark forces still to be found in Escore. With the might of Escore's Dark mages employed on Alizon's behalf, he asserted that Alizon could occupy all of the lands west of the mountains—Estcarp, Karsten, as far south as we cared to extend."

"And just what would these Dark mages of Escore gain from such an alliance with Alizon?" asked Morfew, his hands clenched into fists.

"They would, of course, be proclaimed fully sovereign in all lands east of the mountains," Kasarian replied.

Ouen emitted a muffled snort. "Presumably they already consider themselves sovereign in those areas they control," he stated. "Other folk also share those lands to the east. I cannot believe that the Dark mages tremble for fear that their scattered fiefdoms are at any risk from western invasion across the mountains. As you describe Gurborian's plan, the Dark mages would gain only a gilding of words upon the already existing order of rule."

"Yet I perceive one factor to bear in mind," Morfew observed thoughtfully. "Such an alliance for Escore, should it result in the destruction of Estcarp, could be seen as a gratifying, if overly long-delayed revenge of sorts upon the Old Race for the ancient affront of the First Turning."

I had been watching Duratan, whose stern expression had grown more severe throughout the discussion. "Let us consider another question for a moment," he said in a disarmingly mild tone. "Why should a baron of Alizon openly disclose this previously unsuspected threat to Estcarp? Surely Alizon would rejoice in Estcarp's fall, not choose to warn us in advance of any dire peril."

Each one of us around the table regarded Kasarian warily as we awaited his explanation.

CHAPTER 8

Kasarian—events at Lormt
(7th Day, Moon of the Knife
/Month of the Ice Dragon)

I found this confrontation with enemies who might possibly be manipulated into temporarily useful allies to be as exhilarating as a hunt at full gallop after the split-tusked boar . . . yet I was keenly aware that I was treading upon a sword's edge. Constant vigilance was imperative, even if the enemy of one's enemy did necessarily share some common aims. The interests of one's Line and of Alizon itself had always to be foremost in crafting any would-be alliance.

I reasoned that these scholars at Lormt might well possess information about Escore that I could use to counter Gurborian's efforts. It would not be advisable, however, to reveal to them that Gurborian was plotting to overthrow Lord Baron Norandor. That was purely an internal Alizonian matter, potentially hurtful should Alizon's enemies learn of it prematurely, and turn it to their advantage.

I therefore chose my words with extreme care, emphasizing the potential danger to Estcarp should Gurborian's faction forge an alignment with Escore's Dark mages. The Lormt folk swiftly grasped the implications, I thought, but Duratan, their soldier, inquired why I, a presumed enemy, should warn them in advance? It was a clever question, doubtless intended to expose my motives. Fortunately, I had a ready answer, doubly impressive because it was both plausible and true.

"If Alizon must fight for territory," I told him, "it should be with our own strength. Alizon's barons who hold to the methods proved successful in the past have always shunned magic, whether it was wielded by Escorians or Kolder. I assure you that the Line Sired by Krevonel has consistently opposed any reliance upon magic. This notion of Gurborian's that Estcarp's Witch magic can be defeated by Escore's Dark magic is yet another false idea, worse even than our previous recourse to the Kolder's magic. What benefits did Alizon ever gain from the Kolder? My three elder littermates were all slain in the war with the Dales. Alizon gained nothing from that Kolder-inspired slaughter except some few baubles wrested from the Dales at a deplorable cost, and rivalries among the survivors for inherited baronies."

Another volley of thumps from the old female's staff interrupted me. She wrote furiously on her slate, and pushed it across the table to Morfew. "You say some baubles were taken from the Dales," Morfew read aloud. "Have you ever seen or heard of one particular jewel—an egg-sized, blue-gray stone set as a pendant on a silver chain?"

Bemused, yet startled, I thought that they could refer to only the one such stone. "Baron Gurborian was awarded a jewel of that description," I replied cautiously. "It had been sent back from the Dales early in the invasion, and was considered to be one of the few prime treasures of the campaign."

Although the Lormt folk's expressions were guarded, I could see that they were keenly interested. Why should they care about old booty from the Dales . . . unless the mute female might assert some property claim?

She retrieved her slate and wrote a further message. "That pendant belonged to my family," Morfew read aloud. "I have reason to believe that the stone may be an object of Power. Is Baron Gurborian aware of the nature of his prize?"

I was taken aback. The only stones of Power known to us were those cursed jewels wielded by Estcarp's Witches. If Gurborian's stone was concerned with magic, that would explain the peculiar weakness that afflicted me during and after the Baronial Assembly, when I had been in the same chamber with it . . . possibly even the dreams that assailed me later that same night. But Gurborian appeared totally unaffected, and he had been wearing the frightful object.

"No," I told them honestly, "I do not think that Gurborian at all suspects that he possesses more than a mere jewel. We of Alizon are not . . . familiar with magical objects, and would not likely recognize that aspect unless it was revealed to us."

Morfew stirred uneasily in his chair. "If Baron Gurborian should meet with any Escorian mages while wearing the pendant," he fretted, "they would immediately sense the true nature of the stone."

I slapped my hand on the table to emphasize my words. "All the greater cause," I asserted, "to prevent Gurborian and his faction from arranging any such meeting. I do not know how this particular stone of Power might be wielded, but surely it would be vastly more perilous in the hands of Dark mages. I confide to you now my deepest fear, rendered more harrowing by this word anent Gurborian's jewel: once the Dark mages of Escore have been enticed to cross the mountains, will they choose to retire voluntarily again behind that barrier as before? What shall Alizon do if Escore's magic crushes Estcarp and is then directed against us?" The Lormt folk made no immediate comment, but I detected evidence of dismay in their frozen demeanor.

"I have heard this place called 'Lormt of the Foolish Scholars,' " I persisted, "yet now that I behold you, I see no fools among you. It may be that lore preserved here could help me frustrate Gurborian's efforts. Your land and mine have long considered one another enemies, yet I say to you, both Estcarp and Alizon must now beware of what may fall upon us from the east. Can we not work together to resist this threat? Will you help me search your archives for lore I can use against Gurborian?"

Although I had disturbed them, the Lormt folk showed commendable restraint. I had wondered whether the two females might cower or weep, but both preserved outward calm.

The old sire, Ouen, rose to his feet, and I also stood, along with the others. "You have given us many grave matters to ponder," Ouen said to me. "Your questions are too vital to be answered in haste. Let us all retire now to think, and to sleep. We shall confer again on the morrow."

The Wise Woman motioned brusquely toward the door. "I shall conduct you to a guest chamber nearby," she said.

As I followed her, I noticed that the party remained standing. No doubt they intended to talk further after I had departed. I was not offended, for I should have done the same had we been in Alizon, our roles reversed. I turned at the door. "You honor me with your courteous attentions," I said. "May these night hours bring us wisdom."

To my surprise, Morfew smiled. "I have not heard that admonition since I was a pup!" he exclaimed, then he shook his head, his somber air restored. "I hope on the morrow, Kasarian, that we may have time to discuss those past events concerning my pack. It has been an equally long time," he added, "since I have heard the words 'blood feud.' "

I bowed, and touched my Line badge to him. The Wise Woman closed the door behind us.

CHAPTER 9

Mereth—events at Lormt
(7th Day, Month of
the Ice Dragon Moon of the Knife)

When Ouen bade us to retire, I struggled to my feet, my mind reeling. The thought that my betrothal jewel might be within the grasp of Escore's Dark mages somehow chilled the very marrow of my bones. I felt almost as if Kasarian had slapped my face instead of the table when he exhorted us to prevent Gurborian from meeting with the Escorian mages. I *knew* within myself that we could spare no effort to thwart Gurborian and his henchman; the stone must *not* be lost to the Dark! I had remained standing, heedless of the quiet talk among the others at the table. Nolar took my arm and urged me to sit down.

Quite soon, Jonja returned, announcing that Kasarian was settled in his guest chamber.

Duratan shook his head ruefully. "I seldom feel that Lormt lacks proper accommodations for any guest," he said, "but this night, I would prefer a strong lock on our visiting baron's door, and its key in my hand."

"If Kasarian attempts to skulk about in the dark," Nolar commented with a smile, "he is more likely to fall down the stairs or become irretrievably lost."

"I did warn him about the stairs," said Jonja briskly. "And I made sure his candle was a short one. I do not think he will go far this night."

"Nor shall we." Ouen's tone was grim. "Let us confer briefly before we part. What are we to make of Kasarian's unsettling warnings?"

Duratan stared into his goblet. "How can we dare to believe anything we are told by a baron of Alizon?" he asked. "Their words are notoriously untrustworthy, and they frequently poison their own family members to advance their positions."

I tapped my staff on the floor, and offered my slate. Morfew read aloud my words. "You are wise to be wary. We of the Dales have endured bitter experience of the Alizonders. They are a cruel, devious, and treacherous folk . . . yet we must scrutinize every word of Kasarian's to determine which if any of them might be true. The threat he describes is too serious to be ignored."

Morfew drummed his fingers on the table. "I have been casting my thoughts far back to my days in Alizon," he said. "Some of the noble Lines have preserved more of what you Estcarpians would term a sense of honor than have others. As I recall, Krevonel was one such Line, although much reduced in numbers over the years by battle deaths and murders. I can speak only of the previous generations—this Kasarian is unknown to me, nor do I know his sire's name as yet, but I shall ask him on the morrow when we speak together."

Ouen nodded his approval. "We are indeed fortunate, old friend, that you reside among us. Kasarian may well tell you more privately than he is willing to disclose in our presence."

"He may already have said too much to us," Duratan suggested. "His great fear that Escore's Dark mages, triumphant over Estcarp, might then turn to rend Alizon represents only one of the possible outcomes of a great clash of magics. We would do well to foresee and evaluate a different outcome: if Escore's Dark mages and our Witches should battle to mutual ruin, would not Alizon then be left to capture and hold all three lands?"

"From my knowledge of Alizon," said Morfew, "I perceive another related point. It is likely that Kasarian also belongs to a faction of barons. Just as Gurborian's faction is said to be pressing for an alliance with Escore's Dark mages, so too may Kasarian's faction be waiting to take advantage of any mistakes or reverses. Their goal may be the very seizure of any lands left vulnerable should the primary opponents dispose of one another."

I handed my slate to Morfew. "I do not believe," he read my words, "that Estcarp can dismiss Kasarian's warning, however suspect he may be as its bearer. I must convey to you my intense conviction that the stone of Power must *not* be acquired by any forces serving the Dark!"

Both Jonja and Nolar leaned forward. The Wise Woman spoke first, her voice strained. "I know what mighty deeds can be wrought with Witch Jewels," she said. "An unknown crystal of the size you describe, should it be imbued with Power, might be capable of loosing ruin on a scale that would make the damage of the Turning seem insignificant."

"It is true," Nolar declared, "that some stones of Power can be misused for ill. The Stone of Konnard was meant to aid in healing, yet the Escorian Dark mage Tull twisted its force to produce hideous results." She broke off for a moment, unable to continue. Duratan took her hand without a word. She smiled gratefully at him. "My memories of that awful time still revive past hurts. We learned then that a Dark mage could wrest vileness from an otherwise beneficial object. Had not our Witch stood forth with her jewel, great lasting evil would have been done. As it was, Tull was destroyed, and his effect upon the Stone of Konnard was totally expunged." Nolar looked at me. "If your jewel had been wielded by forces of the Light," she said earnestly, "then it would likely resist being subverted. Certainly, you were not tainted by your association with it, or the crystals and runeboard would have discerned it."

"But a Dark mage with sufficient Power might also be able to corrupt such a stone," Ouen warned. "I believe that we must endorse Kasarian's proposal to thwart Gurborian's alliance with Escore's Dark mages."

"How can we in Lormt possibly affect the maneuverings of a primary baron in Alizon?" demanded Duratan.

I passed my slate back to Morfew, who read for me, "Should there be sufficient lore in your archives concerning Escore's Dark mages, perhaps we could use such in crafting a plan."

As Morfew returned my slate, he observed, "Kasarian has to be our source for current knowledge about affairs in Alizon. My task is to search the archives anent Escore, and I intend to begin at first light . . . or possibly a few hours later."

When Ouen again stood up to dismiss us, his tone was decisive. "We must be alert and probe for Kasarian's true motives. Morfew, we rely upon you to draw him out as best you can. We shall meet here on the morrow and devise a joint plan. For the sake of Lormt—for the sake of Estcarp, we must determine how to meet this challenge. May we be guided by the Light!"

CHAPTER 10

As soon as the Wise Woman withdrew from my guest chamber, I stepped quietly to the door to listen. I could not believe the absence of any lock—the door had a simple latch to hold it shut, but no lock, no key, no means to bar it from without or within. My initial reaction was scorn that Lormt's security should be so woefully lacking . . . then I was struck by a colder, second thought. In a place inhabited by Witchfolk, locks would be unnecessary. The Estcarpians' cursed Witch powers would allow them to set binding spells on any enemies (such as I) within their walls. I snatched back my hand from the door and retreated to sit upon the narrow bed. The Witchfolk might also be able to spy upon me unnaturally, so I must be constantly circumspect. After blowing out the single candle left on a shelf beside the bed, I unbuckled my weaponless belt, removed my boots, and lay down.

I did not think that my thoughts could be discerned without my being aware of such ensorcellment. Silent meditation in the dark, I reasoned, should be safe from observation or intrusion. I reviewed my impressions of my potential allies in order to appraise my chances of influencing their decisions, as well as to assess the dangers each posed to me.

Their soldier Duratan had not troubled to conceal his animosity toward me. I respected his fighting experience, but could not immediately judge the significance of his crystal tossing. Morfew had declared its purpose was to detect any taint by the Dark. How much more information could the peculiar exercise provide? Estcarp's Witches were always female; males were not supposed to possess magical powers. The sole exception known to us in Alizon was the terrible Simon Tregarth, who was said to have come through a Gate from elsewhere. His three whelps bred by a Witch of Estcarp were also magic-wielders of sorts, although fragmentary accounts that reached Alizon held that the female of the three had fled from Witch training, by the aid of her littermates. Alizon preferred to have no dealings with the Tregarth pack, their sire and dam having severely interfered with our aims in the war with the Dales. I resolved to learn more from Morfew concerning the nature and extent of this Duratan's magical talents.

I next considered Duratan's mate, the disfigured Nolar. Was she a true Witch? She admitted accompanying a Witch on the southwesterly journey that had brought about the destruction of a Dark mage. That was daunting news . . . yet I had to smile, lying there in the darkness. What would Gurborian say if he knew that one or more Witches had already vanquished a Dark mage from ancient Escore? My ironic amusement was short-lived. If this Nolar was a Witch of such puissance, I must be doubly wary of her.

I was suspicious as well of the Wise Woman. Although

such females lacked the raw Power of Witches, they nevertheless wielded certain noxious magics. Wise Women in the Dales had several times during the war induced our captured Hounds to babble, to Alizon's sore disadvantage. We had therefore ordered our Hounds to slit the throats of any wounded who might fall into the Wise Women's clutches—thus perished my last littermate.

The third female, the mute Mereth, had come to Lormt from the Dales. I could feel her hatred as plainly as if it were a blazing firebrand—yet she had not openly reviled me in her written messages to the group. I could not understand her appearance. No Dalesfolk had such eyes, skin, or hair. She must possess Alizonder blood, unheard of for a Dales female outside our breeding control. She could not have been whelped in Alizon as a mute, or she would have been killed at once. Perhaps she had been silenced in later years. Might she also be magic-tainted? She unsettled me for too many reasons. I had to learn more about her.

As Lormt's chief scholar, Ouen seemed to be in charge, but Morfew had said there was no ruling council. The others deferred to Ouen as to a sire. Although I could, I thought, dismiss him as a potential fighter, he was of the Old Race and therefore dangerous. In this strange place, he, too, might command Witch powers.

And then there was Morfew. In the past, the Line Sired by Ternak had held influential positions in Alizon. Why would Morfew exile himself far away among enemies? As a noble Alizonder, he had to have deeper motives than the pursuit of powerless learning. Possibly I could gain his confidence to the point that he might disclose to me his true reasons for residing at Lormt.

From his long years at Lormt, Morfew could also enlighten me in the ways of these formidable Estcarpians. It was vital that I persuade them to allow me—indeed, actively assist me in searching Lormt's archives for any hint of Escorian weaknesses.

The lack of available time deeply distressed me. Even now, Gurborian and Gratch were striving to locate Dark mages. My work here at Lormt had to be swiftly productive if I were to have any active chance to hinder them.

A chilling thought occurred to me. Even if I should find useful information at Lormt, how could I return to Alizon in time to apply it? There was also a secondary consideration: would the Estcarpians permit me to leave? Might they not hold me as prisoner or hostage, demanding ransom from my Line? I decided that potential difficulty was less worrisome than my primary predicament. My sole means for presumably immediate travel back to Alizon lay through the terrifying passageway in Lormt's cellar . . . if indeed the magic spell that animated it remained in force. Would the portal beneath Krevonel Castle accept my return, or was its spell set to deliver only from Alizon to Lormt and not in the opposite direction? I could not know until I dared the attempt, provided the Lormt folk would allow me access to their cellar.

I twisted on the bed as I grappled with the many aspects of my plight. At the root of all the questions clamoring for answers lurked a truly gnawing fear. The very existence of an entryway between Estcarp and Krevonel Castle constituted a peril equal to that posed by the Escorian Dark mages. What if a whole troop of Estcarpian warriors—or far worse, a company of Witches—chose to invade Alizon through that portal, assuming that the spell permitted such a transit? In all of Alizon, I was the only one to know of this potentially fatal breach in our closely guarded borders. There was no way to warn the Lord Baron except by personally daring the portal again . . . and what could Alizon do to defend itself? If we sealed off the chamber beneath

Krevonel Castle, might there not be other equally unsuspected horrors poised to open in still other sites?

Apprehensive and frustrated by my crippling lack of sufficient knowledge, I fell into a fitful but dreamless sleep.

Early the next morning, Morfew sent a slightly less elderly scholar (still decrepit to my eyes) to fetch me to him. He directed me across the courtyard to the second, lower stone building near the gates.

Morfew greeted me fairly, and offered simple fare to break our fast—gruel, barley bread, butter, honey, cheese, and ale or cold water to drink.

"I must confess," Morfew confided as he spread butter on a bread crust, "even after all these years at Lormt, I do sometimes miss Alizon's succulent meats." He shut his eyes, and smiled as he recited, "Roast boar, moorhen, haunch of deer, rabbit in pastry . . . ah, well, an old scholar scarcely requires such rich viands. The puddings, though, did linger sweetly on the tongue."

I saw my opportunity to seek answers to some of my jostling questions. "I commend the quality of your honey," I began. "Ours has been bitter of late. Tell me, if you will, why you first came to Lormt, and why you stayed? As one of Ternak's Line, surely, when young, you had firm expectations of advancement?"

Morfew waved his butter knife dismissively. "Although I was an elder whelp," he said with a wry smile, "I was not suited to assume the barony. Kin lists and ancient lore had always interested me far more than hunting or contending with the other whelps for advancement. By great fortune, I chanced to hear of Lormt from a merchant who dealt in scrolls. I set out from Alizon City when I was twenty, and I have never thought of returning. I sought my way to Lormt for nearly ten years, but as soon as I entered these gates, I knew that I had found my true home." His smile faded, and he sighed. "You said last night that my Line had been destroyed in a blood feud. How came that to be?"

"Most of the deaths occurred almost thirty years before I was whelped," I replied. "Our sire related the tale to my elder littermates, who subsequently passed it to me. Shortly before our sire was to be Presented . . ."

"Forgive my interruption," said Morfew. "I recall only some of the famed sires of Krevonel. Which is your sire?"

"I am honored to be sired by Oralian of that Line," I said, touching my Line badge. "I was a fosterling far away from Alizon City when Gurborian ordered my sire's murder. It was over fifty years ago when the blood feud between your Line and the Line Sired by Pagurian reached its climax. As blood feuds go, that one was unusually bitter—I gather that a number of pack alliances had been obstructed by kidnappings and poisonings. Pagurian's forces finally surrounded Ternak's main hunting lodge, and set it afire while its sire was within, Talfew by name. . . ."

"My sire," murmured Morfew, his hands clenched on the scrubbed boards of the table.

"I condole with you," I said formally, "as I must also condole for the two male whelps who were killed in the fire along with Baron Talfew."

Morfew's voice trailed off to a mere whisper. "My only littermates—I had wondered over the years how they had fared."

"You will be gratified to hear that the surviving members of your pack attacked Pagurian's camp. Unfortunately for your Line, they were all killed in the fighting. The Lord Baron of that day decreed that too many of both Lines had died—indeed, no males were thought to be left to Ternak's Line—so he declared the blood feud nullified. He appropriated half of the Ternak lands, and bestowed the other half upon Pagurian's survivors—whose case," I hastened to add, "was persuasive. Most of the ruling baron's hound pack *had* been poisoned, along with his mate, and the linkage to Ternak's official poisoner was clear."

"I remember those of my pack from my early days only," mused Morfew. "Sixty years is a long time to be away. My life is now totally rooted here. The folk of Lormt have become closer to me than those of my own pack ever were."

I was taken aback. "Then you will not present your valid claim for Ternak's lands?" I asked.

Morfew shook his head. "No, young man. I think too much blood has already been shed over that land. I have no interest in it, or in whoever may now hold it. Let it lie where it was bestowed those long years ago. But we have dallied discussing these private pack matters—give me your arm, if you will, and let us hasten to Ouen's study to confer with the others. I must tell you that I have already separated out some of the scrolls I once studied concerning the First Turning. Can you read the ancient scripts of Estcarp?"

"If they differ from what I have mastered," I replied, "I shall apply myself to learn them. Gurborian will not wait for us. He will be progressing with his schemes, and we must stop him."

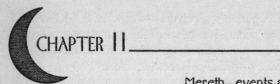

CHAPTER 11 _____

Mereth—events at Lormt
(7th, 8th, & 10th Days,
Month of the Ice Dragon)

During the few remaining hours of that night, I doubt that any of us found ease in sleep. I lay down, but my troubled thoughts denied me rest. Although I was far removed in time and distance from the torments of the Dales' war, I found it still painful to contemplate the necessity of assisting, even working in the same room with an Alizonder baron. Yet if the warning that Kasarian had voiced was true, Estcarp lay in deadly peril. Should Estcarp fall, we of the Dales could not expect the mere expanse of sea alone to shield us, as we had learned to our earlier sorrow.

Kasarian's and the Lormt folk's talk of Dark mages unsettled me. I could contribute no useful lore from the Dales, except to express my intense terror at the notion of such beings. I supposed that I might be of some use in sorting documents, provided that I could read them. My prior acquaintance with old Estcarpian scripts was limited to the small collection of kinship records preserved by Dame Gwersa, together with some few other scrolls I had encountered in my own researches.

My thoughts persisted in returning to my betrothal jewel. That it should even now adorn the chest of a primary baron of Alizon made me clutch my quilts tightly about me to subdue a trembling not wholly provoked by the winter chill. As soon as an opportunity arose, I resolved to query Kasarian about this Baron Gurborian and why he had been awarded my jewel.

At first light, I hastened to the food hall, hoping to encounter Morfew, but he was not there. I ate what was placed before me—it might as well have been boiled wool for all I tasted it—and hurried to Ouen's study.

Ouen opened the door when I tapped with my staff. Nolar, Duratan, and Jonja were already seated at the table. Ouen told me that Morfew had offered to eat with Kasarian before escorting him to join our conference. Morfew had thought it possible that Kasarian might confide in him as a fellow Alizonder, although the old scholar was too honest to hold out much hope on such a brief acquaintance with so wary an adversary.

When Morfew and Kasarian entered the study, we all stood while Ouen pronounced an invocation for guidance from the Light in all of our deliberations. Kasarian appeared bemused, but held his tongue until invited to speak. He immediately requested our decision. Would Lormt allow him to search its archives for, as he phrased it, "weapons of knowledge to be used to deflect Escore's sorcerous dagger raised against us all?"

Ouen gazed at each of us in turn. "I ask you to declare," he invited, "whether you believe that Lormt should open its store of documents to this petitioner. Duratan?"

"I do so believe," Duratan said firmly, "with the stric-

ture that one of us be always present to observe what is
being read."

Nolar nodded. "I agree," she said, "with the proposal
and the stricture."

"As do I." Jonja glared at the Alizonder. "As to the
stricture, I am prepared to serve at any time as one of
Lormt's observers."

I proffered my slate for Jonja to read aloud. "If permitted, I, Mereth, will also serve."

To my surprise, Morfew suddenly chuckled. "What a
grim lot of scholars we appear," he said. "It is true that
the cause for our searching is of the utmost seriousness,
and we must press forward without delay, but consider
the opportunities for discovery! All those previously unknown documents revealed by the Turning—I have been
longing to sort them properly. Now I shall have willing
and able assistants to speed the task. I urge all of you to
join me in the study area near my quarters. I shall instruct the more agile of our helpers to fetch there the materials that we should survey."

And so began our great search of Lormt's archives. To
permit uninterrupted work, Ouen arranged that food and
drink were also brought to us along with the seemingly
unending stream of documents.

During one such brief respite while we were eating, I
queried Kasarian on my slate concerning Baron Gubo-
rian and the jewel, but he feigned to know little about
the matter of the awarding of the pendant. He claimed
that it had been bestowed during the Dales' war, when he
was, as he termed it, "a pup." I did not entirely believe
him, but saw no way to press him at that juncture.

As I had suspected, my skills in interpreting the Estcarpian scripts, especially the ancient ones, were not sufficient to deal with the older documents. Morfew kindly

showed me how to distinguish the writing styles of various periods, with their forms for certain key words, such as "mages" and "Escore," so I could at least assist in the initial winnowing process. Nolar, Duratan, and Jonja were all able scholars, and together with Morfew and Ouen, they sorted through heaps of scrolls, bound leaves of parchment, and fragments. By intense effort, Kasarian appeared to decipher the ancient scripts he had not encountered before, and soon he was proceeding almost as quickly as the Estcarpians. I noticed that Morfew or Ouen were carefully retrieving and examining each document that Kasarian laid aside. At first, Kasarian affected not to see; then he showed his fangs in an Alizonder smile, and simply handed each leaf directly to one of the Lormt folk for their perusal. This continued for a while until Morfew threw up his hands and exclaimed, "We are foolishly wasting valuable time in reading after Kasarian. Either we accept his discernment, or we do not. How say you?"

Duratan frowned, then nodded ruefully. "Our mutual need must outweigh our traditional suspicion. Let him proceed without further oversight. This task before us is too daunting for us to diminish our supply of able readers."

Kasarian wordlessly saluted him, and redoubled his efforts.

We were wearily persisting in our labors two days later when one of Morfew's helpers lurched in bearing a heavy wooden chest blackened by age and dust-snarled cobwebs. He said it had only just been discovered in a remote cellar breached by the Turning. Kasarian peered at the rust-bound hasp, then pried it open handily with a table knife someone had misplaced from our last meal. I happened to be nearby, so I looked inside the chest when he raised its lid.

The top layers of parchment leaves had been damaged by rain or flood. Kasarian lifted them out, disclosing more parchments and several books. As I reached to assist with the emptying, my fingers brushed across a rather small, nondescript leather-bound book. I jerked my hand back instantly—it was as if I had unwittingly stroked a swarm of Anda wasps. Startled, I recalled the similar shock I had felt when I first touched my betrothal jewel.

Kasarian regarded me quizzically, but Nolar rushed to my side. "Have you cut yourself on a splinter, or been bitten by a spider?" she asked, offering to examine my hand.

I shook my head, and wrote on my slate, "I felt a strange sensation when I touched a book in that chest."

Nolar stood quite still while she read aloud my comment. "I, too, have encountered such a wonder here at Lormt," she said, her eyes shining with excitement. "Can you distinguish which book affected you so?"

I deliberately grasped the volume I had dropped back into the chest, and as I did, a surge of mental images nearly overwhelmed me. I fell as much as sat on the nearest bench, striving to retain my senses. Jonja hurried to pour me a restoring cup of wine, while Nolar set a stack of clean parchment before me. Struggling to catch my breath, as if I had run a long distance, I wrote as quickly as I could. All the others crowded closer to hear Nolar read my words.

"We have discovered here," she voiced for me, "the journal belonging to a puissant Escorian mage from that very time a thousand years ago, which Morfew spoke of. I sense the writer's name—Elsenar—and that he possessed the very jewel of such concern to me . . . to us all. It was a stone of great Power. I cannot convey my dread that forces of the Dark now active in our day might seize it for some frightful use."

Jonja had immediately consulted her rune board. Her voice shook with relief when she reported, "There is no taint of the Dark associated with this book. Mage its writer may have been long years ago, but he was of the Light, not the Dark."

"May I see the book?" asked Ouen. He glanced at first one page, then another, and frowned. "Morfew—what do you make of this peculiar script?"

Morfew gazed over Ouen's shoulder. "I regret to say—could you turn that page? Yes, it is quite clear to me that I cannot decipher a word. The hand may be fairly written, but it is in no script known to me."

Nolar and Duratan jointly examined the book, then Jonja, and lastly Kasarian, but none of them could read it. Not being within reach of my staff, I thumped the table with my hand. Ouen handed me the book, its lines of neat script arrayed across the pages, completely unreadable. . . .

I shut my eyes for a moment, and then looked a second time. My hand trembled as I retrieved my message parchment. "I, too, cannot read this script," I wrote for Nolar to read aloud, "but perhaps because of my gift of touch, I can sense in my mind the meaning of these writings. I believe that I can transcribe all that is written here. Pray fetch me more ink and a brighter lamp. I shall begin at once."

At some time, the initial pages of Elsenar's journal had been infuriatingly water-blurred, but when I turned to the first undamaged leaf, the substance of the ancient mage's account was instantly clear to me. As I completed copying each sheet of parchment, Morfew softly read it aloud to the others while I continued to write.

When I glanced up occasionally, pausing to flex my fingers, I could see that the entire Lormt company shared my feelings of excitement mingled with alarm. After more than a thousand years, we were doubtless the first in Estcarp to learn when and whence Alizon had been settled. Kasarian sat rigidly in a high-backed chair, his jaw muscles tight-clenched, his only movement the turning of his signet ring. It seemed to me that when Nolar had read out the name "Elsenar," Kasarian had reacted to it instantly. The general illumination in Morfew's study chamber could scarcely be termed bright, but I vow that the Alizonder paled visibly. Being so fair of skin, he could blanch only slightly, but I do not think my eyes deceived me. He *knew* the name of that ancient mage, and whatever else he knew concerning Elsenar, the knowledge must have been daunting. I wondered whether Elsenar's written revelations surprised Kasarian, or had he already been aware of Alizon's turbulent origins?

I wrote until my fingers cramped. Nolar kindly warmed a basin of water to ease my aching hand. When Morfew grew hoarse, Jonja took up the reading. Elsenar's tale seized us like a fighter's grip on our very throats.

CHAPTER 12

Elsenar—his thousand-year-old
journal transcribed by Mereth
at Lormt (10th Day,
Month of the Ice Dragon)

"...Which we had often done in our collaborative work as Adepts in Escore. I had begun to suspect that Shorrosh might be dabbling in magics perilously edging near the Dark, but when I confronted him, he vowed to me that he had never employed forbidden spells. At the time, his protests of innocence appeared genuine. I resolved privately to monitor all of his activities. We were about to embark upon a most challenging experiment, for we planned to travel to the empty northern lands to essay the conjuring of a Gate. Our arts had revealed to us a place far removed from our world, but threatened by disaster. Shorrosh's magic glass had indicated that killing walls of ice were about to spread across that land. All living things—plants, animals, people—would perish unless they could be removed. The folk of this place called themselves the Aliz. They were a sturdy, aggressive stock, strikingly pale in hair and eyes when compared to the black-haired, gray-eyed Old Race of Escore.

At first, Shorrosh and I were able to conjure only a small portal to link the two worlds. Shorrosh insisted upon daring the passage himself, pointing out that if he should be lost in the transit, I could safely close the portal. That defensive measure proved unnecessary, however, for his initial passage delivered Shorrosh to the primary fortress of the Aliz. When he proclaimed himself to their ruling council, the Aliz mistook his name, hailing him as the embodied Voice of Chordosh, their chief war god. Shorrosh did not correct them, but reveled in their adulation.

Through a smaller scrying glass he had carried with him, Shorrosh reported back to me. The Aliz, he discovered, had no notion of magical Power. That absence of experience contributed mightily to the impression Shorrosh made upon them; his slightest spell or even the most childish of magical entertainments utterly astonished the Aliz. Shorrosh suspected that they might possess hidden magical talents subject to activation and instruction. I warned him not to proceed in that regard, but to leave the Aliz untouched until we had learned more about them.

From his location there, Shorrosh was able to determine that the advancing ice cliffs had not yet approached the more settled areas. We thus were allowed a limited time to organize the rescuing transfers we hoped to provide, once we enspelled a larger portal—a true Gate. We invested substantial energy in our Gate spell. As soon as it was securely framed, Shorrosh led an advance party from Aliz through it into the bleak moorland north and west of Escore.

That first party of Aliz nobles were sorely disappointed by the harsh emptiness of the land, but Shorrosh promised them wondrous improvements to be wrought later by exercise of his magical arts. I feared that he was promising them too much, but I assisted in the spells to raise castles and smaller-scaled living quarters in an area suitable for habitation by active folk. The settlement flanked a navigable river, and Shorrosh soon grandly termed it 'Alizon City.'

Increasing numbers of the Aliz then came through the Gate, bringing with them packs of savage white hunting beasts. Because those alien creatures were generally dog-sized and bred to hunt, I termed them 'hounds,' and the immigrants embraced the name. Indeed, they began to style themselves the Hounds of Alizon, choosing to adopt Shorrosh's name for their new homeland. Along with the packs of hounds, they also brought other living things from Aliz. Several of the animals and plants they attempted to transfer failed to survive, but a few flourished, among them some favorite Aliz food plants, and the small, burrowing animals they called 'shriekers,' which they bred and slew abundantly for their religious ceremonies.

Upon closer association with the transplanted Aliz, I became disturbed by the vigor of some deplorable qualities among them. The nobles were a vain, quarrelsome lot, prone to scheming and treachery. Still, certain of their individuals and families were more responsible and admirable. In the hope of influencing these new Alizonders, I determined to ally myself to one of their major Houses, or as they styled their extended families, 'Lines.' I proposed a wedding alliance with the prominent Lady Kylaina, whose exquisite, ivory beauty was equalled by her keenness of mind. I conjured for her a special castle in Alizon City, in which we established our residence.

During those months of intensive activity, Shorrosh and I had tragically neglected our ties with Escore. A force of Adepts corrupted by service to the Dark had waxed stronger than those of us devoted to the Light had realized. Their meddling with living creatures in Escore had produced horrors that should never have been imagined, much less enfleshed. Alerted too late to prevent the Dark tide of evil from threatening all of Escore, a number of us conferred by glass and agreed to meet far to the south, where a citadel called Lormt was being erected as a rallying point for those of the Light.

I did not at that time consult with Shorrosh, who was back in Aliz supervising further selections of beasts and folk to be transferred to Alizon. Descending into the deepest vaults beneath my castle, I opened a magical postern to Lormt, so that I might assist my fellow Adepts of the Light with both their construction of the citadel and their plans to defend Escore.

While I was gone, Shorrosh shamefully revealed his true allegiance. The Alizonders had complained mightily to him about the desolate lands surrounding Alizon City, reminding Shorrosh of his earlier grandiose promises. He told them that with the aid of various Dark Adepts of his acquaintance in Escore, he could alter the climate and the very land itself to create a bountiful, garden-like expanse. Furthermore, he had been most favorably impressed by several monstrous beasts native to Aliz, which he desired to bring through the Gate to Alizon for hunting purposes, as well as for 'study,' after the depraved fashion of the Dark Adepts. Shorrosh also hinted that he might consent to instruct selected Alizonder nobles in the rudiments of magic.

Because of my nagging suspicions concerning Shorrosh, I had left hidden spells in effect in Alizon City which divulged to me all of these dreadful developments when I returned briefly from Lormt. I confronted Shorrosh in his castle, demanding that he reconsider his recent actions and renounce all of his ties with the Dark. I believe that our escalating clash of wills might have led to a Spell Duel, had we not been obstructed by a jolting exercise of defensive Power raging to the east. We soon learned that a mighty spine of mountains had been raised beginning between Escore and Alizon, and extending far to the south. The forces of the Light in Escore had fatally misjudged the strength of the Dark Adepts, and when those of the Light at last attempted to suppress those of the Dark, many of the Light's best champions were destroyed. Fleeing for their lives, the survivors fought their way westward, relying upon the new mountain barrier to seal off their Dark pursuers, among whom were numbered several of Shorrosh's vile colleagues.

At the time of the disaster in Escore, Shorrosh had been arranging for a major transfer of monsters from Aliz. When he broke off our argument to hurry through the Gate to oversee that impending transit, I seized my opportunity. By secret means, I had only recently acquired a jewel of great power, which I had attuned to my mind so that it was uniquely answerable to my control. I then called upon my jewel to dissolve the Gate to Aliz, thus severing Shorrosh's only means of return to Alizon.

Immediately after destroying the Gate, I summoned to Alizon Castle all of the prominent Alizonder nobles to inform them that there would be no further linkage with Aliz. They were at first incredulous, then indignant. They demanded that the prodigious promises that Shorrosh had made to them must be fulfilled; otherwise, they would consider themselves ill-treated and betrayed. They insisted that I must instruct them in the uses of magic, so that they could subsequently conjure whatever they desired.

I told them that Shorrosh's promises had been false, and I had no obligation to honor them. Because the Gate had been dissolved, Shorrosh could never return to Alizon, so they could expect no further bounty from him. With regard to their being instructed in magical knowledge, I declared that they were not fit to be imbued with it. Because I had vital business to attend to elsewhere, I would soon be leaving, and I warned them, that they would henceforth be obliged to fend for themselves.

I had already spoken privately with my beloved wife Kylaina. We were to be favored with a child in due course, and I urged her to come with me away from Alizon. She declined, refusing to be parted from her people, a sentiment I could understand, but under the circumstances deeply regretted.

Knowing that Kylaina and our child-to-be would have to be kept safe following my necessary departure, I therefore produced a vivid magical demonstration before the Alizonder nobles. I assured them that although I might not appear to be physically present, the spells I was invoking in Alizon would apprise me of any threats to Kylaina and those of my blood descent. Those of my Line would be magically protected from any form of attack. The Alizonder nobles were profoundly shaken by my display of raw Power. With my protective spells invoked, I could safely depart for Lormt.

Returning to my castle, I entrusted to Kylaina the key to the enspelled chamber far below, where I had set my postern to Lormt. I told her that the key would provide access to a magical outlet for escape to be used only by those of our blood, and only in the direst emergency. She vowed that she would safeguard the key and any related instructions as precious secrets to be restricted to those of our Line.

I did not disclose to her the destination of the escape route for two reasons. First, I dared to hope that she would not be forced to use the key. I judged that those of her present Aliz kin should provide her with reliable comradeship, while my protective spells would prevent any violence from touching her while I had to be away. It was possible that, in a fairly short time, the forces of the Light based in Lormt might prevail over the insurgent Dark forces in Escore. Once my work at Lormt was completed, I could return to Alizon and further consolidate the position of Kylaina and our Line-to-be. Second, I did not want my postern ever to be employed as an invasion route to Lormt, should the treacherous Alizonder element somehow learn of the passage and conceive notions of magically-aided aggressive expansion. I precluded that potential danger to Lormt by constructing my postern spell so that only those of my blood could travel by that means; for any other would-be transients, the aperture would not exist.

I bade Kylaina farewell, assuring her that my absence would be as brief as possible, then hastened to my postern to return to Lormt."

[At this point in her transcription, Mereth paused, then wrote with a shaking quill, "When I first touched the key that Kasarian was holding upon his arrival here, I sensed a certain familiarity about it. I now see that I was recognizing the aura of common ownership that now encompasses all three objects: the key, the jewel from my past, and this journal—all belonged to Elsenar. We must necessarily conclude that Kasarian is blood kin to Elsenar, or else he could not have passed through the magical postern from Alizon to Lormt."]

CHAPTER 13

Elsenar—his journal transcription
continued by Mereth at Lormt
(10th Day, Month of the Ice Dragon)

"As soon as I arrived at Lormt, I discovered that an
ominous proposal was being debated among the Adepts
of the Light already assembled there. Lormt's site had
been chosen for its strategic nearness to Escore, permitting a constant magical watch to be sustained in that direction. Since my previous visit, the citadel's walls and
living quarters had been erected by spells, and four great
spheres of quan-iron had been seated at the bases of the
corner towers. The Power inherent in that extraordinary
substance provided the ultimate protection against any
assault by the Dark. Unfortunately—from my point of
view, which was shared by a few other Adepts—the
sheer size and spatial relationship of the spheres tempted
the majority of Adepts to conceive a dangerous plan.
They recommended that such an immense Power focus
be used to create a Master Gate, capable of opening into
multiple destination sites. All of the Gates known to us
from previous experience had linked our world with

only a single destination. The party in favor of this Master Gate project argued that the immense threat from Escore's Dark Adepts demanded that we seek additional sources of Power from other worlds to bolster our defenses and ultimately allow us to regain control of Escore for the Light.

I was not at all convinced that so unprecedented an effort could bring about the results they predicted. The complexity of the spells that would be required necessarily entailed enormous risks of unpredictable repercussions. I stated my reservations before our Council of Adepts, and suggested that we should instead seek closer sources of aid; we could call upon our brother Adepts of the Light in Arvon, across the sea to the west. I proposed that we open a postern to link Lormt to Arvon, but the others would not listen. Because of the success of their recent mountain-raising spells, many of the younger Adepts had become overly confident. They asserted that Arvon's Adepts had little interest in matters relating to Escore. Complaining that it would take time to persuade those of Arvon of our desperate situation, they said such time and energy would be far better employed on their Master Gate effort.

When I saw that I could not sway the disputants to accept my plan, I withdrew from Lormt to a forester's lodge in the nearby mountains. The simultaneous working of spells by so many Adepts at Lormt was creating continuous cross-currents of Power. I determined to act alone, using my jewel to open a postern to Arvon. I had framed my spell and actually begun my transit when the most awful catastrophe occurred.

The main body of Adepts, having descended to the very roots of the Lormt citadel, had invoked a Great Spell, mightier than any ever before attempted by Adepts of either the Light or the Dark. As they had expected, a multibranched Master Gate did briefly form at the quan-iron spheres' Power focus, but the Adepts balancing the intricate layers of spells lost control of the structural flux. An unbelievable surge of Power blasted outward from Lormt, disrupting my comparatively feeble postern spell. I was literally snatched back to the forester's lodge, where I lay for some hours, stunned in both body and mind. As soon as I had revived, I rode immediately to Lormt, where I learned the appalling extent of the disaster that had afflicted us.

There was no one left to testify to the events that had scoured the spell chamber, but apparently, when the Master Gate coalesced in the center of the chamber, it must have exerted an irresistible suction that pulled all of the spell-workers into its maw. The apprentices and retainers who had been stationed in the outer corridor told me that they had been blinded by a blaze of light and deafened by a thunderclap of sound. At that same instant, the Power surge erupted from the chamber, physically dashing them to the floor.

The only Adepts spared to us were those few elderly mages whose bodies had been thought too frail to dare the exertions involved with a Great Spell, and a few others who had shared my distrust of the project and had declined to assist. Even in their tower quarters remote from the spell chamber, they, too, had been rendered senseless by the discharge of Power loosed when the Master Gate vanished.

From a formidable force representing the Light, our company had been reduced to a devastated remnant. I gave what succor I could to the dazed survivors, and dared one magical effort in the spell chamber to establish contact with any of the missing Adepts. The very air in Lormt's lower vault had been drained of all energy. I knew with cold certainty that the Master Gate was unreachable, and all those who had passed through it were lost to us forever.

Once all of us had recovered sufficiently to gather in the great hall, I conferred with the remaining Adepts and apprentices—a pitiful number compared with our former strength. They agreed with me that our only hope now lay in an appeal to Arvon's Adepts of the Light, but feared that no one could be spared from our watch on Escore. With the residual Power of the quan-iron spheres to aid us, we could just barely preserve the same evident force level as before. That was vital, for we knew that Escore's Dark Adepts would have registered the Power disturbance rippling outward from the Master Gate's collapse. They would certainly soon emit questing probes to seek the cause of the disturbance, and to test our remaining strength. As the primary bastion of the Light, Lormt had to appear to be unchanged and impregnable.

Having already once constructed a postern to Arvon, I offered to re-establish that link and essay the mission to seek aid from our brothers to the west. After agonized discussion, the others bade me to make the attempt. Ordinarily, I would have allowed myself a day or more of rest and meditation before I again conjured such an extended postern. In view of our perilously decimated situation, however, I waited only long enough for a fresh mount to be brought before I set out for the forester's lodge."

[Mereth's hand abruptly faltered. She snatched up a fragment of parchment, wrote on it, and handed it to Morfew, who hastily rounded the table to peer down at Elsenar's journal.

Alarmed, Ouen asked, "What is amiss?"

"Mereth can no longer sense Elsenar's message," Morfew said, pulling the study lamp closer to illuminate the opened page. "Master Ouen," Morfew exclaimed, "the hand composing this journal has altered. I can read this script! It appears to be an addition by an apprentice—a distraught apprentice, as well he might be. . . ."

"Morfew," said Ouen in a decisive tone, "pray share your discovery with us before we become distraught."

Morfew was instantly contrite. "Forgive me, dear friends. Could you fetch one more lamp? This scrawl is so ragged that some words are difficult to make out. Thank you. 'Master Elsenar has not returned,' " Morfew read haltingly. " 'It has been . . . three days! Old Master Verdery was taken to the lodge to employ his scrying glass. He detected vestiges of a spell so shattered by intense Power flow that the postern to Arvon which Elsenar had anchored there could not be re-established. We fear the worst—that a Dark Adept in Arvon must have intercepted Elsenar. We can ill bear the loss of one of our few remaining Master Adepts. May the Light defend us!' "]

CHAPTER 14

Mereth—events at Lormt
(10th Day, Month of the Ice Dragon/
Veneration Day, Moon of the Knife)

When Morfew stopped reading and closed Elsenar's journal, we all sat in shocked silence.

Ouen was the first to speak. "It would seem that our present dangers may echo long past events. As in Elsenar's time, Lormt may once again be imperiled by Dark forces from Escore."

Morfew, excited by other aspects of what we had just heard, briskly rubbed his hands together. "I never thought to learn the origins of Lormt," he exclaimed. "At last, Master Ouen, we possess evidence concerning when and why the citadel was constructed."

"And why it was almost preserved untouched during the Turning," Ouen commented. "We knew that our quan-iron spheres were somehow involved, but perhaps an explanation emerges from Elsenar's account. The spheres provided Power for the working of the Great Spell, and for the watch upon Escore. I believe we may reasonably suppose that when Lormt is in any way subject to a magical assault, our spheres have been prepared to produce a protective enclosure spell to encompass the entire citadel."

"Which we certainly observed, to our benefit," Morfew agreed. "Had not the earth subsided following the Witches' Turning, Lormt's walls would have held—but once the Witch-magic departed, our sheltering spell bubble withdrew, and the damages Lormt suffered were entirely due to non-magical causes."

I had by then retrieved my staff, and thumped it to draw their attention. "We may now also understand," Nolar read my words, "how what I had considered to be my betrothal jewel first came to the western lands; Elsenar carried it to Arvon a thousand years ago when he crossed the sea through his postern from Lormt."

"The critical menace we face is here and now, not a thousand years ago," Kasarian declared impatiently. "You have admitted that if Gratch succeeds in arranging an encounter with the Escorians, the Dark mages would be aware of this ancient jewel of Power now possessed by Gurborian."

Jonja nodded grudgingly. "Yes," she said, "even if the jewel was not worn in their presence, the Dark mages would recognize its magical aura lingering from Gurborian's physical association with the stone."

"But Elsenar described his jewel as being singularly attuned to his mind," Nolar pointed out. "Do you suppose that such a personal binding might prevent any other mage from tapping its Power?"

"We must recall that a thousand years have passed," Ouen said. "It is possible that any limitations impressed by Elsenar upon his jewel may have weakened over so long a time. While I feel confident that mages of the Light would not seek to impose their wills upon an object of Power attuned by another, I suspect that mages of the Dark would not likely be bound by any such scruples."

Duratan had been quietly pacing. He moved a chair next to Morfew and sat down, propping his stiff leg upon a document chest. "Two reasonable outcomes suggest themselves in that regard," he mused, "and I do not welcome either one. If the Dark mages can draw upon the Power inherent in Elsenar's jewel, should they acquire it, then the peril to Estcarp would be unbearably increased. On the other hand, if the Dark mages attempted to force their wills upon the stone, and it resisted their efforts, might there not be another immense discharge of Power, such as that caused by the destruction of the Master Gate?"

"It is obvious to me," said Jonja tartly, "that Elsenar's jewel can *not* be allowed to fall into the hands of servants of the Dark. It must be controlled by, or at the very least be held under the protection of those devoted to the Light."

"But how can we achieve that end?" asked Morfew. "We are here in Lormt, and Elsenar's jewel is in Alizon."

"Your question has a simple answer," Duratan replied ruefully. "It is an answer simple in the stating, but far from simple in the achieving: we shall have to wrest the jewel from Gurborian."

"Has Lormt an army at hand of which we are unaware?" Kasarian inquired in a coldly polite tone. "Baron Gurborian is unlikely to surrender his jewel for the mere asking, however persuasively you may phrase your request."

"Perhaps you can suggest a more promising course of action?" Duratan challenged.

Kasarian nodded, ignoring Duratan's sarcasm. "We cannot waste precious time on raising a fighting force or travelling the distance overland to Alizon City," he argued. "If the spell that delivered me to Lormt will also function in the opposite direction, I could return through Elsenar's postern in your vault and attempt to recover the jewel from Gurborian."

The Lormt folk all tried to speak at once, until Ouen raised his hand to restore order. "You would dare such a mission?" he asked the Alizonder.

Kasarian's voice was firm. "I would."

"A drastic reduction in offensive force, would you not say," observed Duratan, "from a prospective army to just the one man? Unless Baron Gurborian customarily marches about alone, and you can provide a well-armed household force to waylay him, I urge that several of us accompany you on this quest . . . to improve our chances for success."

Kasarian stiffened, about to respond, but I thumped my staff to forestall him. All during their discussion, I had been forcing my hand to write. From the moment that Duratan proposed the forceable capture of Elsenar's jewel, I knew that my course of action could not be denied. Although my spirit—indeed, my very body—shrank back from the conclusion that my mind had reached, I knew I had to interpose myself in these crucial deliberations.

I handed my parchment to Nolar, who read for me, "Remember the stricture on Elsenar's postern spell: only those of his blood may traverse that passage. I believe that I, too, must somehow be related to Elsenar; otherwise, why would my mother term his jewel to be our family's betrothal gift from olden times? Could it be that my talent for insightful touch might derive from some measure of previously unknown mage blood? I suggest to you that my appearance weighs in favor of my passage to Alizon—you may have noticed that my hair and eyes could be mistaken for an Alizonder's. Furthermore, I possess one commandable attribute for a potential spy—I can commit no slip of the tongue in the enemy's presence. Besides, should

Gurborian have hidden away Elsenar's jewel, I assure you that I can identify it by touch, even in the dark, if need be."

During Nolar's reading, Kasarian had leaned forward in his chair, his face drawn with dismayed surprise. "You cannot mean," he blurted, then paused, and stared affronted at each of the others in turn. "Surely on so vital a mission, you would never consider dispatching an old, speechless *female!*"

Morfew smiled. "Mereth is not at all accustomed to the sheltered ways of our Alizonder females," he said mildly. "I hasten to inform you that the women of the Dales are every bit as active as the men, in both trade and warfare."

I nearly broke the point of my quill in writing my reply for Nolar to read to Kasarian. "Young man, in my seventy-five years of life, I have likely traveled farther and endured more fighting than you have. I can do more with a staff than merely lean upon it, and during my days as an organizer of war supplies for the Dales, I became a keen shot with a dart gun."

Kasarian did not immediately reply, but his thinly veiled disdain for me seemed to be replaced by an air of wary reassessment.

Ouen again raised his hand to focus our attention. "We have before us," he said, "two proposals: Kasarian's offer to attempt a return to Alizon by postern to act on our behalf, and Mereth's offer to accompany him. We must weigh the virtues and the drawbacks of each offer. I suggest that Kasarian withdraw briefly to his guest chamber to ponder his appraisal and response to Mereth's offer, while we of Lormt abide here to discuss the merits of his offer."

Kasarian instantly stood up, and bowed to Ouen. "I perceive why you are regarded as Lormt's chief scholar," he remarked. "You speak wisely. I welcome the opportunity for a private examination of this . . . irregular proposal."

He turned, bowed to me—to me!—and touched his House badge, then left us, shutting the door firmly behind him.

Jonja waited a moment, then eased open the door and looked down the corridor. "He has gone toward his chamber," she confirmed. "Shall we leave the door ajar?"

"I think not," said Morfew, amused. "Kasarian will likely truly retire to reflect upon the notion—quite bizarre to an Alizonder, I assure you—that a female can be expected to do more than produce strong whelps and mind a household."

I sat very still. I had never before had occasion to think about Alizonder women and how they might live. None had ever been seen during the Dales war; we had assumed that they either did not choose to travel with their men, or were not allowed to do so. Should they be customarily kept as virtual prisoners in their manors and castles, it might be difficult for me to move about freely in Alizon City . . . assuming that Kasarian would accept my company.

Duratan was again fretfully pacing. "How can we dare to trust one Alizonder baron to oppose another such?" he demanded. "Now that Kasarian knows the awesome strength of Gurborian's jewel, might he not try to seize it for the benefit of his own House—or worse, inform the Lord Baron so that he might act?"

Morfew shook his head, all traces of humor banished. "No, I believe that we may rely upon one sure fact: Kasarian would not venture to keep such a jewel in his own possession. The Line Sired by Krevonel was ever one devoted to the old ways. They feared and despised any association with magic. I think we can also trust Kasarian's unswerving hatred for the Line that murdered his sire—such actions are not forgotten in Alizon." His voice shook as he added, "That is why we have been cursed over the years by blood feuds. Deep wounds leave deep and lasting scars that persist over generations."

"Should Alizon loose its fighters upon Estcarp at the same time that we were magically assailed by Escore's Dark mages," Duratan worried aloud, "then our plight would be truly desperate. Our Witches have not yet fully recovered their strength from their mighty exertions required by the spells that caused the Turning."

"I fear that they will never completely regain their former strength," said Nolar sadly. "So many of them were killed or woefully afflicted by the excessive Power they wielded. Even now, the Council in Es City continues to search the land for young girls—even children—to be trained as rapidly as may be in order to reconstitute their numbers."

Jonja glanced warily outside the door, then rejoined us at the table. "Should such an awful double assault befall us," she said, "I would not be surprised if the Witches' Council chose the same tactic resorted to by the Sulcar when the Kolder sent Gorm's mindless masses to capture Sulcarkeep."

Ouen stared at the table, but his eyes were focused upon something other than the wooden surface. "The utter destruction of Sulcarkeep was an act of sorrowful necessity," he said. "May the Light forbid that we of Estcarp ever be driven to such a violent ending."

"Lormt presumably would endure," asserted Morfew stoutly, then he paused, and added, "provided our quan-iron spheres continue to protect us."

"Who would want to exist in a single, isolated fortress surrounded like an island by the flood tides of the Dark?" asked Duratan bitterly.

"In regard to the possible outcome of a mission to Alizon," observed Morfew, "should Kasarian and Mereth succeed in passing through Elsenar's postern, how could they go about securing Gurborian's jewel without being captured or killed?"

"Kasarian will have to formulate a plan feasible for use in Alizon," Ouen replied. "We must then judge whether his plan holds a reasonable prospect for success—as well as whether it provides sufficient protection for Mereth. It disturbs me greatly," he said directly to me, "that because of the postern's stricture, you alone may represent us, risking your life for Estcarp's sake."

My hand was steady as I wrote for him to read, "I am an old woman who had thought her remaining active days were likely few. If this mission should be my last journey, I have no regrets. We of the Dales can never forget what you of Estcarp risked to aid us in our time of need. I have been a trader all my life. Fair service in return for fair service— what honest trader could offer less?"

Ouen's smile softened his usually stern demeanor. "The Dalesfolk have ever been known for their steadfastness and courage," he said. "Jonja, will you fetch back our guest? We need to hear what plans he has devised."

CHAPTER 15

Kasarian—events at Lormt
(Veneration Day, Moon of the Knife/
10th Day, Month of the Ice Dragon)

It vexed me that I had not fully grasped the mute female's potential for disturbance. Soon after we commenced our joint search of Lormt's archives, Mereth poked her writing slate at me, querying me anent Gurborian and why he had been awarded "her" jewel. I thought it advisable to plead ignorance of the details due to my relative youth at the time, thus I did not inform her that the first bestowal ceremony had taken place shortly after my twelfth-year's Presentation to Facellian, the Lord Baron at that time. I had already left Alizon City when Facellian was deposed, so I did not actually see the jewel until its second awarding to Gurborian by Lord Baron Norandor at this just-past New Year's Assembly. Mereth did not press the matter, but I suspected that she did not entirely believe my disclaimer.

When by her unnatural touch, Mereth identified the writer of the ancient journal as ELSENAR, I had to grip the arms of my chair to avoid crying out. I was appalled that she should utter, of all names, *that* baleful name! It was because of the execrated Elsenar that we numbered Alizon's very years by the form "Since the Betrayal." The indelible stain upon the Line Sired by Krevonel had been the tradition that we descended ultimately from Alizon's Lady Kylaina and the treacherous mage Elsenar. It was for that reason that we designated Krevonel as our original Foresire. Reputedly, he had been the elder whelp of Elsenar's siring, but no Alizonder could possibly want to claim Elsenar as Foresire.

By our reckoning, one thousand fifty-two years ago, Elsenar and the equally foul mage Shorrosh had betrayed our Foresires, who had courageously ventured through an ensorcelled Gate into the then empty land of Alizon. That those two ancient and untrustworthy mages proved to have come from Escore (according to Elsenar's fiendish journal) only increased my aversion to Gurborian's present-day determination to seek out more such linkages, courting Escorian ruin for Alizon yet again.

We had always been taught that after the mages had destroyed the Gate, severing all access to our original homeland, they then vanished, abandoning our Foresires with no provisions except for the few hunting animals and food plants they had previously brought through the Gate. Those initial years had been starkly intolerable, but gradually, our Foresires succeeded in devising a new Alizonder society. Except for Chordosh, whose name lingered on as a Moon Name, they set aside their former gods, since their godly powers stemmed from our original blood soil, forever reft from us. To replace the lost gods, they developed over the years a system of veneration of the Foresires, which waxed and waned in prominence and degree of devotion according to the will of each successive Lord Baron. In order to preserve appropriate respect among the packs, the early Lords Baron instituted bodies of official Venerators to carry out the ritual duties required, including the breeding and sacrificing of shriekers.

As I contemplated the ancient origins of our ways, I was jarred to realize that this very day was Veneration Day, Alizon's singular year-day set apart between the ninth and the tenth days of the Moon of the Knife. On Veneration Day, the series of observances culminated in the largest mass sacrifice of shriekers, signifying our recognition of the Foresires. I had never before been absent from those ceremonies.

Isolated at Lormt, I felt simultaneously burdened and challenged by my sudden opportunity to influence the course of Alizon's future existence. Elsenar's journal could not be gainsaid. To my personal distress, the mage's narrative cited not only his redoubtable jewel, but also his key to the postern beneath Krevonel Castle—that very elder's key preserved by the females of our Line. That it should have been originally presented to our Forelady Kylaina by Elsenar caused my fingers to tingle at its remembered touch . . . yet without that key, I should not have been able to travel to Lormt. Nor, for that matter, could I deny that without some measure of the mage's tainted blood, I should not have passed through the postern at all. That was an even more daunting realization—that I must necessarily possess mage blood. I had to brace my body to prevent it from shuddering in the open view of the Lormt folk.

I forced myself to concentrate. In all my study of our Line's lore, I had never encountered word of any such prize as Elsenar's jewel. By Alizonder Line-right, however, it clearly should have descended through the Line

Sired by Krevonel. War booty claim or no, Lord Baron's bestowal claim or no, Gurborian could not retain the jewel: it belonged to Krevonel.

My blood ran cold at the thought. I had heard the whispers about the cursed jewel from the Dales. None could state the full cost in lives associated with it before Lord Baron Facellian seized it. As an Alizonder, I knew that I should experience a blazing desire to claim so great a treasure for our Line . . . but the idea of possessing an object so steeped in magic tore at my vitals like the claws of a dire wolf. Still, I could not deny that Alizon's very future depended upon preventing Gurborian's potential Escorian allies from ever nearing Elsenar's jewel.

The Lormt folk persisted in discussing former unleashings of vast spell powers within and nearby the citadel. Such talk was unsettling. Should these Lormt folk succeed in securing the jewel, might they not surrender it to Estcarp's Witches? I could identify no desirable choice between the two sword edges confronting me. I could not, for Alizon's sake, abide either alternative; neither Escore nor Estcarp could be allowed to control that awful jewel. I therefore offered to attempt the jewel's recovery myself, should it prove possible to proceed back through Elsenar's postern to Alizon City.

Duratan at once challenged my offer, demanding that he and others accompany me, but once again we were interrupted by the Dales female. Duratan's mate read out Mereth's reminder that only those of Elsenar's blood could travel through his postern. To my utter astonishment, she then asserted that *she* should be selected to accompany me! She did present some cogent arguments—that her Witch-like power of touch implied mage blood, and her pack's tradition of owning the jewel linked her to Elsenar.

I regret that I failed to contain my instant reaction of scorn for such a ludicrous proposal. The idea that an elderly *female* would dare to claim a role in high male affairs of state deserved only the laughter of disbelief . . . but I saw at once that the Lormt folk's view was contrary to mine. They did not laugh. Indeed, Morfew informed me that the Dales females were distinctly unlike ours, being as active in affairs as males, which I found a most disagreeable perception, but did not say so.

Mereth herself wrote an acid defense of her war experience, which I realized had to be taken into account, even despite her advanced age. How was I to know the capacity for agility and endurance possessed by these unnatural females?

Ouen then suggested that I withdraw to my chamber to consider Mereth's offer, while they remained to deliberate upon my proposal. I welcomed the chance to reflect upon the disconcerting body of information laid before us in so short a time. I bowed to him, and to Mereth, and hastened through the corridors, striving to impose some order upon my agitated thoughts.

It was evident that I had to revise my appraisal of this Dales female, Mereth. Perhaps her appearance could be explained if her blood had come down through Elsenar's Alizonian alliance. I had wondered earlier if she was part Witch; in one respect, the actuality might prove even worse—she could be part mage! She had not, however, been previously aware of her blood-tie until she read Elsenar's journal, so she was not a trained mage, mistress of many hideous spells. She could, however, sense information by touch, a frightening talent . . . but one that might serve us well in locating the jewel if it should be hidden away. As I reviewed all that I had learned at Lormt, the beginnings of a plan stirred in my mind. When the Wise Woman came to escort me back to the group, I was ready to amend my original offer.

Once I had taken my place at the table, Ouen immediately announced that the Lormt folk had tentatively accepted Mereth's offer, depending upon the details of my plan for retrieving Elsenar's jewel from Gurborian.

I decided to address my proposal directly to Mereth for two reasons. First, out of courtesy to a possible comrade in arms on a potentially fatal mission; and second, out of curiosity to see how she would react.

"I crave your pardon, lady," I began, "for my earlier outburst. I have been trained in the customs of Alizon, and I do not as yet fully comprehend your ways. I did not intend to offend you. I have carefully pondered what you wrote, and if you dare to be bold and resolute, I think I perceive one way by which you might be accepted in Alizon City." I paused, but she merely nodded, and gestured for me to proceed. "In my earliest youth," I resumed, "I was fostered with my sire's elder littermate—"

Morfew interrupted. "These folk are more familiar with the form 'uncle,' " he explained, "just as they tend to say 'brothers' or 'sisters' rather than male or female littermates, and 'family' instead of pack."

I bowed to him. "I thank you for such useful words to increase my understanding of your speech. My . . . uncle, Baron Volorian, still lairs at his manor far to the north and east of Alizon City. His letters first alerted me to Gratch's probes among the mountains adjoining Escore. Volorian is the oldest living male in our . . . family, and is eminent for his intense hatred of any traffic with magic. Since my sire was murdered by Gurborian's hirelings, Volorian has essentially avoided Alizon City, being occupied with his hound breeding, for which he is also duly famed. None in the City now would likely recall him well enough to doubt you, lady, should you appear, posing as Baron Volorian."

The Lormt party stirred in their chairs, obviously dismayed by my suggestion. Having launched my initial thrust in what I had to view as a duel with words instead of swords, I hastened to press my advantage. "You are much the same size and age as Volorian, lady," I said to Mereth. "Your hair, of course, would have to be properly shortened and perhaps brightened. Your lack of voice, however, does pose a problem."

Morfew unexpectedly smiled. "I discern a simple solution for that difficulty," he observed. "Could we not say that a winter ague has temporarily quenched your uncle's voice? It is a common enough ailment among us here at Lormt—our Master Pruett is kept busy in his herbarium through all the winter months, brewing soothing syrups to restore lost voices."

I was favorably impressed by his quick wit. "That would do very well. I could explain my current absence from Alizon City," I continued, "as a sudden journey in response to a summons from Volorian to confer with him at his manor."

"But you just said that Volorian has avoided any possible contact with his brother's murderer all these years," the Wise Woman objected. "How could you now devise a way that the two of them could meet without blood being shed? I gather," she added, nodding toward Morfew, "that you Alizonders cherish your feuds."

"It is precisely because of the depth of animosity between our two Lines that my plan has such promise," I retorted. "Gurborian avidly desires to attract more prominent barons to his faction. We could intimate that if sufficient reasons . . . and payments . . . were offered, then the Line Sired by Krevonel *might* be persuaded to join Gurborian's faction. I could assert that Volorian insisted upon returning secretly with me to Alizon City to conduct such delicate negotiations personally. Gurborian would not dare refuse such an opportunity. I believe that he would even risk coming to Krevonel Castle itself to attempt to win our support by his false enticements. We could then dispose of him and seize the jewel, provided we could somehow spur him to bring the jewel with him, thus sparing us both the hazard and the trouble of seeking it at his castle."

CHAPTER 16

Mereth—events at Lormt
(10th Day, Month of the
Ice Dragon/Veneration Day)

When he was brought back to the study room, Kasarian addressed a brazen proposal to me, with an odd mingling of both arrogance and courtesy. He declared that I was of a suitable age and size to disguise myself as his uncle, Baron Volorian, who had fostered him as a child.

I was appalled by Kasarian's proposition. How could I possibly pose as an Alizonder baron? I had already felt utter revulsion at my own notion which required me to go among our Dales' worst enemies in even the most inconspicuous, surreptitious fashion, but this hideous plan entailed my assuming a visibly prominent role. I forced myself to attend to the continuing discussion.

"If our initial overture to Gurborian is composed skillfully enough," Kasarian resumed, "Gurborian would feel obliged to investigate the validity of our receptiveness. Once we tempt him into Krevonel Castle, we can maneuver adroitly for the best opportunity to kill him. Gurborian has always been as wary as a cornered split-tusked boar. He would be unlikely to succumb to any consumable poisons. If I could position myself near enough to him, a dagger thrust should be more certain. . . ." His voice trailed off as he became aware that the others around the table had drawn back in obvious distaste. "I see that Alizon's common modes of action differ from yours," Kasarian remarked, evidently more intrigued than offended by our reactions. "Do you not resort to killing under pressing circumstances such as these?" he asked.

"We do not often have occasion to weigh various methods of killing in advance," said Ouen dryly, "except during councils of war."

Duratan's expression remained somber. "In this instance," he commented, "the Alizonian way may have to be considered. If Gurborian is customarily on guard against sudden attacks, it will be far more difficult for us to take him by surprise."

I thumped my staff and extended a written question for Nolar to read to Kasarian. "Would Gurborian recognize Volorian's script?"

Kasarian appeared startled by my query, but after a moment's thought, he shook his head. "No," he said, "I can think of no reason why they should have exchanged writings in the past. Volorian dispatches few letters—only to me, and to other noted breeders of hounds."

Nolar accepted and read my related proposal: "Could we not bait our trap with a message ostensibly written by Volorian? Suppose Volorian demanded to know the truth of Gurborian's intentions concerning Escore, and offered, under convincingly stringent conditions, to pledge his Line's backing for Gurborian's plot?"

"An admirably clever thought, lady," Kasarian acknowledged. "Knowing that Gratch had encroached upon our lands, Gurborian must assume that Volorian is aware of his suspicious activity near our estates. He should indeed be drawn to respond to such an approach."

"Regarding the setting of conditions for a meeting of mutually mistrustful barons," mused Duratan, "Volorian could insist that Gurborian come secretly to Krevonel Castle at a discreet hour—midnight, say—with a minimal number of bodyguards. I trust that Gurborian does employ bodyguards?"

"A dozen or more," Kasarian confirmed. "Gurborian has accumulated many enemies."

Nolar's eyes brightened. "It may be that I perceive a way whereby Gurborian might be persuaded to bring Elsenar's jewel with him to Krevonel Castle. Since Morfew's winter ague has silenced Volorian's voice, the baron would reasonably order Kasarian, his brother's son, to speak for him. And," she added triumphantly, "Volorian could make it a condition for the meeting that Gurborian wear his jewel from the Dales. He could claim that Kasarian had taken a fancy to it, and its presence and implied potential availability as a bribe might sway his opinion in Gurborian's favor."

Morfew reached for quill and ink. "I can easily indite that message in the proper Alizonian style." He scribbled busily, then read to us, " 'Gurborian: I have heard curious rumors and reports concerning certain of your recent plans. What is the truth of the matter regarding your furtive incursions along the Escorian border? Packs of our puissance should unite into one overwhelming force, not splinter our strength by opposing one another. Is it not time that we set aside our Lines' past enmities? If you have contrived a scheme with promise, I might, for carefully negotiated considerations, rally Krevonel to your faction. Come to Krevonel Castle at midnight. Bring no large retinue, but I would hear from your agent Gratch, who I know has been sniffing about my territory. Discussions of such moment should be held circumspectly by pack elders. Since a winter ague has quenched my voice, however, Oralian's whelp will accompany me to speak in my stead. A private word for your ear alone—the whelp has taken a fancy to that bauble of yours from the Dales. Bear that in mind when you arm yourself for the excursion. His opinion could be persuasive, especially among the younger whelps of our Line. I await your reply. Volorian."

Kasarian showed his fangs in a wolfish grin. "Morfew, I commend the shrewdness of your composition. It strikes the perfect tone to prick Gurborian's ears." His expression reverted to his more usual semblance of keenly focused regard. "I do foresee one other obstacle," he said. "Yonder female's paws cannot be mistaken for those of a proper baron and Master of Hounds."

Morfew emitted a snort that I took to be a suppressed laugh. "The seamstresses of Lormt," he said, "ably directed by our Mistress Bethalie, can craft ornamental gloves suitable for even baronial use. Surely an elderly baron suffering from ague would choose to glove his hands warmly for a clandestine meeting in an old castle at midnight."

"Your ingenuity is inspiring, Morfew," Ouen observed appreciatively. "We must also address the matter of diverse speech. Do you think it will be possible to teach Mereth sufficient Alizonian so that she can react acceptably to what might be said during a conference with Gurborian?"

"If the lady will permit," Kasarian offered, "I can endeavor to instruct her in our basic speech."

"The two of us can assist her," Morfew declared. "She must master our script as well, so she can write brief comments on her slate as Volorian would, in order to communicate with his nephew. 'Nephew,' " he added for Kasarian's enlightenment, "is the Estcarpian term for a brother's or sister's son."

I nodded to each of them, and wrote, "I thank you both. Let us set about these tasks at once. I possess a few words of Alizonian, and I know the script for some trading terms, but I achieved that limited understanding many years ago. My memory will require much refreshing and additional instruction."

"As for her hair. . . ." Jonja had been looking from me to Kasarian, and then back to me. "Kasarian is right. Mereth's hair needs to be a paler, yet brighter hue if she is to survive close scrutiny by Alizonders."

Nolar had been quietly pondering. "I am familiar with many preparations of bark or nut shells to darken hair," she said, "but I cannot immediately recall any treatment that causes hair to lighten to the silver-white we require. I shall ask Master Pruett—he knows more about herbs than any person in all of Estcarp. If such a substance exists, he will know of it, and likely have three different forms of it tucked away in his herbarium."

"Pray inquire of him for us," Ouen requested, and Nolar rose from her chair.

Jonja also stood. "By your leave, I can alert Mistress Bethalie to assemble her most skilled glovemakers." At Ouen's gesture of approval, she followed Nolar from the room.

Ouen pushed back his own chair. "Your study of Alizonian should be as undisturbed as possible," he said. "I shall arrange for food and drink to be brought here, as we did for our work in Morfew's rooms. We will rejoin you presently, after you have had time to progress. Despite the gravity of the threat from the north, we cannot neglect Lormt's necessary activities."

Duratan smiled ruefully. "Master Wessell has been chasing after me through every corridor, waving his provisioning lists. I had hoped to elude him in here, but this would be a good opportunity to confer with him."

Once they had departed, Morfew gathered together several blank sheets of parchment, and invited me to take the chair beside his. Kasarian retained his place across the table from us.

As the hours passed, I was exceedingly relieved that I could not physically speak the wretched tongue. The more I listened to Morfew and Kasarian growl and snarl at one another, the more they sounded like a brace of quarrelsome hounds. Spoken Alizonian grated upon my ear . . . and my memory. I had thought that I had buried those memories, but jagged shards from the past stabbed my mind, unbidden, no doubt prompted by the hateful speech of our Dales' bitterest enemies.

I thumped my staff, and gestured toward the flask of ale. Kasarian leaped up to pour me a measure. I shut my eyes for a moment, then forced myself to copy yet again the shapes of the script letters that I had to master. I was gradually achieving some facility, but my hand was again aching from the intensive exercise.

Nolar returned first, bearing a welcome tray of porridge, cheese, bread, and fruit. Jonja arrived soon afterward, noting that Mistress Bethalie herself insisted upon coming to measure my hands for the baronial gloves.

Nolar briskly swept aside our parchments to make room for the food. "I described to Master Pruett our need for some means to match the Alizonder hair color," she reported. "He regretted that he could not attend to you personally, Mereth, but he is engaged in a most delicate extraction of essences that he cannot abandon. He assured me, however, that this decoction of silver nettles should produce most satisfying results." She withdrew from her skirt pocket a flask of murky liquid that exuded a sharp scent even though its stopper was tightly wrapped with dried grass.

Jonja eyed it dubiously. "I should not care to apply that to *my* hair," she stated firmly. "Common nettles I know well enough, and how they will restore hair color, but these silver nettles from the high mountain meadows are far harsher in their juice and in their stings! Surely such an extract would be too strong to apply to the scalp."

Nolar nodded. "From my own herbal experience, I raised that very objection, but Master Pruett vows that his regimen for purifying and cooling the decoction quite diminishes the more noxious elements of the plant. Still. . . ." She glanced at me, and smiled. "If Mereth will allow us, I would feel easier if we cut off a lock of hair and tested that first."

Jonja plucked from her belt scrip a sturdy wooden comb and a small knife. I let down my hair, curious to see whether its already white hue could be bleached by Lormt's herbs to the singular silver-white shade characteristic for Alizonders.

We duly peered at the lock Jonja placed on a saucer, while Nolar dampened it with water, then added a few drops from Master Pruett's flask. Jonja stirred the strands with her knife, and rinsed them in a second saucer.

"Master Pruett advises that we apply the nettle extract in a solution with mild soap," Nolar said. "The lightening process will take somewhat longer, but will be gentler to the skin."

"I would not have believed it," Jonja admitted, "but this extract of Pruett's does produce the desired hue. If you agree," she added, turning to me, "I can trim your hair to the length and style worn by this Volorian."

Kasarian had been watching us with great interest. "The last time I saw Volorian," he remarked, "his hair was trimmed much like mine. He wears his perhaps a trifle shorter at the back of the neck, since he seldom fights in a helmet. I practice frequently with blade and spear," Kasarian explained, "in order to maintain my speed of thrust. Some fighters must pad their helmets, but since my hair is dense, I require no padding."

"I welcome your attentions and advice," I wrote for Nolar to read aloud. "At your convenience, I place my hair at your disposal."

That afternoon sped past in a blur of activity. Just as we were completing our hasty luncheon, an energetic woman of middle age rapped at the door. Nolar introduced her as Bethalie, Lormt's mistress for all forms of needlework. She spread a square of thin cloth on the table before me, and with a stick of charcoal, deftly marked around my outstretched fingers. From a capacious pocket in her smock, she produced a well-worn strip of linen barred with evenly spaced lines of stitching, which she stretched around and along every possible dimension of my hands. Having carefully noted each measurement on a corner of the cloth, she bobbed her head, gathered up her materials, and promised to bring me a pair of cloth test-gloves as soon as her seamstresses could cut and stitch them.

Jonja was lighting the candles and Nolar was about to serve our evening meal delivered by one of Morfew's assistants when Mistress Bethalie bustled through the door. She explained that these relatively flimsy cloth gloves would be unstitched to provide patterns for cutting the leather versions. Humming a quiet tune to herself, Mistress Bethalie tightened a tuck here and loosened a seam there. "It may take two days," she announced at last. "The final gloves must be appropriate for a baron of Alizon. I have three embroiderers marking out the ornamental designs for the gauntlets."

True to her word, two days later at midmorning, Mistress Bethalie appeared at Ouen's study door looking highly gratified. Walking directly to the table, she extended to me a pair of hideous red-purple leather gloves, their gauntlets encrusted with tortuous swirls of silver thread so closely stitched that I expected the surface to be as stiff as a turtle shell. When I thrust in my fingers, however, I discovered that the leather was as soft and supple as fine wool. I had never in all my years possessed finer made—or more garish—gloves. I removed one for Kasarian's inspection. He examined it with every appearance of genuine approbation.

Bowing gracefully to Mistress Bethalie, Kasarian said, "I have seldom touched a finer prepared piece of leather, or seen more elegant decoration. Baron Volorian himself would wear these gloves with pride."

He turned away to exclaim to Morfew about the stitching, and I heard Mistress Bethalie murmur to Nolar, "I promised our chief tanner last year that someday I would rid him of that vile mistake he made in dyeing. He wagered with me that no man in Lormt would endure such an appalling shade of leather. I believe that I can now honestly claim my wager, for these gloves have been worn, albeit briefly, at Lormt. It seems that their appearance appeals solely to Alizonders."

In the past, I had prided myself upon my ability to juggle several tasks, compressing into one stretch of time a number of trading activities that had to be accomplished simultaneously. The next several days at Lormt reminded me most forcefully of the strenuous trials for both mind and body that had assailed us during the time of fighting in the Dales, and to an even greater degree in the awful years following the war. I had been aided then by others who shared my burdens; now I also had supportive assistance, but so much depended upon my personal exertions. I raced through the crowded hours, listening to and writing Alizonian, sitting for my hair to be cut and bleached silver-white, trying on piece after piece of clothing that Kasarian selected from Mistress Bethalie's stores to outfit me as Baron Volorian.

Kasarian himself brought up the subject of weaponry. One morning when I had finally been fitted with matching breeches, tunic, and boots that would serve until we could substitute the distinctive high-sided Alizonian style, he declared, "Volorian must be properly a ed."

Without saying a word, Duratan crossed the study to unlock the small cabinet mounted above Ouen's desk near the window. He took from its shelves all of the weapons he had removed from Kasarian's body, and placed them on the table.

The Alizonder instantly arose to restore each item to its designated place on his belt or up his sleeve or tucked inside his boot tops. He preserved a deliberately impassive facial expression, but when he wriggled slightly to settle his gear in place, I suddenly recalled a similar motion. Doubt's old dog had given just such a gleeful squirm whenever his master buckled on his favorite cart harness. I realized that except when he slept (and indeed, I suspected that Kasarian slept with his knives within close reach), he probably had never before been deprived of his personal weapons for so many days as his current visitation to Lormt. I knew that I should have felt ill at ease had someone taken away my slate, chalk, or tally sticks—how much more vital to an Alizonder's sense of well-being must be his constant awareness of his personal weapons? Possibly the only time they would consider going unarmed would be in a place they knew to be utterly secure . . . if such a place could exist in Alizon, where treachery could be confidently expected from one's own closest family members.

As I watched Kasarian, I could not avoid noticing the stark contrast between him and Duratan. Duratan's body, too, had obviously grown accustomed to the weights of sword and dagger, and had been hardened in their use . . . yet during my observations of him at Lormt, Duratan had seemed most serenely content while wielding a quill or searching through old documents. By comparison, for all the pallor of his coloration, Kasarian called to mind the shadows of the night rather than the light of day. He was like a lean, sharp-toothed hound trained to lunge for an enemy's throat, I thought, then decided that he embodied elements of wildness beyond those of even a war hound. With his uncanny agility and quickness of balance, Kasarian more closely resembled a prowling wolf, always poised to spring, always deadly.

Kasarian had noticed that I was watching him. He touched his belt and said, "As Volorian, lady, you will also have to wear such weapons. In recent years, however, he has exchanged most of his daggers for training gear with which he works his hounds. For our would-be meeting with Gurborian, he would definitely equip himself with full armament. If we do emerge in Krevonel Castle, I have there ample stores of weapons for you, as well as a proper pair of boots." He walked around me, scrutinizing me from all sides. "I commend you, lady," he said. "Did I not know better, I would vow that you were a true baron of the blood."

"And one who regrettably still requires more practice in understanding the quickness of spoken Alizonian," warned Morfew. "It is vital that you be prepared to respond to sudden queries, Mereth, with no suspicious hesitation. Let us rehearse again the kinds of phrases that you are likely to hear."

For what seemed endless hours, I feared that I would never grasp what they were saying, but finally my ears discerned the important words which I could not dare mistake. We frequently labored far into the nights. We were constantly aware that at any moment, Gurborian might be succeeding in locating a Dark mage from Escore.

I was both deeply relieved and keenly daunted when on the twentieth day of the Month of the Ice Dragon, after nine days of furious effort, Morfew pronounced me sufficiently prepared for our purposes to deal with both spoken and written Alizonian. Ouen received Morfew's report with evident gratification. "I believe that we can risk no further delay," Ouen declared. "We have accomplished all that we can here at Lormt. Let us now discover whether Elsenar's postern will accept these two would-be travelers. May the Light favor our enterprise!"

CHAPTER 17

Kasarian—events at Lormt
(19th Day, Moon of the Knife/
20th Day, Month of the Ice Dragon)

I had to concede privately that these Lormt folk were formidable plotters. Although they clearly disliked my proposal that Mereth should impersonate Volorian, once they had weighed our perilous situation, they began to offer inspired suggestions for implementing my plan. Initially, they appeared to be repelled by my various strategies to kill Gurborian if he could be lured to Krevonel Castle; then Duratan acknowledged that violence, however repugnant it was to them, might have to be employed. I wondered to myself how else they expected to acquire Elsenar's jewel except by violence, but I did not utter the comment. We Alizonders knew to our sore cost that Estcarp's male fighters were deadly in open warfare. I had to trust that they could be depended upon to wield a blade in defense of their own bodies, even if they shrank from planned assassination. Besides, if Mereth alone could accompany me, I could not rely too heavily upon her prowess with weapons. I should have to dispose of Gurborian myself.

I was considerably relieved to be allowed to resume my confiscated armaments. My uninvited residence at Lormt had been distinctly uncomfortable without their familiar weights and shapes close to hand. I informed Mereth that once we reached Krevonel Castle, I would provide the proper boots and arms to make her fully presentable.

The three of us—Morfew, Mereth, and I—toiled diligently for days until we felt reasonably certain that Mereth could pose as Volorian and not be swiftly exposed as an enemy pretender.

On the Nineteenth Day of the Moon of the Knife, Ouen judged that we must delay no longer, and led our party to the same vault into which I had been so abruptly thrust only thirteen days before. Duratan strewed his uncanny crystals on the stone paving. The blue gems among them fell into a tight oval pattern, as if they had been deliberately set in a cluster. I beheld no significance in the array, but he and the others evidently viewed the display as some sort of positive omen.

Morfew voiced the question that had also occurred to me. "Can we expect Elsenar's postern to function only at that same hour of the night? It may be that the activating spell is time-linked. I was not present when the magical opening was visible, but Ouen pointed out for me the stone over which the access area formed, and we marked that stone for any future reference. I understand that all of you observed a disturbance in the air—a glowing light suspended above the floor. My eyes are not as keen as they once were, but I currently see nothing out of the ordinary about this space above the marked stone."

The Wise Woman frowned at her rune-board. "Nor can I sense the flare of raw Power that initially drew us here before the postern opened. Do you feel aught,

Nolar?" Duratan's mate shook her head, and the Wise Woman turned to Mereth. "Perhaps if you touched Morfew's marked stone," she requested, "you might detect some information beyond our sensing."

Mereth stooped and ran her fingers lightly over the expanse of paving that Morfew had indicated, but her witchly insight failed her on that occasion. She wrote on her slate that the stone produced no images in her mind.

Ouen reached in his belt scrip and withdrew . . . the elder's key! "It may be that this key is needed as part of the spell," he observed, extending it to me. "Were you holding the key in your hand at Krevonel Castle when you first became aware of the postern's opening?"

I hesitated, reviewing my recollections. "Yes," I confirmed, "I was holding the key, but my back was turned away from the center of the room. My eye was attracted by the strange light suddenly waxing behind me."

"If only we knew more about how the ancient mages set their spells," Duratan's mate fretted. "No doubt they could conjure the opening whenever they required it, using special words or gestures."

"I certainly employed no words or gestures," I retorted, "nor did I know whither I was going."

Morfew had been staring at the marked stone. "Perhaps," he said thoughtfully, "if Kasarian stood upon this spot and envisioned the postern-linked chamber in Krevonel Castle, then the force of his mental focus might summon the access point."

The Wise Woman nodded. "Assuming that the postern will accept more than one transient at a time," she cautioned, "we dare not risk any physical separation of the two travelers. If Mereth and Kasarian clasp hands, surely that contact would keep them together during the journey."

Remembering the unsettling disorientation of my passage, I judged it wise to warn Mereth beforehand. "My initial transit was tumultuous," I said to her, "rather like being severely buffeted by a winter gale. The Wise Woman speaks reasonably, but a mere handclasp alone could be dangerously inadequate. I had best lock my arms around you, lady, while bearing the elder's key as I did before, should that be a necessary element for the working of the spell. Come, let us stand close together, and fix our minds upon our urgently required terminus."

Mereth tucked her staff through her belt, and after some slight hesitation, placed her arms around my waist. Taking the elder's key in my right hand, I reached around her cloaked shoulders, grasping her body firmly against my chest.

"The chamber which we would enter," I declared aloud, "is that magic-secured lower vault beneath Krevonel Castle." I closed my eyes to concentrate upon the bare stonewalled space as I had last seen it . . . the age-roughened wooden door with its bronze-silver lock. . . .

"It's coming!" The Wise Woman's abrupt cry startled me. When I opened my eyes, an eldritch oval of curdled light was soundlessly expanding only an arm's length away from our position.

"Hold fast, lady!" I ordered, then lifted her off her feet, and plunged both of us through the shimmering expanse.

CHAPTER 18

Mereth—events at Lormt, then at
Krevonel Castle (20th Day, Month of the
Ice Dragon/19th Day, Moon of the Knife)

"I forced myself to approach Kasarian and put my arms around his slender waist. He was apparently not equally repelled by me, for he seized me so tightly that I could scarcely breathe. A shattering thought struck me—no male had hugged me so fervently since my beloved Doubt, achingly long years ago. That I should have to submit to this indignity from an Alizonder was almost more than I could bear, but even worse lay ahead.

I clung frantically to Kasarian, the only solid, warm object in a pitch-black, freezing, roaring chaos. I could feel his heart hammering through his tunic, but he held me unflinchingly. I do not know whether I dared to breathe, or if one could breathe in that awful space. Just as instantly as we had been afflicted, we emerged into another stone-floored chamber. Our only light source was the postern opening itself, and as it rapidly diminished, then vanished, we were left in complete darkness.

"Can you stand, lady?" Kasarian's voice came from

near my ear. He had eased his enveloping clasp so that my feet were again firmly on the floor, but he kept one arm around my shoulders. "She cannot speak," he muttered to himself in Alizonian, then added to me, "Squeeze my hand if you can stand unaided."

I felt for his hand, and pressed it. I was somewhat lightheaded, as if feverish or only half awake, but I believed I could hold myself upright if I did not try to move.

Kasarian released me. Shortly afterward, I heard a scraping sound nearby. Abruptly, I could see that he had struck a spark with his tinderbox, and was squatting to kindle a burnt-out torch, possibly the one he had left behind when he came to Lormt. The flickering torchlight disclosed a bare, windowless room with only one massive door. I leaned upon my staff while my dizziness receded.

"Before we leave this chamber," Kasarian warned, "we must plan carefully. It would be best for you to be seen by the fewest possible people. I cannot show myself here without being at once attended by Gennard, who has been my body servant since I was whelped. Having previously served my sire's littermate, he is the sole person at Krevonel Castle who knows Volorian by sight. I shall tell him that you are a baron engaged upon a secret visit to the City; he will ask no prying questions. We can also rely totally upon Bodrik, my castellan, who came to Krevonel five years ago from our coastal estates. Yes, those two shall be the pair to serve us. Do not be disturbed by the scar on Bodrik's face—he was wounded two years ago in a skirmish with brigands from Karsten." Kasarian paused, then added, "Bodrik has often clashed with Lursk, Gurborian's Master of Arms. The two of them preserve a wary truce while both

Gurborian and I are in the City. I shall entrust the dispatch of Volorian's message to Bodrik. He will contrive to achieve our desired ends: secure delivery of Morfew's summons into Gurborian's hands, while avoiding unwelcome attention by outside observers."

I withdrew my slate and chalk from an inner pocket of my cloak. Limited both by the slate's small available surface and my store of Alizonian, I strove to compress my host of questions into the briefest form. I wrote, "Will not your servants seek our horses?"

Kasarian read my words, and showed his teeth in a wolfish smile. "I rejoice, lady, that our rough transit has not addled your wits," he said. "If we are to assert the secretive nature of your baronial mission to the City, then we should not arrive conspicuously, with a mounted troop. As the Master of Krevonel Castle, I alone know and use the many secret passages allowing entrance and exit without notice by friend or foe. My staff will assume that we used such a passage—which, after a most abnormal fashion, we did." He fell silent for a moment, than stated, "You will have to inspect my hounds; no visiting baron, most especially Volorian, would fail to do so. Have you ever had occasion to see or touch one of our hounds?"

I clutched my slate tightly to prevent him from seeing the tremor that pulsed through my hands. "From distance," I finally managed to write, "only twice, during war." I shuddered inwardly at the memory of those two awful events.

During the early years of the war in the Dales, the Alizonder invaders had brought with them a number of ravening packs of their namesake beasts, which they loosed upon our defenders. The Alizonders' hounds were like no dogs such as those we knew and employed ourselves for hunting or warfare. From Elsenar's journal, I now knew that the original hounds had come through a mage's Gate with the first Alizonders. All we of the embattled Dales had known was revulsion and terror for the lean, white creatures that savagely ran down our fleeing men, women, and children. Once the blessed Sulcars succeeded in harrying and intercepting Alizon's supply ships, the barons gradually withdrew their precious hounds as too valuable to be slain at sea or by our darts or swords. Volorian, I recalled, was supposed to be a noted breeder of the vile creatures. I would have to compel myself to view Kasarian's hounds.

Staring at me speculatively, Kasarian must have sensed my reluctance. "I shall fetch to you a recent pup from my prize bitch," he declared. "Before you encounter the entire pack, we must determine how your scent affects them. Come, let us repair to an upper chamber. I have much to tell you while we dispatch and wait for Gurborian's reply to our message." He thrust his key into the great lock, and swung back the door.

We proceeded through corridors and up stairs whose dusty surfaces had recently been disturbed by the marks of only one pair of boots. Unlike the sober gray stones of Lormt, Krevonel Castle's stones were a glistening buff-brown color, but the scale of the Alizonders' construction was equally impressive. I noted a strange similarity between these underground ways and those beneath Lormt . . . until we gained the more habitable upper levels. The farther we climbed, the more sumptuous the decorations and furnishings became. Possibly because of their own physical paleness, the Alizonders seemed to adorn their living quarters with brilliant—even jarringly bright—colors.

Twice, far ahead of us in the corridors, I glimpsed

white-haired figures clad in dark blue livery, but as soon
as they noticed our approach, they scurried out of sight
around the next corner or through the nearest door. One
figure alone did not retreat, but marched purposefully
across a vast reception hall to meet us. He was a tall,
gaunt, older Alizonder, whose pale blue eyes reminded
me of Morfew.

Kasarian nodded brusquely to the man, as if he had
expected to encounter him. "You will serve our guest
and me in the north tower room, Gennard. Send for Bodrik to meet us there at once."

As he bowed to Kasarian, Gennard touched his House
badge. "Welcome back, Master." He turned toward me,
repeating the bow and the gesture. "Krevonel Castle
welcomes you, Worthy Baron," he said in a voice neither
subservient nor fearful. If he had served Kasarian since
the baron's childhood, I assumed that he must be a capable survivor . . . and that he felt secure in his position.

I imitated Kasarian's nod, and strode after him, for he
had already moved toward a distant door. We climbed
yet more stairs. I was deeply relieved when Kasarian finally entered a room and offered me an ornate chair. We
had scarcely seated ourselves before a different Alizonder appeared at the open door.

"Enter, Bodrik," Kasarian invited, and the man he had
described to me as his castellan approached us.

Somehow, I had expected that all Alizonders would
look alike. So far, Kasarian's castle staff did share the
same distinctively pale hair and skin, and they were all
outfitted in the same neat blue livery ornamented with
white piping and braid. When viewed face to face, however, the individual Alizonders appeared as different as
any two Dalesmen would. Bodrik's features were not as
finely cut as Kasarian's, and he was stockier and broader

of shoulder than his master. His eyes were a clear green, like the early leaves of spring, but what drew my gaze was the livid scar that branded a diagonal slash from above his left eyebrow across the bridge of his nose, extending down his right cheek.

Touching his House badge, Bodrik bowed to Kasarian. "Krevonel welcomes your return, Master," he said in rumbling tones, the growl of his Alizonian more pronounced than Gennard's or Kasarian's.

"Krevonel is honored by the arrival of this Worthy Baron," Kasarian proclaimed, nodding deferentially toward me. "His name and presence, however, must not be revealed to outsiders, since his purpose in the City must be achieved in utmost secrecy. He has traveled a far distance, despite a winter ague that has presently quenched his voice. He will make known his orders to you in writing."

As Bodrik bowed to me, he said, "I am yours to command, Worthy Baron."

"The Baron's first command is that you convey a private message to Baron Gurborian," Kasarian said, holding out the leather-wrapped packet containing Morfew's cunningly phrased summons. "Take this at once to Lursk, for his immediate delivery into Gurborian's hand. We require an equally discreet reply. Depending upon the nature of Gurborian's response, I shall have further instructions for you."

"It shall be accomplished, Master. Lursk is drinking today at the Hooded Crow. Your message will be in Baron Gurborian's hand within the hour." Bodrik bowed again to each of us, then hastened from the room.

Gennard must have been watching for Bodrik's departure, for he entered right away, bearing a carved wooden tray crowded with flagons, covered dishes, and open containers. With the ease of long practice, he swiftly set out an array of food and drink on a side table. He would have commenced to serve us, but Kasarian held up his hand.

"We shall not require you to serve," Kasarian said. "I prefer that you attend to a different task. In our haste to reach the City, we did not encumber ourselves with baggage. During his guesting with us, the Baron therefore relies upon our wardrobe for his needs."

Gennard surveyed me. "If the Worthy Baron will allow me, I can fetch to his guest chamber a selection of robes from your sire's store, Master."

"An excellent idea," Kasarian approved. "He is much the same size as Baron Oralian. Bring the clothing and suitable boots to the chamber next to mine. We shall repair thither after we have eaten and conferred. Be sure also to fetch a supply of writing chalk. The Baron's voice has been temporarily silenced by an ague, and he must write his orders upon a slate that he has brought with him."

"As you command, Master . . . Worthy Baron." Gennard bowed to us both and withdrew.

Kasarian moved a table between our chairs, and began to transfer the dishes. "I do not permit the affairs of Krevonel Castle to be conducted in the lavish fashion favored by some other barons," he remarked. "I became accustomed to the simpler fare and style of service provided at Volorian's estates. Now that I am Master of Krevonel, I maintain that style, rather than indulge in pointless rounds of banqueting." He carefully poured a dark red liquid into a silver flagon, then paused before offering me the cup. "I must caution you," he advised, "about this bloodwine of ours. We have never allowed any of it to be taken beyond Alizon's borders; it is restricted solely for baronial use. I suggest that you sample it . . . sparingly, until you fully appreciate its character."

I accepted the flagon warily. In my years of trading experience, I had tasted many vintages, some thin and sour, others strong and heady. This Alizonian wine had a pronounced bouquet, somewhat acrid, but not offensive. I took a very small sip. It tasted like no other wine I knew—at the same time, both strangely sweet and salty. As soon as I swallowed, I felt it bite like a potent, long-fermented cider. I set the flagon on the table, taking a deep breath to clear my vision. Kasarian was watching me over the rim of his goblet. I fancied I could detect a certain glint of amusement in his eyes. I wrote firmly on my slate, "Best I not drink much of this. Makes eyes water."

Kasarian nodded, evidently entertained by my reaction. "I shall have to serve bloodwine to Gurborian and Gratch when they come," he said. "We can excuse your failure to join us as occasioned by your loss of taste due to that same deplorable ague that has taken your voice. To accompany this meal, try this cordial made from white hedgeberries—much blander, yet thirst quenching."

As he served each dish, Kasarian described it for me, and tasted a sample himself. I could not help recalling that both he and Duratan had cited the Alizonders' penchant for poisoning one another. Doubtless Kasarian was attempting to reassure me of the wholesomeness of his viands. I chose to eat items familiar to me—some poached fish, a leg of wild moorhen, rabbit in pastry, some cheeses. Kasarian urged me to taste a dish of what appeared to be steamed roots served with a cream sauce. He said it was another Alizonian speciality, never offered to outsiders. I found it so highly spiced that I doubted that many outsiders would desire to eat it, but I was spared from having to write my opinion of the dish, since he devoted his attention to slicing a glazed fruit confection. He would have pressed further dishes upon me, but I hastily wrote that I could eat no more.

Kasarian passed me a silver bowl containing moistened cloths so that we might wipe our hands. "I shall leave you briefly now," he announced, pushing back his chair, "to fetch the hound pup. Gennard may return to clear away our finished meal. If his presence perturbs you, you can survey the City from our windows until he leaves."

As Kasarian had predicted, soon after he left the room, Gennard did come back. He bowed to me, then started stacking the dishes on his tray. I nodded to him in what I hoped was an acceptably dismissive baronial style, and walked to one of the slit windows to look out upon the city of my enemies.

Because of the winter cold, heavy wooden shutters padded with wool had been secured across the windows. I unlatched one panel and swung it back. The sunlight was impeded by a layer of high clouds, so that my first view of Alizon City was appropriately drained of color. I was dismayed to behold the extent of the sprawling settlement. Ranks of roofs crowded one against another as far as the eye could see. From its commanding perch on an elevated rocky ridge dominating all other buildings loomed a monstrous fortress that had to be Alizon Castle, seat of the infamous Lord Baron. High up as I was in the Krevonel Castle's tower, I could see the glitter of metal flashing from the helmets of the sentries patrolling the fortress walls.

The frigid draft through the open window numbed my face, but I was already chilled from within. The realization that I, a lone Daleswoman, should be standing in clear sight of the very Kennels of the Hounds of Alizon pierced me like a knife thrust. I was aghast when tears I could not feel because of the cold suddenly splashed down on my sleeve. I contrived, while closing and fastening the shutter, to rub a fold of my cloak around my face. I did not turn around until I heard Gennard close the door as he left the room. I chided myself severely. Loneliness and weariness could not excuse so dangerous a lapse. I doubted that Alizonder barons often indulged in tears—unless they were writhing in poisoned agony.

The door opened abruptly, and Kasarian entered, carrying a squirming white bundle in his arms. I hastened to sit on a nearby bench so that he could place the horrid creature in my lap. It was an extremely young beast, but already long of leg and well-muscled for the chase. I tried not to disclose my repugnance, but settled the hound with my gloved hands.

I was surprised by the softness of its short white fur. Its head was very narrow, with keen yellow eyes deep-set above a pointed, questing nose. Its curiously flared ears folded back flat against its skull except when they pricked erect to listen. The needle-sharp claws, like those of a cat, could retract into the foot pads; I soon discovered that its teeth were even sharper when it nipped me even through Mistress Bethalie's gloves. Kasarian's hands, I saw, also exhibited fresh toothmarks and scratches.

He observed my gaze, and laughed—the first time that I had heard him laugh. I suppose I had expected Alizonders to bark like their wretched hounds, but Kasarian's laugh was a natural sound of genuine pleasure.

"Exceptional spirit!" Kasarian exclaimed, wiping away a streak of blood from his wrist. "Both his sire and dam are fine beasts, as this one will be in time. Due to the silver in his coat, I call him 'Moonbeam.' " He rubbed his fingers gently behind its ears, and the beast twisted its muzzle around to lick his hand.

I was astonished. Could these murderous hounds actually inspire affection? Was an Alizonder capable of such feelings?

Kasarian compounded my surprise by assuming an uncharacteristically defensive manner. "Few other barons name their hounds," he conceded, "but I have found that some hounds respond to training more energetically when singled out. Volorian introduced me to the practice, for he always named his primary hounds, the better to maintain correct breeding records. While they are pups, of course, hounds are more amenable to handling. Moonbeam clearly welcomes your attentions."

I realized that I had unconsciously begun to stroke the creature, and to my amazement, although the sound it made was rougher and more grating, it purred, almost like a cat.

Rising from his crouching position by my feet, Kasarian reverted to his more usual arrogant manner. "I rejoice that your scent does not infuriate Moonbeam," he said. "Since you have handled him, his scent will cling to you, which should aid in your acceptance by the adult pack. Let us now restore Moonbeam to the Kennels."

As we started toward the door, Gennard appeared. "I have placed a selection of Baron Oralian's clothing in the chamber adjoining yours, Master," he reported.

"Having examined Moonbeam, the Worthy Baron presently desires to inspect the balance of my pack," Kasarian declared. "We shall assess your choices upon our return from the Kennels."

Long before we reached the Kennel area, I could hear

the dreadful clamor of the hounds. Moonbeam whined excitedly from his perch in Kasarian's arms. We descended several steep ramps, stopping only when our way was blocked by a heavy iron grill anchored firmly in the stones on either side of the passageway.

Kasarian called out, "Wolkor!"

A burly Alizonder hurried out of the shadows to unlock a hinged gate panel fitted at one side of the grill. "Moonbeam's dam be sore vexed, Master," he complained. " 'Twas needful to double leash her."

Kasarian shifted Moonbeam into the other man's eagerly extended arms. "They shall be parted soon enough when he joins the training pack," Kasarian said.

I followed close behind the pair of them through a narrow passage that opened out into a spacious courtyard. The Alizonder carrying Moonbeam darted aside beneath an archway leading back into the Kennels.

"Wolkor has served me as Hound Master for many years," Kasarian observed to me. "I had to bribe his former master to secure his release, but I have found none better at tending whelping bitches. You can judge his prowess by the excellent condition of my pack."

I do not know how I endured the next hour. Like most nursling animals, Moonbeam had possessed—to some limited extent—the attraction of vulnerable helplessness. To be forced now to survey the grown hounds with every appearance of approval made my flesh crawl.

Having restored Moonbeam to his mother's custody, Wolkor paraded before me individuals, braces, triples, and surging packs of hounds. My worst memories from the Dales war rushed back into my mind as the thin-flanked, ghostly white bodies strained against their leashes, weaving their snake-like heads from side to side, snapping and snarling. Whenever Kasarian bellowed some encomium above the din, I nodded appreciatively. I had to believe that the hounds accepted me as an authentic Alizonder, for their vicious exuberance was not directed in any corporate attacks on me.

Finally, as I was beginning to feel giddy from the dust, noise, and peculiar odor of the hounds, Kasarian called to Wolkor, "We shall distract you from your duties no further. I look forward to the whelping!"

Taking my arm, Kasarian led me back through the twisting passageways into the castle. "You did very well, lady," he murmured, when we were safely alone in one of the castle's endless corridors. "Volorian himself could have looked no wiser—except he would have forcefully evaluated every hound. I had to explain your lack of voice. Wolkor is convinced that you are a famed hound breeder." That obviously ridiculous assumption made Kasarian smile. "You may yet deceive Gurborian, lady—I begin to think that you may!"

Gennard was waiting for us outside an intricately carved door in one of the upper halls. The bedchamber within was regally appointed. On a wide table beside the canopied bed, Gennard had laid out a profusion of elegant cloaks, tunics, breeches, and soft leather boots.

With a low cry of recognition, Kasarian picked up a tunic of vivid green velvet, closely embroidered with gold thread. "I remember this," he said slowly.

"Baron Oralian preferred that color," Gennard remarked. "I thought that perhaps the Worthy Baron. . . ."

"Just so," Kasarian interrupted. "We shall consider your selections. You may retire."

Once Gennard had shut the door, Kasarian held out the tunic to me. "I was five when my sire last wore this, just before his murder," he mused. "It is unlikely that

Gurborian would recall it. Try it on, together with these proper boots."

I was relieved that only outer garments had to be exchanged, since Kasarian showed no intention of leaving the room. The genuine Alizonian clothing and boots fit me passably well.

While I dressed, Kasarian had paced back and forth. When my outfitting was complete, he surveyed me critically and nodded. "I commend you," he said. "No man could deny that in such garb, you present the appearance of a true baron." Suddenly he tensed, motionless except for a deliberate inclination of his head. Had he been one of his appalling hounds, I thought, his ears would have pricked up, he was listening so intently. From immobility, he erupted into a blur of motion, snatching a knife from his belt with a horrid facility, and throwing it with the sureness of a striking snake toward a shadowy corner where the brocaded bedskirt brushed the carpet.

I flinched inadvertently at the thud of the knife's impact, which coincided with a shrill animal cry of pain.

Kasarian bent to retrieve his knife, jerking it free from a fold of fabric, and disclosing the body of a large brown rat he had impaled against the wooden bedstead.

As he walked toward the door, Kasarian drew a strip of cloth from his tunic pocket to wipe his knife blade before resheathing it. Opening the door, he called Gennard, who appeared so quickly that he must have been waiting nearby. Kasarian gestured at the carcass and said, "An extra morsel for Wolkor's evening feeding." Gennard tidily grasped the dead rat by its tail, bowed to us, and withdrew.

Kasarian must have sensed my disquiet, for he surveyed me speculatively. "Have you no rats?" he asked.

I countered on my slate, "Have you no cats?"

He read my words, and smiled. "I have heard of such beasts," he remarked. "They are kept, I believe, to hunt rats and mice within inhabited structures. Our hounds are superb ratters, but are far too high-spirited and valuable to be allowed to run loose indoors. They must be reserved for hunting truly significant game. For controlling vermin, we find that a ready knife is quite adequate . . . and the sport instructs the young, exercising the agility of both hand and eye." His smile faded. "We may have scant time left before Bodrik returns with Gurborian's reply. Pray sit down. You must be informed of certain matters before Gurborian and Gratch arrive—for I cannot believe that they will avoid falling into our trap."

CHAPTER 19

Kasarian—events at Krevonel Castle
(19th Day, Moon of the Knife/
20th Day, Month of the Ice Dragon)

I was not at all certain how well Mereth would accommodate herself to our Alizonian food and drink, particularly to those singular items which we never allowed beyond our borders. It was vital that her reactions not betray her before Gurborian. I knew that she would have to accustom herself—if that were possible—to our potent bloodwine, which was always served copiously at any baronial meeting. Mereth sipped the portion I poured for her with commendable caution, then wrote that it made her eyes water, and she preferred to avoid drinking much of it. I deemed it prudent to accept her superficial response; she could not be seen by Gurborian to choke upon or swoon from imbibing our primary baronial drink. I suggested that we would ascribe her otherwise inexcusable rejection of the bloodwine to her loss of taste due to the ague.

Mereth appeared to experience no other difficulty with our Alizonian food. In case she might be suspicious of the presence of poison, I tasted some of each dish to allay her fears, then left her briefly to fetch my hound pup Moonbeam, who had been whelped early, between the year's two regular Whelping Moons. He already showed considerable promise of becoming a pack leader like his sire. When I placed him on Mereth's lap, she held him acceptably. Even when he nipped her hands through her gloves, she refrained from striking him. She was, of course, incapable of crying out, but I was favorably impressed by her forbearance. To my considerable relief, Moonbeam freely endured Mereth's presence and attentions—indeed, he actually rumbled in response to her stroking! I trusted that his scent would cling to her sufficiently to assuage the pack when we proceeded to the Kennels.

I was most gratified by the fine display of my pack arranged by Wolker, my Hound Master. When all of my beasts had been shown to their best advantage and we rose to depart, Wolker whispered to me that Krevonel's Kennels were honored to be inspected by such an experienced visiting authority. His reaction encouraged me to think that Mereth might just possibly deceive even Gurborian.

Upon arriving at the guest's bed chamber, Mereth dressed herself with admirable dispatch, requiring assistance with only the bestowing of weapons. Arrayed in one of my sire's complete outfits, she could easily have been mistaken for a genuine baron. I had been carefully weighing in my mind how much to reveal to Mereth. I could not know what Morfew might have told her about Alizon and our ways. Although he claimed to have been cut off from news of Alizon during all his years of exile in Lormt, I was not certain whether that was a deliberate attempt to deceive me. I decided that in order for Mereth to be properly wary of Gurborian and Gratch, she had to be more fully informed about their reputations. Because Volorian was well aware of Gurborian's plotting, Mereth dared not appear surprised by facts known to Volorian. It was now therefore vital that I disclose to her Gurborian's and Gratch's intentions to depose of Lord Baron Norandor.

"I must warn you first about Gratch," I began. "He is a shadowy figure, much dreaded due to his mastery of rare poisons. Little is known about his past except that he escaped from his birthsite on Gorm shortly before the island fell to the Kolder thirty years ago. Doubtless his intense hatred for the Kolder stems from that time. Ten years ago, he appeared in Alizon, and after assessing the relative prospects for advancement among the primary barons, allied himself with Gurborian. I had just assumed the mastery of Krevonel Castle when word began to circulate that Gratch had become Gurborian's principal advisor, contributing to and participating in all of his schemes. A year or so after Lord Baron Mallandor's accession, both Gratch and Gurborian retreated to the Reptur Line's estates along the coast. They conducted their plotting in general seclusion there for some five years, allowing Mallandor's suspicions ample time to cool."

Mereth held up her hand, and scribbled on her slate. "After war, Mallandor replaced Facellian," she wrote. "Why would Mallandor suspect Gurborian? Was he not friend?"

"Gurborian had openly supported Mallandor's overthrow of Facellian," I confirmed. "That was the chief reason why Mallandor rewarded Gurborian with the jewel we now know to be Elsenar's."

"But you said at Lormt you did not know details about gift of jewel," Mereth objected on her slate. "You said you were only pup at time."

I could not entirely suppress my amusement at the gullibility of the Lormt folk. "When you first inquired," I said, "it was not advisable to divulge the full extent of my knowledge. We Alizonders learn early that information can be as precious as gold, and should be as closely guarded. It is now necessary that you be thoroughly informed about the foes we must vanquish.

"At Lormt, I spoke the truth to you—a limited portion of it. As a twelve year old whelp-of-age, I had been presented to Lord Baron Facellian. Volorian accompanied me to that New Year's Assembly to stand in my murdered sire's stead, then we returned to his manor where I had been fostered. Shortly after we left Alizon City, Facellian was overthrown and executed for losing the Dales war. Mallandor bestowed the jewel upon Gurborian as partial payment for his support, but soon realized that Gurborian's loyalty to him as Lord Baron might be no more trustworthy than it had previously been to Facellian. Gurborian prudently withdrew to his coastal estates to allow Mallandor's doubts to subside. Even after Gurborian returned to Alizon City five years ago, he deliberately shunned the Lord Baron's close scrutiny. To disguise the true intentions of his travels, he occasionally pleaded for leave from court to attend to various matters at his estates.

"When I established my residence here at Krevonel about ten years ago, I had heard about the initial awarding of the jewel to Gurborian, but I had not seen the gem until it was for the second time bestowed upon him by Norandor at this New Year's Assembly just past. To my knowledge, Gurborian had never publicly displayed the jewel after he first received it from Mallandor. I had wondered why he had refrained from wearing such a rumored prize, since he is famed for his lavish show of baubles, but I concluded that during those intervening years, Gurborian likely dared not remind Mallandor of the reason for his possessing it. After all, one successful overthrow of a Lord Baron might lead to thoughts of another such removal . . . and indeed, we now know that Gurborian was already scheming to depose Mallandor.

"Three years ago, when Estcarp's Witches forestalled Karsten's impending invasion by their horrendous magical assault upon their southern border's mountains, Mallandor longed to attack Estcarp while it was distracted and vulnerable. The Witch-spells sealing their northern border with us held firm, however, preventing any incursions from Alizon. Mallandor then witlessly acceded to the pro-Kolder faction's arguments, resulting in last spring's bungled raid into Estcarp led by Esguir, his trusted Hound Master. When all the remaining Kolder were killed and the Witchlings had escaped back into Estcarp, Gurborian recognized his opportunity. He united Mallandor's enemies in a plot to elevate Norandor, Mallandor's littermate—brother, as you say—to the throne. To recompense Gurborian for his essential aid, Norandor then officially conferred the jewel upon him for the second time—although only for his lifetime's use. Esguir and Mallandor were, of course, fed to the hounds."

I was interrupted by the sudden grating of Mereth's chalk. She held up her slate for me to read her scrawled query, "Fed to the hounds?"

"Surely Morfew has described to you our traditional method of disposing of failed Lords Baron and traitors to Alizon," I replied. "Obviously," I hastened to add, "the bodies are *never* given to the better hounds because of the poison residues."

Mereth's hand faltered slightly as she wrote, "Poison?"

"All prominent barons and their primary retainers must guard themselves against being poisoned by regularly consuming small amounts of the more usual poisons," I explained. "The practice naturally renders the human bodies unfit for houndmeat. Traitors' bodies are fed to only the less able hounds, so that their illness or death would not diminish the effectiveness of the pack."

I regarded Mereth closely for any other signs of deplorable weakness, but aside from her initial hand tremor, she seemed to have recovered her resoluteness. "One of Norandor's men, Sherek, has been lately named the new Hound Master," I resumed, "to Gurborian's bitter disappointment. Gurborian had mistakenly assumed that he could influence Norandor by bribery and coercion. Soon after Norandor's elevation to the throne, Gratch came forward with the cursed notion of seeking an alliance for Alizon with the Dark mages of Escore to replace our former, failed alliance with the Kolder. With Gurborian's approval, Gratch probed about in the mountains near Volorian's estate this past summer, occasioning those letters from Volorian that first alerted me to the Escorian threat.

"I must tell you that I have private reasons I may not discuss which convince me that Gurborian and Gratch intend to depose Norandor, if they can secure sufficient backing from other disaffected barons. Volorian suspects as much—ever since the murder of my sire, he has harbored boundless enmity for Gurborian. You must bear that enmity constantly in mind during your impersonation. Despite the fair words of Morfew's message, Gurborian will not be easily persuaded of Krevonel's willingness to ally with him. You and I must appear to be both outwardly cold—as he will expect—and yet plausibly prevailed upon by the strength of his arguments to accept his proposals."

Looking bleakly determined, Mereth nodded, then wrote yet another query on her slate. "If Volorian known for rejection of all magic, how can I in his place . . ." She hesitated, groping for a usable Alizonion word, I presumed. After a pause, she finished the query, "bend to endorse any alliance with Escore?"

"The potential for irresistible gain should overwhelm our objections, or so Gurborian will likely insist," I predicted. "If I appear to press you forcefully on behalf of the younger whelps of the Line of Krevonel, then your skillfully timed change of attitude may satisfy them. Your initial revulsion toward Gurborian's suggestions can moderate into reluctant acquiescence. Under the circumstances, we are compelled to risk all—we must say anything necessary to pry Elsenar's jewel away from Gurborian. As soon as the stone is within our grasp, we must withdraw as rapidly as we can, to convey the jewel through the postern to Lormt, where it will be safely beyond the control of Gurborian or the Dark mages."

Bodrik should have returned by this time, I thought, unless he had encountered difficulties in delivering our message. I chastised myself for my impatience. Gurborian would weigh each word Morfew had written, and surely take equal pains—and time—in composing his reply.

I glanced at Mereth. She did not appear to be unsettled or visibly nervous, but it might be well to keep her occupied so that she would not have time to brood or indulge in fretful female imaginings. "You are suitably garbed for our baronial meeting," I said, "but I am not. Come through into my quarters and refresh yourself with another . . . feebler wine while I array myself."

CHAPTER 20

Mereth—events at Krevonel Castle
(19th and 20th Days, Month of the Ice
Dragon/ 20th and 21st Days, Moon of the Knife)

As Kasarian described to me the two enemies we were likely to confront, I blessed my long years of trading experience that enabled me to listen without exhibiting any outward signs of my true feelings. My beloved Doubt had often accused me of cultivating a facial expression of bland indifference. He was forced to concede that at times, I could extract better prices than he because the other merchants could not discern which particular goods I especially desired.

Listening now to Kasarian, I was appalled by the history of repeated intrigue and murder that he recounted. It was all the more chilling in its impact because of his matter-of-course style of speaking. I found it horrid to contemplate that for him and all the other Alizonder barons, their chosen way of life had grown out of such a bloody tradition.

When Kasarian mentioned Gorm, I felt a surge of painful memories. We Dalesfolk had once conducted a lively commerce with that island stronghold offshore from Estcarp. In my early years of trading, I had established fruitful ties with many merchants based in the warehouses crowding Gorm's ports. Moored like a great vessel of rock in Estcarp's coastal bay, Gorm was sheltered from all but the rare north-westerly storms by the peninsular arm crowned by Sulcar-keep, the Sulcar fleet's home port. During my first overseas voyage with Uncle Parand so many years before, our ship had anchored for a time at Sippar, Gorm's primary city, which also served then as Estcarp's main port.

Thirty years ago, all the golden days of prosperity had come to a shattering end. While Hilder, Gorm's Lord De-fender, languished near death, his second wife, anxious to secure her regency on behalf of their young son, secretly summoned the hideous Kolder to back her rule. The very night that Hilder died, the Kolder swept in from the sea, not as allies, but as merciless invaders. Most of Gorm's in-habitants suffered an unspeakable fate, forced to fight as mindless slaves for the Kolder until they were killed by their own grieving former friends from Estcarp and Sulcar-keep. Following Sulcarkeep's tragic, deliberate destruction by its own defenders to prevent its seizure by the Kolder's forces, Estcarp's Witches, aided by the famed Simon Tre-garth, used their magic to launch a successful invasion of Gorm, exterminating all the Kolder lairing there. Ever since, the haunted island had been abandoned, mourned by all who remembered its fair past.

I now learned from Kasarian that Gratch, Gurborian's prime henchmen, was one of the few who escaped from Gorm shortly before the Kolder doomed the island. Unlike the Gormfolk I had known and respected, Gratch was evi-dently a wicked schemer, no doubt attracted to Alizon where his murderous talents would be most fully appreci-ated. Because of Gorm's betrayal into the Kolder's hands, Gratch loathed the Kolder, and thus aligned himself with

Gurborian, who, for different reasons, shared that detestation for the foreign instigators of the war with the Dales.

I was startled when Kasarian confided that Lord Baron Mallandor had suspected Gurborian of conspiring against him. I had understood that Mallandor had relied upon Gurborian in their violent overthrow of the previous Lord Baron, Facellian. Kasarian boldly admitted to me, however, that he had not told me the entire truth at Lormt concerning the circumstances of Gurborian's receipt of Elsenar's jewel. The wretched baron had actually been awarded the stone on two separate occasions by two different Lords Baron!

I was numbed by Kasarian's factual recital of the murderous intrigues and betrayals that saturated the Alizonian court. I hoped that he did not notice how my hand shook before I steadied my chalk when I queried him regarding the hideous double execution of a disgraced ruler and his underling who were literally *fed* to the hounds. It was as well that I could not speak, for I do not know what damaging words I might have blurted out—yet what words could have conveyed the depths of my affronted disbelief? I shuddered inwardly to think that countless generations of Alizonders had preyed upon one another in so cruel a fashion. It was difficult to grasp how Alizon had survived for so long when outright murder was a commended tactic for baronial advancement.

Clearly, Gurborian exemplified the most deplorable Alizonian traits. He had benefited from each major act of treachery, but not all of his schemes had succeeded. The execution of Mallandor's Hound Master had left vacant that powerful Alizonian office of primary war baron. Gurborian attempted to sway the appointment by means of bribes and intimidation, but the new Lord Baron Norandor had ignored Gurborian's machinations and installed one of his own men as Hound Master.

Kasarian warned me that Volorian had long been aware of the extent of Gurborian's ambitious plotting. When I posed as Volorian, I should have to reflect his enduring animosity toward the murderer of his brother; Gurborian would expect it. Both Kasarian and I, in fact, would have to strive to convey a plausible change in our established attitudes, from entrenched opposition to grudging acceptance of Gurborian's proposals. When . . . if we did obtain Elsenar's jewel as a necessary bribe to secure Krevonel's backing, Kasarian admonished me to disengage as quickly as possible, so that the jewel could be carried safely to Lormt, out of danger of discovery by the Dark forces of Escore.

As if struck by a sudden thought, Kasarian fell silent. He observed that he was not appropriately dressed to confer with Gurborian and Gratch, and invited me into the adjoining bedchamber. I had an initial fleeting impression of sober elegance. Dark blue wall hangings softened the expanses of bare stone, and I glimpsed a canopied bed draped with a matching blue brocade occupying a raised dais against the far wall. Before I could fully survey the room's furnishings, however my attention was exclusively engaged by one of the most terrifying sights I had ever beheld. When I half-turned as I passed a shadowed alcove, I found myself at the mercy of an enormous golden-eyed monster rearing up to attack me. I nearly fell, lurching backward and to one side in what I expected to be a futile effort to evade the nightmare's fangs and claws. Had I possessed a voice, I should have cried out in despair . . . then I abruptly realized that the beast had not moved.

Doubtless alerted by his sensitive ears as well as his swordsman's eye for movement behind him, Kasarian spun on his heel, one of his belt daggers ready in his hand. When I gestured at the monster, he laughed aloud. "I should have warned you in advance about Krevonel's most noteworthy trophy," he said, sheathing his dagger as rapidly as he had drawn it.

Plucking a torch from a nearby stone embrasure, Kasarian raised it to illuminate what I could now see was a gigantic wolf-like creature whose thick-furred hide had been preserved and mounted upon a hidden framework to mimic the effects of a living, lunging predator. Kasarian was a tall man, but the rampant creature's outstretched front paws loomed above his shoulders. He regarded the horror with an expression that I had seen only once before, when he had brought me his hound pup. It seemed impossible to believe, but he was genuinely proud, even . . . fond of this monster.

"So few sightings are reported nowadays," Kasarian mused. "My sire's sire killed this dire wolf many years ago during a hunt in our northern mountains. The craftsman who mounted the skin achieved a splendid effect with the eyes, don't you think?" He waved the torch from side to side. I tried not to shudder as the glittering eyes appeared to shift within the massive skull. "Pure gold orbs with black stones inset for the pupils," Kasarian explained. "They provide a most lifelike impression." He sighed regretfully. "I have never had the fortune to sight a dire wolf myself," he said. "My sire once told me that he had encountered unmistakable tracks, but the winter weather was too severe for his hunting party to pursue them. Still, we cherish this excellent specimen which not even Gurborian can match, for all his wealth and power."

I welcomed the goblet of fortifying wine that Kasarian poured from a silver ewer on a side table, and was equally grateful when he offered me a cushioned chair. He then strode to the door to shout for Gennard to attend him in his robing chamber.

My pounding heart had slowed to a more reasonable pace by the time Kasarian returned. I had to admit that he made a striking figure in midnight blue velvet tunic and hose, white leather belt and boots, and with an even more elaborate gold baronial chain suspended across his chest.

He had scarcely seated himself when Gennard thrust open the door. "Master," he called urgently. "Bodrik has been wounded."

Jumping to his feet, Kasarian demanded, "Where is he? Was he able to return to Krevonel?" Before Gennard could answer, we heard an approaching clamor in the outer corridor, and suddenly Bodrik himself reeled into the room, closely pursued by several liveried servants scrambling to assist him. Krevonel's castellan had been sorely battered. A blood-soaked rag had been wound around his neck, and his formerly spotless livery was torn and streaked with more blood. He fell to his knees at Kasarian's feet, and tried unsuccessfully to raise his right hand to his chest where his House badge had been nearly ripped away. "Arm slashed," he muttered.

Kasarian immediately knelt, steadying Bodrik with a firm hand to each shoulder. "Gennard," he ordered, "Send for Wolkor, then fetch a basin of water and bandages. The rest of you, away to your duties."

The other servants hastily withdrew, Gennard close on their heels.

Bodrik shook his head slowly, as if dazed. He fumbled with his left hand inside his disheveled tunic. "Lursk is dead, Master," he said hoarsely.

I snatched up the wine ewer and filled a goblet to hand to Kasarian, who held it to Bodrik's lips.

"Rest a moment," Kasarian advised. "Wolkor is coming to attend to your wounds."

The wine seemed to revive Bodrik. As he drank the full measure, some color returned to his blanched face. Kasarian set aside the emptied goblet and lifted his castellan into a chair. Bodrik's labored breathing eased. He managed at last to extract the message packet with his left hand, and held it out to me. "Baron Gurborian entrusted me with this reply to be given only into your hands, Worthy Baron," he said, his voice clearer and stronger than before.

Accepting the bloodstained packet, I peered questioningly at Kasarian, who drew one of his belt knives and reached across to cut the packet's binding straps. "How came Lursk to die?" he asked.

There was no mistaking Bodrik's reaction—he showed his Alizonian fangs in a triumphant grin. "Whilst we waited for Baron Gurborian to compose his reply, Master, Lursk and I fell to arguing in the courtyard."

Kasarian nodded gravely. "I trust," he said, "that you promoted the duel to facilitate my orders?"

"Aye, Master. I thought an open clash with Lursk would guarantee a direct audience for me with Baron Gurborian." Bordrik looked at me. "Before I entered the Master's service," he said, "Lursk killed my younger littermate in Canisport. I thank the Worthy Baron for this opportunity to settle my Line's account with Lursk."

I acknowledged his statement with what I hoped he would view as a nod of approval. I had been in Alizon for only a matter of hours, and already one death had resulted. What a dreadful place this was—filled with violent hounds, legendary monsters, and murderous barons.

Kasarian held the message packet stationary for a moment. "How came you to survive once Lursk was dead?" he inquired in a dangerously calm voice. "Surely there were others present in Reptur's courtyard."

"Lursk's men would have killed me," Bodrik replied with earnest conviction, "had it not been for Lord Gratch. The noise of our struggle attracted his attention. He came out of the balcony, quill in hand, just as Lursk foolishly overbalanced and I ran him through. The others were set to attack me, but Lord Gratch ordered them to seize me and bring me before Baron Gurborian at once. The Baron was not pleased to hear of Lursk's death, but he said to Lord Gratch that the opportunity provided by Krevonel's message could not be lost due to misdeeds by underlings. I spoke up then, Master. I told him that I had settled a private score with Lursk—our duel had naught to do with Krevonel or Reptur. He said I had best stay out of Reptur's reach henceforth, then ordered me to deliver his reply before he changed his mind and killed me himself."

Kasarian smiled unpleasantly. "Should the occasion arise that I must dispatch another message to Gurborian," he remarked, "I shall take care to send a different messenger."

Gennard returned with bandages and a basin of water just as Wolkor arrived carrying a well-worn satchel bulging with ointment jars and herbs that I presumed he kept to treat injured hounds—or Alizonders. Fortunately, in one sense, this was far from my first experience with severe battle injuries. I had helped our Wise Women during the harrowing years of the Dales war, so I was not outwardly shaken by the sight of blood and mangled flesh. I took the bandages from Gennard and spread them out on a nearby table ready to be folded to the required dimensions.

Wolkor and Gennard swiftly removed Bodrik's tunic and the remnants of his undergarment. Besides the still undisclosed wounds on his neck, he had suffered a jagged sword cut down his right forearm. To my surprise, Wolkor threaded a delicately curved needle with what appeared to be a length of waxed thread. While Gennard pressed together the edges of the slash, Wolkor sewed the torn skin as neatly as any seamstress, then sponged the area with wine before bandaging it.

Leaving them to examine Bodrik's neck, Kasarian

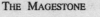

pulled Gurborian's reply from the packet. He held the document out deferentially for me to read, but I could make scant sense of the elaborately swirled Alizonian script.

"I vow, Worthy Baron," Kasarian observed to me, "that Gratch's hand has become more decorative since the last time I saw it. Let us seek a better light by which you can advise me of your response." Taking my arm, Kasarian firmly steered me to a table near the looming dire wolf, well out of listening range of the other Alizonders.

"Gurborian, through Gratch's quill, expresses himself with his usual pretense," Kasarian said, fetching an extra candle to illuminate the writing. " 'Volorian,' " he read in a low, sarcastic voice, " 'I rejoice that you honor Alizon City with your presence. We have sorely missed your counsel these many years—I have often thought what valuable contributions you could make to advance Alizon's interests. Now you grace me with your most noble invitation to attend you. I shall be delighted to arrive at the time and place you specified, accompanied solely by Gratch and a minimal party of guards. Your suggestion truly stirs my interest. I dare to hope that both our Lines may benefit greatly from our meeting. Pray extend my most cordial greetings to Kasarian, whose loyal service I have long admired. I eagerly await the set hour. Gurborian.' " Kasarian paused, then bared his teeth in a feral smile. "Morfew has earned a large medallion to attach to his baronial chain," he said. "Our quarry has taken his well-worded bait. Come, let us set our arrangements in order."

At our approach, Bodrik insisted upon rising to his feet. He appeared to be fully recovered from his ordeal.

"Wolkor," Kasarian said, "you may return to the Kennels. Tell the steward you may draw a flask of bloodwine."

Grinning, Wolkor bobbed his head and slapped his House badge with enthusiasm. As soon as he had closed the door, Kasarian turned to Bodrik and Gennard. "We shall be receiving Baron Gurborian this midnight," he informed them. "The Worthy Baron and I shall confer with him and Lord Gratch in the green audience chamber. Since this is to be a secret meeting, they will be accompanied by only a few bodyguards. Bodrik, are you fit to serve as my Armsmaster?"

To demonstrate his restored capacity, Bodrik flexed his right hand and sketched a vigorous swordsman's flourish. "Aye, Master," he asserted. "Krevonel's prime troop can overmatch any of Reptur's lot."

"See that they do," Kasarian ordered. "It is possible that some . . . disagreement may arise between our two parties. Your picked troop will deal with Gurborian's guard. The Worthy Baron and I will attend to Gurborian and Gratch."

"Shall I bring your sire's sword from the Armory, Master?" Gennard inquired.

"Yes, take it to the audience chamber," Kasarian replied, "along with proper refreshments for the four of us. The Worthy Baron and I will take a light supper here. You will fetch our repast before you attend to the arrangements in the green room."

Bodrik had not been gone long when Gennard duly delivered yet more trays of rich Alizonian food, which he was prepared to serve, but again Kasarian dismissed him to "see to your more important duties below."

Kasarian shut the door behind him, observing briskly to me, "Your imposture would be revealed if Gennard saw you eating. Your flat Dale's teeth betray you. You must therefore guard against showing your teeth to Gurborian and Gratch. It is as well that Volorian's supposed ague prevents you from consuming the prepared refreshments."

I choked down a bit more of the Alizonian food, vow-ing to keep my mouth shut tight throughout the baronial meeting.

At last, Kasarian led me downstairs to a wide hall. He stopped before towering double doors that opened inward upon a spacious room whose walls were draped with vibrant green tapestries glistening with gold-threaded patterns. Three substantial iron cressets set in floor mounts provided illumination in addition to the candles flaring on the large table at the room's center. Gennard had arranged a lavish cold supper on a long trestle table against a side wall. He had also placed a sheathed silver-hilted sword on the conference table.

Kasarian at once grasped the sword, drew it with his left hand, and executed a sudden flurry of lunges and mock parries. As I had suspected, he handled the weapon with expert ease. Evidently satisfied with the blade, he sheathed it, then peered keenly at the wall hangings. Behind one of the great carved chairs, vertical folds of fabric covered a niche in the stone wall. Kasarian concealed the sword in the narrow space. After rearranging the tapestry, he turned to address me. "I warn you to avoid being scratched by any baronial blades—it is customary for all such to be dipped in poison. You did say you could wield your staff; can you also use a sword or dagger?"

I shook my head, and wrote on my slate, "Dart gun and staff—not sword. I could stab, if close." I touched the hilt of one of the daggers at my belt, but Kasarian frowned.

"It is likely best if you attempt to stay out of dagger range," he said "Besides, all of us will be obliged to disarm—ostensibly—before our meeting begins. I have no doubt that both Gurborian and Gratch will carry hidden weapons, just as they will suspect the same of us, but custom is custom. They will not consider your staff to be a weapon, of course. Alizonder barons do not fight with staffs."

"Dalesfolk do," I wrote firmly.

Kasarian grinned. "So I have heard." Instantly, he resumed his serious mien. "When Gurborian addresses you," he said, "you must write on your slate as rapidly as you can, but in such a way that neither Gurborian nor Gratch can clearly see the results. I alone will interpret for you. That way, I can answer concerning matters which you might not know. Do not be fearful of Gorborian's or Gratch's lordly manner—you are Baron Volorian of the Line of Krevonel, and as such, you defer to no man save the Lord Baron himself."

Bodrik appeared at the open door. He had donned a high-collared tunic to cover the bandage at his neck, and seemed fully alert and able to fight, should such action be necessary. "The Reptur party has arrived, Master," he announced.

"We shall meet them in the hall," Kasarian replied.

As I followed him toward the double doors, I noticed a heavy wooden beam lying along the interior wall beside the theshold. I had no opportunity to query Kasarian about it.

Just outside the doors, four of Kasarian's armed retainers were rigidly drawn up in a line behind Bodrik. They faced four equally well-equipped Alizonders garbed in gaudy ocher livery piped with black. A sense of mutual hostility hung in the air as strongly as if a bottle of rank scent had been spilled on the stone paving between the two groups. Kasarian coldy ignored the underling intruders, striding out into the middle of the hall to intercept their approaching masters.

I immediately recognized Gurborian, having glimpsed him during my earlier vision at Lormt. He was a broad-shouldered, stocky man, with a wider face than Kasarian's, flatter cheekbones and a more prominently hooked nose. His eyes were a murky green, reminding me of a pottery glaze that had gone wrong in the firing. I was repelled by the ostentation of his costume. His bloodwine-red velvet tunic was slashed with black satin inserts, whose seams were ribbed with pearls. The gold filigree chain draped across his shoulders glittered with red gems, as did the several rings he wore on both short-fingered hands. Even his black high-sided boots were decorated with gold inlays. He was not, however, wearing Elsenar's jewel. If he had brought it with him, he had tucked it away out of sight.

The taller, thinner figure carefully keeping a pace behind him had to be the infamous Gratch. Like most folk from Gorm, he differed in coloring from the Old Race. With his wheat-yellow hair and blue-green eyes, he appeared out of place among the paler Alizonders. His features were fine cut, but as he drew closer, I could see lines of dissatisfaction around his mouth, as if he often scowled. His tunic was made of a dark red-brown corded fustian whose color and texture reminded me unpleasantly of Bodrik's clotted bandages. The links of his neck chain, while discreetly smaller and less ornate than his master's, were still clearly fine gold.

I could not avoid comparing the two opposing parties. Next to Gurborian and his men, the men of Krevonel looked severely plain. Kasarian had mentioned that he preferred a simpler style of life than some other barons; I now understood better what he had meant.

I quickly decided to imitate as best I could the outward demeanor of the most arrogant man I had known, a merchant from Karsten who had infuriated Uncle Parand with his haughty airs. I therefore measured Gurborian with an offensively unimpressed glance.

Gurborian showed his fangs in a patently insincere

smile, and proclaimed, "When I received your message, Volorian, I knew that only a matter of urgent significance to Krevonel could lure you away from your hounds at so crucial a time."

I scribbled busily on my slate for Kasarian to "read" my reply. He deftly held the slate out of Gurborian's view while relaying my presumed remarks. " 'What better time for a covert meeting? I have not missed the First Whelping since the war overseas. No baron would expect me to desert my pack just now.' "

"An adroit stratagem," Gurborian complimented me, "but might not word . . . sift out concerning your absence?"

"Certainly not," Kasarian retorted. "Volorian's Hound Master is completely reliable. No whisper concerning this meeting will ever be heard—at least, not from Krevonel."

"Nor from Reptur, I assure you," Gurborian heartily asserted.

Kasarian wiped my slate with his pocket cloth and returned it to me. "Let us now disarm," he suggested, "so that we may commence our discussion."

The four of us deposited a daunting array of knives upon the hall table outside the audience room.

Since I was both the eldest and the ostensible instigator of the meeting, I stalked into the chamber first, claiming the highest-backed master's chair for myself. Kasarian waited for our two guests to enter, then closed the doors and stooped to raise the wooden beam whose purpose I had not known. I now saw its intended use, for he dropped it into iron brackets bolted on the inside facings of the double doors, effectively barring us within, while also shutting our armed retainers out.

CHAPTER 21 _____

Kasarian—events at Krevonel Castle
(20th Day, Moon of the Knife/
21st Day, Month of the Ice Dragon)

As I preceded Mereth downstairs on our way to the audience chamber where we were to meet with Gurborian and Gratch, I weighed in my mind her reactions to events earlier that night. She had clearly been shaken by her unexpected confrontation with the dire wolf in my bedchamber, but, surprisingly, she had not fainted from fright. Considering that she had never before beheld such a beast, and must have initially assumed it was alive, she had responded well, lunging to one side while gripping her staff to ward off its attack. I was favorably impressed by her steadfastness—most unusual for a female. Later, she had also proved undaunted by the sight of Bodrik's wounds when he returned injured. Indeed, she had offered useful assistance, pouring a timely cup of wine for him, and displaying an obviously experienced hand with the bandages. I judged that those actions provided evidence that her service during the Dales war was likely worthy of respect.

When Bodrik reported that he had killed Lursk, Gurborian's Master of Arms, it was as well I could confidently trust my castellan. Otherwise, I might have been reasonably concerned that Gurborian had contrived, by bribe or threat, to shift Bodrik's allegiance to Reptur, and send him back to Krevonel as a spy. I knew, however that Bodrik was sworn to me by an unbreakable blood oath. He had taken a notable risk in tempting Lursk to duel on Reptur's ground, but his rashness had been rewarded. Immediately after Lursk fell, Gratch had intervened to prevent the Reptur troops from killing Bodrik. As Bodrik had calculated, he had been ushered directly to Gurborian, who rightly recognized that the loss of His Master of Arms was of far less import than the potential opportunity to woo Krevonel's alliance with his faction. Instead of killing Bodrik, Gurborian had allowed him to return to Krevonel, bearing Gratch's penned response to Volorian's invitation. As we had hoped, Reptur would come to Krevonel at midnight.

I dispatched Gennard to arrange a suitable repast in the green audience room, and to take there my sire's poisoned sword. By Alizonian custom, conferring barons always disarmed before entering a meeting room, from which all mere retainers would be excluded. These measures had been originally intended to reduce the incidence of outright armed clashes between mortal enemies, but over time, would-be combatants tended to provide themselves with concealed weapons in case active offense or defense became necessary within the locked chamber.

Bodrik announced Reptur's arrival. I was gratified by my castellan's choice of four armsmen to stand for Krevonel. I recognized three of Reptur's four armsmen—able fighters all, but not equal to our troop.

Gurborian and Gratch had arrayed themselves handsomely. I watched Mereth closely for any betraying signs of intimidation, but was greatly heartened when she assumed a most convincingly magisterial demeanor, reminiscent of old Baron Moragian.

As soon as the four of us had disarmed in the hall, Mereth marched directly to my sire's chair at the head of the oval table within the audience chamber.

I deliberately turned my back on them in order to secure the interior beam in place to bar the doors. I had relied upon Gratch's choice of chairs—ordinarily, he would never have consented to sit with a door to his back, but he had to assume our barred double doors precluded any surprise entry. Moreover, he was right-handed, and had to be lured by the direct proximity afforded for a knife thrust toward Mereth. My sire's sword was conveniently within my reach behind the chair across from Gratch, to Gurborian's left and Mereth's right.

Gennard had prepared a tray for us on the conference table. Moving to my desired chair, I shifted the three gold goblets and poured a generous measure of Krevonel's best bloodwine for our guests. They naturally waited for me to sample my own portion before tasting theirs.

Gurborian frowned at Mereth's empty hands. "Can it be," he inquired, "that you shun this excellent vintage, Volorian?"

Mereth achieved a remarkably rueful, close-mouthed grimace as she scribbled on her slate, then presented it for me to read. She had written, "Frustrated due to ague. Cannot taste food or wine properly."

" 'I can scarcely express my frustration,' " I read

aloud. " 'This ague has robbed me of my taste so that I cannot properly appreciate food or drink.' "

Gurborian relaxed somewhat in his chair. "What a pity," he said. "When your taste returns, you must prevail upon Kasarian to send some casks of this wine to you. I find it quite laudable. Don't you agree, Gratch?"

"Most assuredly, my lord," Gratch dutifully responded.

Mereth rapped her staff upon the floor, and made a peremptory gesture at Gurborian, who laughed sharply.

"You always were impatient, Volorian," Gurborian said, "as direct with words as with swords." He turned back to Gratch. "Pray explain to the Worthy Baron what a singular opportunity awaits him and Krevonel when they ally with Reptur to promote our new venture."

Whatever else one might say about Gratch, one would scarcely characterize him as direct in any matter. I recalled Volorian had written that if Gratch's object in prying near our estates was to spy upon Escore, it was a wonder he had approached the actual border region—it would have been more like him to take ship to Karsten and worm his way around by the most devious possible route. I was intensely curious to hear how Gratch would try to lure us into denying our Line's traditional utter rejection of magic. It was not surprising when he chose to approach the subject obliquely.

"We cannot, of course, enhance the already formidable reputation secured by the Line of Krevonel," Gratch said earnestly to Mereth.

Mereth nodded, as if acknowledging an accepted fact.

"It appears," Gratch continued, "that you no longer care to participate in the active conduct of affairs at Alizon Castle, being fully occupied, no doubt, with your renowned breeding efforts at your country estate."

Mereth nodded again, and drummed her gloved fingers restlessly on the table top.

Undaunted, Gratch forged ahead, creeping nearer to the nub of his argument. "My lord and I have carefully considered what enticements we might offer to encourage a certain . . . change of mind on your part," he said. "We knew that the virtues of our proposal would appeal to your keen military judgment, but oftentimes extra . . . factors can speed one's decision."

Mereth thumped her staff suddenly, startling Gratch into a slight stammer. "W-worthy Baron?"

She scrawled one word on her slate. I held it so both Gurborian and Gratch could see the boldly written query, "Terms?"

While she wiped the slate, I added. "And in return for what action by Krevonel?"

Gurborian had propped his chin on one beringed hand, his expression passive, but expectant. He was—at least for the present—evidently content to let Gratch speak for him.

Gratch sipped thirstily from his goblet. "I understand," he said, "that the Worthy Baron's pack is lacking in only one champion strain—the bloodline held exclusively by Baron Bolduk." His voice took on a wheedling note, as if he were trying to induce a newly weaned pup to put its head through a spiked collar for the first time. "Quite recently, Baron Bolduk actively embraced our proposals. Should you join our faction, it is most likely that he would favorably entertain your request for breeding rights."

Mereth subjected Gratch to a withering stare, rightly implying that so flagrant a bribe—without previous explanation of the reciprocally required action—was too contemptible to deserve comment.

It seemed a suitable time to divert their attention to me, and possibly trick them into saying more than they intended. "Speaking of Bolduk's Line," I remarked, "I heard lately that the younger whelp died quite suddenly during the New Year's Assembly . . . on the Sixth Day, was it not? Doubtless the old Baron was sorely grieved."

Gurborian affected a doleful outward expression, but his eyes glinted with satisfaction. "Just so," he said. "I hastened to his side as soon as the sad news reached Reptur. As I had suspected, their old feud with Ferlikian was behind the death. Baron Bolduk was most appreciative of my condolence." He addressed Mereth directly. "You will want to confer with him, I am sure, since both of you have long held similar attitudes regarding certain . . . matters. You will find that Bolduk has completely revised his former convictions now that he has assessed the rewards promised by our venture."

Mereth wrote briefly and to the point. I simply voiced her command: " 'Detail this venture.' "

Gurborian nodded to Gratch, who dipped a finger in his bloodwine and drew a scarlet streak across the table top. Once he had added a few more such lines, I saw that he was sketching a crude map of Alizon's borders.

"Since our ill-advised alliance with the Kolder has been destroyed," Gratch declared, "my lord and I have devoted ourselves to determining the most advantageous new course to expand Alizon's dominion. For too long, we have been thwarted by the Estcarp's hags' detestable spells that hinder our free movement southward. Here—where the Forbidden Hills trail off into the trackless Tormarsh—the Lord Baron has persisted in probing over the years, but the Witchspells have prevented passage of more than a pitifully few spies. Some moons ago . . . " Gratch paused, looked keenly at Mereth, and added, "as you were evidently aware, Worthy Baron, I journeyed near your estates to pursue inquiries in the mountains bordering on Escore." He marked two spots with his finger. "Here . . . and here, my lord sought word of certain powerful forces which might assist us in scourging Estcarp . . . ."

"You dared to consider consulting the vile Mages of Escore?" I interrupted. It was not difficult to feign intense dismay, given the appalling nature of the Escorian threat.

"Calm yourself, Honorable Kasarian," Gurborian purred. "It has been said that you are a swordsman of notable skill. Would you refuse to employ the sharpest blade available merely because you disapprove of the decoration on the hilt? I urge you to weigh the obvious advantages of our strategy. Who else can counter—indeed, overpower—Estcarp's hags? The sole strength of the Witches lies in their magic. Why should we not enlist even more puissant magic on our behalf? As a scholar, you must know that in the far past, it was the Mages of Escore who first drove the Witches over the mountains into Estcarp."

Gratch leaned forward, stabbing his wine-stained finger at the area of his map that represented Escore. "Like Alizon," he asserted, "Escore does not forget past insults or past foes. For a thousand years, Escore, too, has been border-blocked by Estcarp. Their Mages likely still cherish hopes for further revenge."

"How say you, Volorian?" Gurborian inquired. "Surely you do not mourn the destruction of the Kolder—unreliable foreigners who failed miserably in their campaigns against the hags. Escore is nearby, and centuries-steeped in Power. Should we not seize so promising a means to enlarge Alizon's borders while also avenging the honor of our Foresires?"

Mereth surveyed Gratch's map, then wrote on her slate for me to read, "Krevonel has always hated magic. How can this plot help Krevonel?"

I nodded, as if in firm agreement, and "read" aloud, " 'You know very well the position our Line has always taken regarding magic: it is an abominable practice, *never* to be accepted. How can you propose that Krevonel consider allying with such disgusting foulness?' "

"But no magic shall be wielded within Alizon itself," Gratch quickly averred. "The full force of Escore's fury will be directed entirely against Estcarp."

Mereth regarded him balefully, scribbled briefly, and flourished her slate at me. I had to admire her spirit—the genuine Volorian could have reacted no better. I read her words as they were written, since they were perfectly chosen. " 'And if Escore should prevail against Estcarp, then where next do they turn for prey?' "

Gratch sputtered, and flushed a dusky red.

Gurborian laughed aloud. "I had wondered whether your years away from court might have dulled your wits," he exclaimed. "I see they remain as sharp as your hounds' teeth. You pose a fair question. Until we complete our negotiation, I cannot supply the particulars, but you may be assured that Alizon will emerge with full dominion over all lands to the west of the mountains. I will not settle for less."

"Can you confide to us the names of those negotiating for Escore?" I inquired.

Gurborian shook his head. "Alas, no. Our contacts must for the present remain secret. It is their imperative condition, you understand."

"But you are dealing with acknowledged Mages," I persisted.

"Of course," Gurborian snapped. "Those with minor skills would be of scant use to us."

Mereth passed me her slate. Again, I read it directly aloud. " 'How do you plan to control Escore's Mages? Will they not attempt to enslave Alizon with their foul magic?' "

"No, no," Gurborian objected. "You misunderstand the thrust of our argument. We shall deal with only the most powerful enemies of Estcarp, those Mages whose desire for revenge is greatest. We shall assure them that once they have swept away the hags, Alizon will occupy and administer the whole of Estcarp. Their own sovereignty to the east of the mountains will be complete; we guarantee not to challenge it. Think of the advantages for them: a stable border, steadfast Alizon guarding their western approaches—perhaps we might even indulge in some limited trade to our mututal benefit."

I pretended to be impressed. "That does sound eminently rewarding to both sides," I admitted. "The Lord Baron must have commended you when you presented the proposal to him."

Gratch hesitated, pouring himself more bloodwine. "As to that," he began to say, but Gurborian interrupted.

"Norandor has not yet been advised regarding our venture," Gurborian said. "We prefer to be able to present him with the complete results of our negotations."

"So you have not yet actually found the Mages you seek," I stated, forcing him to commit himself . . . or lie.

"It is a delicate procedure." Gurborian signaled for Gratch to refill his goblet. "Our efforts proceed concurrently, like a brace of hounds questing after two separate scents. Gratch has been pursuing our potential Escorian linkages, whilst I have been enlisting barons to our cause. Each effort strengthens the other. The Mages will be the more impressed by a large faction of like-minded barons, just as the barons will be similarly impressed by the experience and power of the Mages with whom we deal."

"I should think," I observed tentatively, "that locating Escorian Mages would be a difficult, indeed dangerous undertaking."

As I spoke, I watched Gratch closely. Oftentimes, folk who boast of their mastery of a skill like poisoning fail to recognize that others may also stumble upon useful scraps of poison lore of which they may be unaware. Among Krevonel's ancient manuscripts, I had found a description—annoyingly pierced by vermin's teeth—of a certain rare root which, when dried and powdered, was promised to loosen a guarded tongue. Having acquired and powdered such a root, I had cautiously sampled a few grains to gauge whether the flavor could be noticed in wine, and also to test its effect on an Alizonder, since the document had originally been seized in a sea raid on the shipwreckers of Verlaine. Aside from a slight warming of the blood, I detected no other effect on me, but I thought it worthwhile to try the potion on Gratch, whose home isle of Gorm was near enough to Karsten to render him perhaps vulnerable. I had therefore tipped a pinch of the root powder from my signet ring's hidden compartment into Gratch's first goblet of bloodwine. It was gratifying to see that his breathing had noticeably quickened, and a film of sweat was glistening on his forehead. I awaited his reponse to my statement with special interest.

"There are more mages and would-be mages lurking about in those border mountains than you would believe," Gratch blurted. "Of course, most are worthless, self-deluded fools. I mind one I came upon this past summer—an old recluse who had brewed a potion supposed to stimulate the body to great feats of strength and endurance. He was so enamored of the effect he felt when he dipped his fingers in a basin of it, that he had his apprentice fill a bath with the potion so he could immerse his entire body."

"Such a potion could be of great value to soldiers," I acknowledged. "The mage was mightily affected, I trust?"

Gurborian scowled. "The old fool died outright from excessive excitement," he said bitterly, "and his witless apprentice was so frightened that he turned out the tub, scrubbed the floor, and burned the only directions for mixing the potion."

"What a loss," I commiserated.

Gurborian waved his hand dismissively. "Only a minor disappointment when measured against the range of our accomplishments. An assurance for the future greatness of Alizon is within our very grasp." He regarded me keenly. "You cannot deny that your word wields weighty influence upon the younger whelps of your Line. What more dazzling prospect could you set before them than an Alizon whose borders extend into . . . even beyond Karasten. I should certainly prize your counsel and leadership in the triumphant days to come." For an instant, his fingers hovered near his tunic pocket as if he intended to reach inside, then he hesitated, and merely extended both his hands flat on the table. "In addition to the high position I would guarantee you," Gurborian continued, "it might be possible that other rewards. . . . "

But Gratch had been staring fixedly first at Gurborian's hands, then at Mereth's gloved hands, and abruptly he exclaimed, "Hands! I knew I had heard something about Volorian's hands. The left hand—during this summer, you lost parts of two fingers while separating your hounds. Why are your hands concealed in those gloves?"

"The ague produces frequent chills," I intervened, but it was too late. Before I could prevent him, Gratch seized Mereth's left hand and snatched off that glove, revealing her full complement of fingers—as well as her gender.

While Gratch glared as if he had uncovered a venomous toad, Mereth jerked her hand free from his grasp. Gratch bellowed, "A *bitch's* hand—this is not Volorian!"

CHAPTER 22

Mereth—events at Krevonel Castle
(21st Day, Month of the Ice Dragon/
20th Day, Moon of the Knife)

As soon as Gurborian had seated himself, I became aware of a curious sensation emanating from his end of the table. And then I *knew* as if my fingertips had brushed the very stone: Elsenar's jewel was concealed upon Gurborian's person. Never before had I felt such a certainty, or detected an object's presence without physically touching it.

It was impossible for me to alert Kasarian that Morfew's devious message had succeeded. Gurborian now had to be pricked into openly presenting the jewel as his crowning enticement.

I had to be aware of judging the attraction of a bribe by the Dales' standards. As an experienced trader, I had already assessed the wealth of the House of Krevonel. Its castle fittings might be spare, but they were all of the highest quality. My association with Kasarian caused me to doubt that lavish riches or sensual pleasures would appeal to him. The other Alizonder barons craved brute power—or in Volorian's case, pre-eminent mastery of those accursed hounds.

When Gratch sought to take advantage of that weakness by proposing access to hound breeding rights, I stared scornfully at him as if he were proffering me a tub of rancid butter. Undeterred by my negative reaction, Gratch drew a rough map on the table top with a finger dipped into his bloodwine. I had to suppress the urge to shudder at the raw memories that action evoked. The table's wood was pale, bleached like the Alizonders themselves. Against that ivory surface, the wine's crimson streaks ran like real blood, reminding me unbearably of other long-ago tables covered with wounded Dalesmen. I forced myself to concentrate on Gratch's hateful voice. His Alizonian was tinged with a Gorm accent which he constantly strove to disguise.

My heart lurched when Gurborian actually began to reach for his tunic pocket, but he hesitated, spreading his hands flat on the table. Jarred from his wine-soaked reverie, Gratch peered from Gurborian's hands to mine. Before I could evade him, he stripped off my left glove, roaring that I was not Volorian, but a *female*.

We all leaped to our feet, seeking positions of advantage. I discarded my right-hand glove so that I could take a firmer grip on my staff.

Just as Kasarian had predicted, both Gratch and Gurborian had smuggled in concealed weapons—Gratch pulled from his pocket as small a dart gun as I had ever seen, while Gurborian drew a thin-bladed dagger from his sleeve. Kasarian immediately snatched his hidden sword from behind the wall tapestry.

Even despite his copious bloodwine consumption, Gratch still moved with unsettling agility. He lunged toward me, snarling, "Out of my way, useless female!"

In backing away from him, I caught my boot heel against the chair leg, throwing myself off balance. Gratch struck at my shoulder as I swayed, shoving me to the floor. He desired a clear dart shot at Kasarian, who was completely immersed in his life-or-death duel with Gurborian. I knew Gratch's darts had to be poisoned, probably rendering any bare-skin impact deadly.

Gratch did attempt one shot, but Kasarian's keen side vision must have registered our movement, for he dodged to one side even as Gratch lifted his gun to fire. Unwittingly, Gratch stepped within range of my staff. I reached up from my prone position on the floor and smashed the staff across his forearm, sending the dart gun careering over the stone paving. Colliding with the table support, the gun rebounded toward me. I snared it with my staff, seized it, and fired point-blank at Gratch's looming face, as he was diving to retrieve his weapon. The dart lodged beneath his left eye. He gave a horrid shriek as he fell atop my legs, but I kicked out and rolled away from him, under the table. In case he pursued me, I spun around as quickly as I could, but I need not have troubled on Gratch's account. His dart poison must have been instantly lethal. Gratch lay where he had fallen, his eyes still staring in disbelieving horror, his limbs twitching like those of a beheaded lizard. It occurred to me that he had never expected a "useless female" to fight back.

CHAPTER 23

Kasarian/Mereth—events at Krevonel
Castle, and later at Lormt (20th Day,
Moon of the Knife/21st Day,
Month of the Ice Dragon)

Kasarian

As Gurborian engaged me in an aggressive pursuit around the room, I heard the impact of Mereth's body against the paving stones, but I could spare no more than the briefest of glances in their direction. Gurborian furiously pressed his attack at that point, and I was forced to transfer my full attention to our dispute. It could not have been more than a moment or two later that Gratch screamed. As I retreated toward the conference table to survey Mereth's situation, I tossed one of the chairs in Gurborian's path to obstruct him.

I could not immediately see Mereth, but Gratch was dead, lying half under the table, his face contorted. I had to assume that Mereth had somehow acquired his dart gun and shot him—a most unexpected but welcome action on her part. I had no time to search for Mereth, being again assailed by Gurborian. In case Mereth was alive and hiding under the table, I drew Gurborian toward the far end of the chamber. As we fought our way past the barred doors, a volley of blows rang out against them from the corridor side. Bodrik's force was doubtless engaging Reptur's quartet. I felt confident that Krevonel would prevail in that encounter; I had to be equally certain that I was the victor on my side of the doors.

Mereth

As I caught my breath, I realized that along with the clash of blades inside the room, I could also hear definite sounds of conflict outside in the hall. The two Alizonders were warily circling one another in the far end of the room. I shivered at the thought that with both sword and dagger blades poisoned, even the slightest scratch might be fatal. I crept nearer, hoping to trip Gurborian with my staff, but like Kasarian's, his huntman's senses alerted him to my stealthy approach. Dropping his dagger to free both hands, Gurborian toppled one of the iron cressets to block Kasarian's way, and grasping a heavy chair, he rammed it toward me, forcing me back against the stone wall.

I tried desperately to squirm to one side, but the chair arm cruelly impacted my thigh. The pain was so severe that my sight clouded for an instant. When my vision cleared, I saw Kasarian wrench the supper-laden trestle table away from the wall and sling it side over end, sweeping Gurborian off his feet. Kasarian hastened to release me from the crushing weight of the chair. As I collapsed to the floor, the entire room seemed to slide sideways in the most sickening fashion. I had somehow held on to my staff, which was fortunate, for Gurborian, having regained his footing, was skulking behind Kasarian, raising a broken chair arm over his head. I managed to deliver a glancing poke to Gurborian's ribs, partly deflecting his stroke so that the length of wood smote Kasarian's upper right arm and shoulder instead of his skull. Gurborian snarled at me, and viciously kicked my outstretched leg. I felt the bone crack. He likely would have assailed me further, but Kasarian, surely halfstunned by the blow he'd taken, whirled around, interposing his sword, which he had transferred to his left hand.

Gurborian hesitated, backing away from Kasarian's naked blade. "Your right hand appears quite limp," he observed with a savage grin. "Can it be that your arm is broken?"

Kasarian smiled equally unpleasantly. "So paltry a blow could produce only a transient numbness and possibly a minor bruise," he said, executing a complex flourish with his blade. "Arms Master Shivar insisted during my earliest training that I develop expert skill with either hand. Do not indulge in any false hopes that you have disabled me."

Gurborian growled several Alizonian words which I did not know, but their import was obviously insulting. Kasarian's expression hardened. He regarded Gurborian with icy scorn, and declared, "You bring disgrace upon the Line Sired by Reptur."

Suddenly, I smelled the sharp scent of scorched or burning fabric. Coals from the overturned cresset had ignited torn chair upholstery, Gurborian's cloak, and a tangled tablecloth ripped loose during the earlier phase of the duel. To my immediate distress, bright flames were feeding along the debris, drawing ever nearer to my injured legs, which I could not move no matter how hard I tried. Desperate, I waved my staff to attract Kasarian's attention.

Kasarian

As Gurborian warily retreated from my sword's reach, he cast unforgiveable aspersions upon my sire's breeding, thus providing more than ample grounds for slitting his throat had I not already determined to kill him.

From the corner of my eye, I sensed a frantic movement. Unable to attract my attention by crying out, Mereth was waving her staff. The cresset's spilled coals had ignited debris scattered on the floor, and a line of fire was licking toward her. At once, I slashed a panel of tapestry from the wall and cast it, tentlike, over Gurborian. I knew that even such a heavy fabric would not contain him for long. Although somewhat hampered by my numbed right arm, I cast aside my sword, seized the overturned trestle table by its edge, ramming it over against the far wall to squeeze the swathed Gurborian behind it.

I could then turn to assist Mereth. There was no time to skirt around the mounting flames fed by Gurborian's discarded cloak and other wreckage. I reached directly through the fire to haul Mereth to safety. Using Gratch's unburnt cloak, I smothered the worst of the flames and dispsersed the remaining coals and debris.

Mereth

Kasarian sped to assist me, thrusting his bare hands unflinchingly through the flames to grab my boots and pull me away from the mounting danger.

Having untangled himself from Kasarian's impediments, Gurborian emerged like a wounded boar from its den, his eyes wild, blood welling from a scrape on his forehead. He had retrieved his dagger, and lumbered toward us, intent upon striking Kasarian while he was distracted with my rescue. Alert to his approach, Kasarian executed a tumbler's roll, snatched up his own sword, and leaped back to guard me.

In his single-minded frenzy to penetrate Kasarian's defense, Gurborian dashed at us, but stumbled when his foot struck one of the fallen goblets. Instantly, Kasarian lunged, slicing Gurborian's outflung hand. Unable to check his forward progress, Gurborian fell heavily. He lay motionless on the floor for the space of a heartbeat, then gave a chilling cry. As he rolled over, we could see that in addition to the sword cut on his hand, he had impaled himself upon his own dagger. In obvious agony, Gurborian pleaded in a choking voice, "Kill me, I beg you—this blade is steeped in flesh-rot poison!"

Kasarian warily neared his fallen foe, but not close enough to come within dagger reach. What he saw prompted him to take three rapid steps and pierce Gurborian through the heart. After withdrawing and wiping his sword, Kasarian dropped to one knee beside Gurborian's body. When he stood up, I saw for just an instant the glitter of something silver in his hand before he thrust it into his tunic pocket and hurried back to me.

Had my leg pain not been so overwhelming, I would have smiled at the disgusted expression on Kasarian's face. Our violent combat had produced deplorable disorder. I had seen enough of his living quarters to know that Kasarian preferred everything around him to be maintained neatly in place. He was now obviously far more annoyed by the disarray and damages to his audience chamber than by his own injuries.

He stooped to lift me up. Having previously experienced his raw strength first hand during the postern transit, and now having seen his fighting energy, I was surprised by his gentle touch. He eased me into the only unbroken chair, then turned toward the barred doors.

I brushed tears of pain from my cheeks as I watched with trepidation. We could hear no further sounds of battle from the hall outside, but we could not know which force of retainers had triumphed—Krevonel's or Reptur's.

Kasarian

No further sounds of combat emanated from the hall, but I felt it was still advisable to proceed prudently. I eased the bar out of its supports. Then, sword in hand, I quietly opened the right-hand door.

It was as well that I forbore from rushing out into the hall. Bodrik was poised just outside with a poleax, ready to strike our enemies, had they prevailed. I complimented him on his preparedness. He reported that all of Reptur's men were dead, along with two of ours.

"Come within," I ordered. "We must hasten to dispose of our primary guests. Baron Gurborian unwisely chose flesh-rot poison for his dagger, so observe the necessary precautions."

Bodrik glanced at what was left of Gurborian, and smiled. "The safest way to transport yon carrion to the river will be to wrap it in some of the downed tapestry cloth," he said. After appraising the chaotic state of the chamber, Bodrik added, "Gennard will be sore vexed, Master. He dislikes spills and stains, so he does. I wager he'll complain of the damage as well." "Gennard can attend to the cleaning in the morning," I observed. "Be sure none of the poison soaks through when you lift the . . . residue. Gratch's body will not require special handling; his darts were evidently prepared with smother root. I shall be occupied attending to the Worthy Baron's injuries. We may be obliged to consult a bonesetter."

Bodrik saluted Mereth respectfully, then departed to

assemble his work party. I lifted Mereth in my arms and carried her as quickly as I could to the nearest passageway leading to Krevonel's vaults.

Fortunately, my right hand had recovered from the effects of Gurborian's blow. Had Mereth not so ably employed her staff to deflect his stroke at my head, I should likely have been killed. It was frustrating not being able to ask her the extent of her bodily injury. She had shut her eyes, but I did not know whether she was wearied or had swooned from pain or weakness. I dared not stop to request that she write upon her slate. Having broken bones myself in falls during hunts and melees, I presumed she must be enduring considerable pain. I attempted to proceed as fast as I could with the minimum of jarring. Even so, the journey to the postern chamber seemed interminable. I was particularly gratified that due to forethought, I had slipped down earlier in the evening to kindle the slowest burning torches. We were therefore assured of a minimal lighted path had we been forced to make a hasty—or fighting—retreat to the postern once we secured Elsenar's jewel. Striding with Mereth in my arms, I had no free hand to carry a torch or taper.

When I at last reached the lowest corridor, I had to lay Mereth down in order to extract the elder's key and unlock the door to the postern chamber. Recalling how that door had shut behind me before, I had to assume the same magic could again protect our backs once we had entered the room. It was still deeply unsettling to behold the heavy door swinging shut and locking by itself, but I was almost immediately distracted by the formation of the eerie floating patch of light signaling the postern's opening. Carrying Mereth, I stepped through, hoping that the Lormt folk would be aware of our coming.

Evidently, Ouen had ordered that someone be present

in Lormt's cellar at all times. When I emerged, one of the elderly scholars was standing nearby, his face stricken with fright and amazement. I cudgeled my wits for the proper Estcarpian words. "Do not stand there, man," I told him. "Fetch a healer!"

Speechless, he snatched up his lantern and scurried toward the distant door, but before he had proceeded very far, was met by two figures hurrying toward us.

Alerted by their unnatural talents to the postern's activation, Duratan's mate and the Wise Woman were approaching at a fast walk that quickened to a run when they saw that Mereth was injured. Dispatching the scholar to inform the others, they assisted me in laying Mereth on one of the wooden benches. "What happened to her?" the Wise Woman demanded.

"It was necessary to fight," I replied. "Gurborian and Gratch are dead. I believe Mereth's leg is broken."

The Wise Woman had been delicately feeling Mereth's body and limbs. "Also some ribs," she snapped, "and who knows what else." She glared at me as if she held me personally responsible.

"Were you wounded in the fighting?" Duratan's mate asked, raising her lantern to shed more light on me.

"A mere bruise or two," I said. "Attend to the lady— her injuries are more severe."

Mereth suddenly opened her eyes and fluttered her fingers. "I think she wants her slate," Duratan's mate observed. She turned to Mereth. "Is that what you wish?"

Mereth nodded vigorously. By great fortune—or perhaps the force of long habit—Mereth had retained her slate and chalk in her tunic pocket. The Wise Woman extracted them, while Duratan's mate supported Mereth to a sitting position so she could write. I lifted a lantern to provide illumination.

CHAPTER 24

Mereth—events at Krevonel Castle and Lormt (21st Day, Month of the Ice Dragon/ 20th Day, Moon of the Knife)

The gnawing agony in my injured right hip combined with the searing ache in my left knee to distract me from noticing the unsettling effects accompanying our postern transit. I knew I had returned to Lormt when Nolar spoke to me and Jonja retrieved for me my slate—only slightly cracked—from my tunic pocket. I had become increasingly aware of another sensation overriding my pain. I recognized with a start that it was the same mental pressure I had earlier felt at Krevonel's conference table, except it now waxed even stronger.

I remembered the flash of silver in Kasarian's hand when he stepped back from Gurborian's body. Seizing my remaining sliver of chalk, I wrote on my slate for Kasarian to read, "You found the jewel. I sense its presence. Let me see it."

He hesitated for an instant, then slowly drew out the chain. The brilliant blue stone I had discovered at

Vennesport so long ago at last dangled before my eyes at Lormt.

Jonja gasped audibly. "It is truly an object of great Power," she whispered.

Nolar peered thoughtfully at the jewel. "I feel something akin to the puissance of my own Stone of Konnard," she said. "Perhaps this jewel, too, possesses similar healing properties that might relieve Mereth's pain."

Kasarian dropped the pendant into my outstretched hand. The instant it touched my flesh, all other sensations diminished as if cast into the depths of a bottomless well. My mind reeled as a strange, insistent voice addressed me. Before I became incapable of acting, I managed to thrust my hand into my pocket, unclenching my fingers and breaking my contact with the jewel.

I snatched my slate, and wrote for Nolar to read, "Elsenar has enspelled a message within his jewel—an urgent plea for aid. I long to write it for you, but my hand grows unsteady. Can you carry me to a bed? I fear that my pain is such that I may swoon at any time."

Jonja emitted a derisive snort. "A plea for help that has waited a thousand years to be heard can wait a few more hours—or days. Your leg and the rest of you needs a healer's attention. What can be delaying that scholar? He should have notified Ouen by now."

My vision was beginning to darken again, but as often happens in times of great strain, minor irritations can assume undue significance. I abruptly realized that my hands were bare, and managed to scrawl, "Pray express my apologies to Mistress Bethalie. In the struggle with Gratch, I have lost both her fine gloves."

"Good riddance," Nolar said firmly. "They were atrocious to look upon." She turned her head away toward the distant door, and smiled with relief. "Be of good cheer—Duratan is bringing the litter we used to transport Master Kester when he fell and broke his hip."

Her voice unaccountably receded, as if she had moved far away, then swooping darkness obliterated all further sensations.

My next awareness was of a ravishing smell of herbed broth. I opened my eyes to find myself in a bed of glorious softness, propped against a bank of pillows. Nolar was sitting nearby, stirring a pot suspended over the fireplace coals.

I raised my hand and slapped the bedclothes to attract her attention. She hurried to my side at once, bringing a pannikin of broth and a horn spoon. No wealthy merchant could have savored the finest banquet fare more than I did that simple broth. I gestured for my slate, but Nolar would not give to me until I had drunk the last drops of nourishment.

I saw at once that my poor old slate, companion for so many hazardous leagues, had been replaced by a fresh slate mounted in a sturdy wooden frame. Nolar handed me a piece of chalk, and I wrote, "How long have I been asleep?"

"Nearly half the day," Nolar replied. "It is more than an hour past midday, and all of us are most grateful for the respite after last night's exertions. Although," she added with a mischievous smile, "we are markedly curious to hear Elsenar's long-delayed message. When you are certain that you feel strong enough to convey it, Master Ouen wishes to be informed. Since this room will not comfortably accommodate our full assembly, he suggests that chairs might be placed in the hall."

I wiped my slate, and wrote, "Pray tell Master Ouen that I, too, am most anxious to learn whatever Elsenar sealed within his jewel. I cannot know in advance the extent of his message, but if you will fetch me parchment and ink as before, and a table we may position across the bed, I shall try to transcribe Elsenar's ancient plea."

Within the hour, my bedchamber had been converted into an audience chamber. Morfew claimed a cushioned chair near my bed, the better to hear the reading. Nolar insisted upon sitting next to me, where she said she could most easily read the pages I wrote and also provide any refreshments I might require. Ouen sat beside the door, while Jonja and Duratan placed chairs just outside the door in the hall. Kasarian preferred to stand at the foot of the bed.

While I had slept, in order to attend to my bodily hurts, Jonja and Nolar had removed my baronial clothing, replacing it with a long-sleeved, high-necked linen nightgown which was far more comfortable. They had bandaged my aching ribs, and my knee, and had applied a wondrous poultice to my hip, which both warmed and numbed the area. I felt considerably more alert, with far less pain than I had upon my return through the postern.

Oralian's green velvet tunic had been carefully draped at the foot of the bed. I did not have to touch it to know that Elsenar's jewel remained within its pocket where I had left it. I motioned for Kasarian to hand me the tunic. When I had first grasped the jewel in Lormt's cellar, my impressions had been confused and fragmentary due to the strain of my injuries. I had to hope that Elsenar's spell would allow me a second opportunity to receive his message now that I could devote my entire attention to it.

I shook the chain and pendant out upon the table positioned above my lap, then deliberately seized the jewel in my right hand. Like a rush of icy mountain stream water, the enspelled voice of Elsenar poured into my mind.

CHAPTER 25

Elsenar—his enspelled message
transcribed by Mereth at Lormt
(21st Day, Month of the Ice Dragon/
20th Day, Moon of the Knife)

"Greetings, Child of Mind. However distant in time you may be, I know that you will heed my call and come to my aid. Hear now the tale of my plight. I am Elsenar, Mage of the Light. I conjured a postern from Lormt to the land of Arvon across the sea in order to seek assistance from like-minded mages there in meeting the perilous challenge from the Shadow emanating from Escore. My first attempt was disrupted by the unprecedented forces loosed at Lormt by our mages's disastrous efforts to conjure a Master Gate. The momentary existance of my postern probe to Arvon, however, was detected by a Dark Adept there, one Narvok, who was himself seeking to open a Gate, but lacked sufficient Power. He lay in wait for me, and when I later launched my second spell, he twisted my postern's opening to his lair so that I was drawn into a Duel of Power as soon as I emerged. My jewel afforded me insight into Narvok's intentions. I immediately framed a spell to pitch him through his half-opened Gate and seal it behind him—but he, in turn, discerned the inestimable value of my jewel, and by tapping Power from his Gate spell, for an instant, he succeeded in stripping the gem from my grasp.

Before Narvok could seize his prize, however, both of us were overcome by a third and far greater Force. Unknown to either of us, the place where we contended had been a Site of Power in the distant Elder Days. The energy of our spells had stirred the residual Force to awareness of us. It fastened upon my jewel, dashing the gem from Narvok's control to the stone floor beyond my reach, while simultaneously expelling Narvok through his Gate, and disintegrating the portal once the Dark Adept had passed through it.

Lacking my jewel in hand, I was at a great disadvantage, seemingly unable to communicate with the aroused Force. I felt myself beginning to be swept back toward my postern's opening to Lormt—but the excess of Power unleashed in that place was more than either my modest spell or its framer could bear. My very being was reft in twain; one part of me was ejected through some portal beyond my knowledge, while the rest of me was englobed, as in a drop of amber, within the walls of that place. Yet I was not truly physically present there, for I sensed that my fragmentary essence was so insubstantial as to be invisible. Still, my jewel was physically present, and because it was so intimately linked to me, I could bespeak it by mind-call. Through it, I entreated the Force of that place to examine both my jewel and what remained of me, to determine that I intended it no ill will, and was not of the Shadow as Narvok had been.

At once, I was subjected to a pitiless appraisal that probed my inmost being. To my extreme relief, the

Force ruled me acceptable . . . but in its dealings with Narvok and me, all of its Power reserves stored through the ages had been expended. Its mind-touch fading, the Force expressed genuine regret for causing my sundered condition, then to my horror, it ebbed away, diminishing beyond my mental reach.

Lacking physical substance, I could not touch my jewel, even had I been capable of movement. In one sense, my suspended state was fortunate, for I required neither food nor drink in my bodiless condition. I could only wait for someone to enter the place, someone whose mind I could address by means of my jewel. I had no way to know what span of time elasped. I was entrapped in what appeared to be an underground vault, but it might lie beneath an inhabited castle or an abandoned ruin. Flares of light released during our Duel of Power had revealed a stone staircase in a far corner of the chamber, but that rose to a landing and twisted so that no outer light penetrated to delineate day from night . . . or, as I was to find to my dismay, season from season.

When at last a figure finally stumbled into the chamber, its heavy outer clothing was laden with snow! I caused my jewel to pulse with a bright light so that it would both provide illumination and attract the intruder's attention. At once, the figure threw back the fur-rimmed hood of its cloak, exposing an unmistakably female face.

As she drew nearer to gaze upon my jewel's waxing brilliance, I used that thread of visual contact—for she was no mage nor even mage-trained—to call to her mind. I employed the simplest of commands: "Come to me." She was receptive to my mind-call, and once she reached down and grasped the gem in her bare hand, I achieved a strong mental link with her.

It was instantly apparent that she could not act to free

me, for she possessed neither the knowledge nor the Power to wield my jewel. During my immurement, I had considered such a likelihood; I could scarcely expect that the first person to enter my prison would be an Adept. I had also considered a possible strategy to employ should my first potential rescuer be a female untutored in magic.

It would have been unspeakably shameful to use my Power to force this woman against her will—only those of the Dark would dare such evil. I therefore described to her my desperate situation, and proposed my remedy— that only with her free consent, I would, by my magic, sire a line through her body so that one day, the resulting empowered Child of my Mind could return to this place, able to wield my jewel and release my enspelled fragment.

I sensed an immediate turmoil in her mind. The very thought of magic repelled her—a most curious reaction which I had not foreseen, but I could not know what alterations in attitudes might have occurred while I had been entrapped. Simultaneously, however, she was also fiercely attracted by the possibility of childbearing. Throughout the three years of her marriage, it had been her ardent desire to bear sons by her husband, but no children had been granted to them.

After intense deliberation, she told me frankly that she was accustomed to weighing all the costs and benefits of any proposed course of action before committing herself.

I was most favorably impressed by her prudent demeanor. Should she consent to subject herself to my spell, this woman of forceful character would serve as an admirable mother for my rescuer-to-be. Since she could not perceive my invisibly ensorcelled remnant, in order to assuage her understandable fears, I provided her with a vision of my previous physical appearance.

I further assured her that the action I requested was not to be viewed as a betrayal of her wedding vows. I entreated that she and her husband foster the child of my mind as if it were their own. Indeed, in an additional attempt to ease her aversion to my Power, I suggested that I could, for a set time, veil her memory of this entire incident. From her first intimation of pregnancy, I wanted her and her husband to consider and then rear the child as their own. I did insist that when the child reached a practical age to be able to commence my rescue, she would regain her clear memory of this encounter so that she could impart directions and advise in the planning. I explained to her that if she did choose to help me, she must agree to take my jewel with her, for it would maintain my magical protection over her and the child, insuring that both would survive.

"She pondered my offer, then affirmed her willingness to assist me. She did ask that I perform the temporary obscuration of her memory. To account for possession of my jewel, I proposed that she would remember it as a valuable gift received from a secret source, and that would safeguard it for the child's coming of age (should it be a male), or betrothal gift (should it be a female). When that time came, her full memory of our bargain would return; she would present the jewel and its accompanying obligation to the child of her body and my mind.

"Upon her agreement, I expressed my profound gratitude, and at once commenced my initial incantations. To promote introspection and the development of a reflective nature, I set strictures to produce a child mute from birth, who should also be gifted with the insightful touch, allowing instant future recognition of my jewel, mind to mind.

"Know therefore, Child Who-is-to-come, that I, Elsenar, your father, implore you to hasten hither to free me. You must seek guidance to this place from your mother, the Lady Veronda of the Dales. . . . "

CHAPTER 26

Mereth—events at Lormt
(21st Day, Month of the Ice Dragon/
20th Day, Moon of the Knife)

At first, Elsenar's mental voice totally dominated my senses, but gradually I recovered an overlapping awareness of my Lormt surroundings. I found that I could briefly lay the jewel aside while I wrote Elsenar's words for Nolar to read aloud. I wished that the others in the room could "hear" the degree of urgency underlying Elsenar's magical communication. Somehow I knew beyond any doubt that there could be no possibility of deceit in such a message. The emotional overtones were stark—Elsenar had been convinced that his sole hope for rescue depended upon the response of his enspelled plea.

I glanced up for an instant. Lormt's party of listeners were thoroughly engrossed by Elsenar's account of his unnatural incarceration. As I resumed my transcribing, Elsenar's words "to produce a child mute from birth" echoed through my mind. I was gripped by an icy sense of foreboding. I forced my fingers to continue to wield my quill until two unbelievable phrases assailed me like the lash of a whip: "I, Elsenar your father," and "your mother, the Lady Veronda of the Dales."

Had I possessed a voice, I would have cried out in utter consternation. I did not feel the jewel drop from my nerveless fingers as a tide of darkness swelled within me, blotting out all sensations.

Afterwards, the others told me that quite abruptly, I seemed to stop breathing, and fell back against the pillows. While Jonja chafed my hands, Nolar fetched her nearby satchel and thrust a handful of crushed herbal leaves under my nose.

I was jolted from my swoon by a bracing, acrid scent that made me sneeze. As soon as I opened my eyes, I motioned for the press of figures to move away from my bedside so that I could orient myself and catch my breath.

I struggled desperately to make sense of what must be true, yet seemed unthinkable. Elsenar the mage *was* my true father . . . but until my mother had sought refuge amid the ancient ruins beyond Ferndale, Elsenar had been trapped there for a thousand years. I had found the answer to the vital question I had journeyed so far to ask; I now knew my true father's identity. As an exceedingly unsettling secondary discovery, I had also acquired yet another unexpected addition to my kinship list, albeit one more distantly removed in time. I had been sired by Elsenar almost seventy-six years ago, but a thousand years earlier, he had sired the foundation for the House of Krevonel. Kasarian was thus a peculiarly time-displaced kinsman of mine! With a trembling hand, I reached for a new sheet of parchment, and wrote the last astonishing words of Elsenar's message, to which I added my kinship deduction.

When Nolar read the words, Kasarian's face blanched

to such a degree that I almost believed he might swoon. Instead, he resorted to his habit of furiously twisting his gold signet ring. When he spoke, his voice was hoarse, as if his throat were dry. "How can we know," he began, then stopped and poured himself a measure of barley water from the jug Nolar had prepared for me. At any other time, I am sure that an Alizonder baron would have spat out such an insipid brew, with appropriate imprecations. It was a telling indication of Kasarian's distraction that he drank a full goblet without a murmur. I doubt that he knew what he had swallowed. The moisture, however, did restore his voice to its usual firmness. He resumed his unfinished question. "How can we know where to seek our common . . . Foresire [the very word seemed sour in his mouth] if his postern to that place of his imprisonment has been magically destroyed? Surely your lady mother is dead and cannot direct us as Elsenar had intended."

I hastened to write, "Even if that ancient postern still existed, we would have no way to locate the site near Lormt where Elsenar conjured it. No, as we embark upon any effort to succor Elsenar, we must pursue our journey to the Dales by ship, horse, and possibly on foot. I was not yet twenty when my mother died, but I recall many walks with her during my early years through the unnamed valleys near my birthplace. I believe that I can identify the very site of Elsenar's immurement. My mother once pointed out to me some ancient stone ruins within which she had sheltered, she said, from a winter storm before my birth the following summer."

I stopped writing, suddenly aware that my grasp was bending the quill near its breaking point. Like a sheaf of brittle leaf fragments tossed by an icy wind, previously unexplained segments of memory abruptly formed a coherent pattern.

As one reared in a large family, my mother had longed for sons to assume her Clan's trading responsibilties. She had trained me, her only child, to be useful despite my physical limitations. Could it be that her substantial trading successes had been achieved because of the magical influences of Elsenar's jewel? It now seemed reasonable that those strange dreams that had affected both my mother and me had been prompted by the jewel's close presence.

I wondered if my mother had begun to regain her memories of her encounter with Elsenar before she departed upon her last, fatal trip. With searing insight, I confronted the harsh truth from our past: the heaviest strokes of evil fortune had befallen us when we became separated from the jewel—when it was first stored away, then lost in the looting of our treasure room at Vennesport. My mother had been swept away to her death, while I had suffered the torments of the war against the Dales. Now that Elsenar's jewel was once again in my hand, I was obliged to act upon his appeal for kin-aid.

Another shard of memory intruded, piercing me like a dagger thrust. Painfully long ago, I had shared my private feeling with Doubt, writing for him in our secret script expressions of the emotions I could not voice. Compelled now to unburden myself, I scribbled furiously, "Intolerable frustration! To be confined in this feeble body that can no longer sit a horse or climb a mountain track! Elsenar's geas from the past was directed to *me*—I was deliberately bred to fulfill this charge! When my mother was ready to give me Elsenar's jewel as my betrothal gift, she would have been empowered to explain the circumstances of her agreement with him. With the assistance of my prospective husband, I should have been able to undertake the mission to set Elsenar free . . . but my mother died before I became betrothed, before she could tell me about Elsenar's plight. Blood oath binds me to honor her commitment, but in my present condition, I cannot contemplate such a journey. My predicament is unbearable!"

I paused again, reluctant to continue, but unable to ignore the only other answer to the conundrum. Once more, I had to force my hand to shape the words for Nolar to read aloud. "Yet I can perceive one remaining alternative."

After hearing my words read, Kasarian nodded slowly. "I also bear the blood of Elsenar," he said in a grave voice. "Would you permit me to attempt this quest in your stead?"

Duratan intervened. "You cannot seriously propose to travel in the Dales," he objected. "Although more than twenty years have passed, the wounds Alizon inflicted upon the Dales have still not entirely healed. You would be far likelier to be met with a sword edge than a journey cup."

Kasarian regarded Duratan as if he were a particularly willful hound refusing to follow a clear trail. "I am accustomed to living with a sword edge ever near my throat," he retorted. "Why should that circumstance hinder the making of reasonable plans? When I alone can satisfy the stricture, the conclusion is obvious: I must go."

"But can you so easily abandon your baronial duties in Alizon for such an extended journey?" Nolar inquired. "Besides, troubling questions must arise concerning Gurborian's sudden disappearance. Might you not be suspected of some complicity?"

Kasarian shook his head impatiently. "I answer only to the Lord Baron, and then only if I witlessly fail to make sufficient preparations in advance. Gurborian provoked many powerful enemies. Before I left Krevonel Castle, I ordered Bodrik to dispatch in two days' time a persuasive letter to the Lord Baron suggesting four plausible causes for Gurborian's abrupt absence. I further informed the Lord Baron that I should be engaged for a period of weeks in a needful evaluation of my most distant estates. I shall not be expected in Alizon City until I choose to return there."

From her position in the hall, Jonja half rose from her chair. "Why would you commit yourself to this quest?" she demanded. "You have made clear to us your utter aversion to objects of Power. Do you expect us to believe that you would personally bear Elsenar's mighty jewel over the vast distance to surrender it to its very master?"

"You speak plainly to me," Kasarian replied. "I shall be equally forthright. No, I do not welcome the burden of this accursed jewel, yet it belongs to my Foresire, who, if he presently exists, commands it be restored to him. I perceive this journey as an imperative duty to our Line of Krevonel. I also venture to suggest that it would be advantageous for our collective interests should our factions be strengthened by the backing of so puissant a mage. Surely he would incline toward granting that boon to his rescuer."

While Kasarian spoke, I had reluctantly reached my own decision. I handed Nolar my written comments. "The ruins you must seek," she read aloud, "lie near the border of the Waste, the whole breadth of the Dales inland from the sea coast. You may encounter severe peril in nearly every inhabited area."

Kasarian surveyed me ironically. "Lady, not long ago, I would have said that no foreign cur from outside our borders could live to penetrate Alizon City . . . yet you did." Addressing the others, he added, "I have observed that the wits of you Lormt folk can be sharp beyond my previous imaginings. If you can craft a credible tale to explain my presence in the Dales, I shall willingly journey under its protection." Pausing, Kasarian smiled suddenly, which softened the harsh angles of his face. He turned back to me and said, "You dyed your hair to improve your disguise, Lady. Could not mine be similarly darkened to placate the hostile eyes of the Dales?"

"I must say," Morfew observed wryly, "I was not at all certain that Mereth could successfully impersonate an Alizonder baron. It is an even more difficult prospect to believe that you can deceive discerning Dalesfolk into accepting you as one of their own. You are far too pale all over, young man—you would have to soak your whole body in a bath of oak bark extract."

"Perhaps not." Nolar's quiet voice drew our attention to her. "Have not children been sired upon Daleswomen by Alizonders?" she asked. "Kasarian might claim to be such a halfling."

My hand trembled as I wrote, "I know of no such unfortunates who were . . . allowed to live. During the war, many Daleswomen took their own lives rather than bear children of shame."

Kasarian had been listening intently, his head inclined a little to one side like an inquisitive hawk watching the grass below for signs of an unsuspecting mouse. "I was four when the invasion began," he said. "To my knowledge, no mixed-breed pups were ever brought back from the Dales. It may be, however, that I can suggest a circumstance under which a mixed-breed of my age could reasonably claim existence. Formerly, Alizon dispatched raiding vessels which at times returned to port with captive breeding stock."

Jonja's eyes widened. "You cannot mean that you used captured women . . . ." Her voice trailed off into appalled silence.

"Rumors of such events have reached us," Ouen remarked coldly. "We had hoped they were mistaken."

Kasarian did not appear at all perturbed by our obvious revulsion. "Do not you Estcarpians breed with the Sulcar at times to invigorate your lines?" he inquired. "We barons, of course, have always preserved our pure blood, but among the common folk, captured outside females have produced useful servants and workmen. Could I not represent myself as one such?"

With a heavy heart, I wrote, "In years past, some of our trading ships have been, we thought, lost at sea. We assumed that they had been sunk in storms, but . . . ." I could write no further. It was too painful to contemplate what horrid lives our tradefolk must have endured had they been taken to Alizon to serve as brood mares.

Nolar did not hide her repugnance when she declared, "We of Estcarp deplore and reject any form of slavery."

Kasarian shrugged. "It has ever been so in Alizon," he said. "The strong exploit and rule the weak."

"As important as such matters are in the lives of our people," Ouen asserted sternly, "we cannot at present address our divergencies. Whether we view this Alizonian practice as traditional or offensive, it exists, and perhaps we can make use of it in a constructive manner."

"Suppose. . . . " Nolar looked at me with a rueful expression, as if she understood my barely restrained grief. "Suppose," she resumed, "we say that Kasarian's mother was aboard a trading vessel from the Dales—perhaps a

coasting ship blown far enough out to sea to be intercepted by an Alizonian raider. Reared as an oppressed servant, he would have schemed to escape whenever an opportunity arose."

"I can contribute the opportunity," Jonja offered. "Three years ago, when Karsten clashed with Estcarp, all our lands were in an uproar. If ever a flight from Alizonian captivity could have succeeded, it would have been then, while the border with Estcarp was beset with thrusts against the spell barriers."

Morfew rubbed his hands together. "And I foresee the necessary linkage to Lormt," he exclaimed. "Kasarian could have slipped into northern Estcarp and apprenticed himself to a wandering trader whose travels led the pair to Lormt. But what excuse can we offer for Kasarian's dangerous foray into the Dales—surely not that he seeks Dales-kin of his presumed mother?"

I had finally controlled my internal turmoil of memories, and was able to write upon my slate, "Let us take account of the knowledge we possess. I know the Dales, and I know trade. As Morfew's suggested apprentice, Kasarian could undertake a journey for his master. Among Lormt's countless documents, surely there must be maps of the Dales. Let us say that upon one such old map, the merchant found a reference to a possible source for something valuable in trade . . . but not too valuable." I stopped to think while Nolar read, then wrote my conclusion. "I know the perfect material: lamantine wood. It is prized, but not so much so that a venture to seek it would attract brigands. It is also to our advantage that the area where Kasarian must pursue his search is near the Waste, which will likely discourage any offers to accompany him. Futhermore, I can write letters to my Sulcar friends to secure Kasarian's sea passage, and to tradefolk in the Dales to request their aid to him along his way inland."

"A most plausible tale indeed," Morfew pronounced when Nolar finished reading my parchment. "How say you, Kasarian? Can you pose as merchant's apprentice?"

During the reading, Kasarian had at first looked highly skeptical, but then his expression had grown more thoughtful and less doubtful. "I can try," he said. "I have scant experience with trade," he admitted frankly, "other than my periodic reviews of the steward's accounts for Krevonel Castle, and my dealing in hounds." Kasarian turned to me. "You will have to instruct me, Lady, regarding such matters, as well as assist me with the speech of the Dales."

"An accomplished scholar, Irvil of Norsdale, came here some years ago to engage in kinship studies," Ouen said. "His joints stiffened so during the winters that he found further travel too painful and asked to reside with us. He will gladly teach the spoken tongue of the Dales."

"Before we embark—again—upon such strenuous activities," Morfew observed plaintively, "can we not consider at least a brief respite for food? My aged stomach reminds me that the hour for supping has come . . . and gone."

Jonja stood up. "We have chattered too long as it is," she proclaimed. "Mereth requires rest after her ordeal. Out, all of you, and do not trouble her again until morning."

I lifted my quill to write a protest, but Jonja plucked it from my grasp. "Out!" she commanded, and like a flock of singularly meek sheep, the whole troop, except for Nolar, filed out of the bedchamber.

"Before I retire to the chamber next door," Nolar promised me, "I shall warm another cup of broth for you, and replenish your barley water, since Kasarian unaccountably drank your supply. Should you need me during the night, you can ring this little bell suspended on a cord from the bedstead."

Although my mind longed to weigh and assess the events just past, as well as the burgeoning prospects for the morrow, I found that I could scarcely keep my eyes open after I had drunk the second cup of broth. Nolar sensed my desire to keep Elsenar's jewel close by me . . . but not where I might accidentally touch it barehanded in my sleep. She dropped the chained pendant into a small leather bag she took from her herb satchel. My last vision from that momentous day was a fading glimpse of Nolar's sleeve as she gently tucked the bag out of sight under my pillows.

CHAPTER 27

Kasarian—events at Lormt
(20th and 21st days, Moon of the Knife/
21st and 22nd Days,
Month of the Ice Dragon)

When I listened to the reading of the message enspelled in the jewel, I had to bite back a cry of denial at
the revelation that Mereth had been sired by Elsenar
upon a Dales female name Veronda. Krevonel, the Foresire of my own Line, had been sired a thousand years
previously by Elsenar. We had suspected earlier that
Mereth had to possess some of Elsenar's blood, however
attenuated, because of her acceptance under the stricture
of his postern spell, Her Line's claim to the jewel also
argued in favor of some kinship linkage ... but by his
ghastly magic, Elsenar was not just Mereth's distant kin.
He was her very sire! I had to accept the incredible;
Mereth and I belonged to the same direct Line. That
recognition took my breath away.

With an effort, I forced my attention back to the final
words of Elsenar's message. I had to admire his devious
reasoning and foresight in bespelling Mereth to be mute,
but he had not been able to control what subsequently

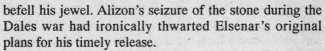

befell his jewel. Alizon's seizure of the stone during the Dales war had ironically thwarted Elsenar's original plans for his timely release.

I did not express aloud my profound doubts that Elsenar could still be alive and capable of being rescued. I had to concede, however, that reason could not always be relied upon when magic reared its vile head.

When Morfew complained that we had talked well past the common hour for supping, the Wise Woman abruptly commanded us all to leave the bedchamber so that Mereth could rest.

I welcomed the interruption, for I needed time to plan and reflect. After stopping by Lormt's dining hall, I withdrew to my chamber, carrying with me a loaf of bread, some deplorable gruel, and a flask of ale.

The problem of Elsenar burned in my mind. The opportunity appeared irresistibly tempting: if I could somehow contrive to free the ancient mage by restoring to him his jewel, then Elsenar should grant abundant rewards to me as his rescuer. On the other hand, the prospect of facing a living mage, especially one of such notorious reputation, was unspeakably horrid. What could I do to defend myself against the very monster present at Alizon's dawning and personally responsible for the Original Betrayal? Instead of rewarding me for freeing him, Elsenar might blast me on the spot . . . or far worse, return to Alizon by his sorceries and seize total control of the land. How could a mortal man stand against such unnatural Power? And yet . . . taking risks had always been the Alizonian way, and potential gains had to be balanced against only possible threats that might never materialize.

Constrained by the cramped dimensions of my bedchamber, I managed sufficient exercise to verify that my swordsmanship had been unimpaired by my slight injuries. I then blew out the candles and lay down. Feeling somewhat weary from the day's exertions, I slept dreamlessly.

It was midmorning of the next day before the Wise Woman allowed us to gather again in Mereth's bedchamber. Somewhat restored by her rest, Mereth appeared less haggard. She had already drawn a crude map to show us where lay the ruins beneath which she believed Elsenar had been trapped. She had also drafted letters for me to carry to certain Sulcar ship masters at Etsport, Estcarp's chief port since the destruction of Gorm.

I was examining Mereth's map when yet another of Lormt's host of elderly males arrived at the door. Although his ruddy skin had lightened with age, as had his hair, he was evidently a Dalesman. Morfew hailed him as Irvil, the kinship scholar Ouen had named to us. It was a telling indication of the lack of proper organization at Lormt that Irvil had been totally unaware of Mereth's presence within the citadel. He at once erupted in a spate of Dales speech which was far too rapid for me to comprehend more than a few scattered words.

Mereth seemed outwardly unaffected, but I noticed a tear spilled down her cheek. She scrubbed it away with her sleeve, and wrote a private greeting to her countryman on her slate.

After reading it, Irvil turned to me and said in Estcarpian, "I am told that you have urgent need to learn the speech of the Dales. I never thought to speak to an Alizonder . . . but Master Ouen requests that I talk with you."

Irvil was easily old enough to be my sire's sire, which meant he likely harbored ill feelings from the time of the war. I bowed to him, and touched my Line badge. "I would not impose upon you if the need were not urgent," I said. "Both Alizon and Estcarp face a common threat which, if unchecked, would likely endanger your Dales. My proposed voyage to the Dales may assuage that threat. I thank you for your forbearance and assistance." Irvil's grim expression eased, as if my words had mollified him.

Mereth thrust her slate at him, and he read aloud, "'We shall divide our time between instruction in both speech and trade, since Kasarian must master the rudiments of each.'"

Morfew smiled. "Pray do not entirely submerge your Alizonian accent, young man," he advised me. "You must remember that the only Dales speech you would have learned as a pup would have come from your mother; until you escaped into Estcarp three years ago, you would have spoken chiefly Alizonian."

Nolar rose and advanced toward me. "I claim an hour of your time to dye your hair. Shall we attempt the transformation this afternoon? I must consult with Master Pruett concerning the proportions for the herbal mixture. I will call for you when my preparations are complete."

Duratan moved to accompany his mate. "It is just as well," he remarked at the doorway, "that you can admit to an Alizonian father, since otherwise your pretense would be ruined every time you opened your mouth."

"May you swiftly impart the knowledge that is required," Ouen exhorted Mereth, Irvil, and me. "Pray inform me if I may provide any aid. All of Lormt's facilities are at your disposal."

Thus began a daunting week of constant application. Morning, noon, and evening, I listened, and wrote under Mereth's and Irvil's demanding tutelage. Bearing Mor-

few's warning in mind, I did not attempt perfect mimicry
of the sounds of the Dales speech. In truth, the tones
were difficult to match, being softer and quite different
to the ear from Alizonian.

As she had promised, Duratan's mate marched me to
her lair later that first afternoon. She had me sit upon a
stool beside a stone basin in which she stirred an acrid
fluid. After wetting my hair with water, she poured cup
after cup of the odiferous rinse over my head—nor did
she neglect to darken my eyebrows, using a soft brush
dipped in the dye. Both of us were well-soaked by the
time she pronounced me possibly presentable. She
warned me that once-set, the dye would not fade for a
long time. It would not do for the color to lapse during
the sea voyage. I must confess that I started at the sight
of my image reflected in a silver tray. For an unsettling
instant, I thought I was beholding a stranger. No baron
would have allowed such a dark-haired, disreputable ruf-
fian into his living quarters as a guest . . . but Duratan's
mate smiled at me, and said I made a barely passable
halfling.

Between our strenuous study meetings, Mereth composed additional letters to be given to her kinsmen and
other traders in the Dales once I landed at Vennesport.
We pored over maps together for hours while she supplied me with descriptions of the land I must traverse
and the likely arrangements that must be made for me to
secure supplies and hire suitable horses.

The First Whelping Moon commenced while we labored. Mereth termed it the Month of the Snow Bird,
and indeed I had seldom seen heavier snows than those
burdening the mountain fastnesses surrounding Lormt.

I was soon beset by Lormt's chief provisioner, a bald,
talkative Estcarpian named Wessell, who fell upon me

like a yammering hound pup. He proved to be surprisingly efficient, however, in choosing and assembling the travel gear I required. He also presented me with a small box of lamantine wood, which he praised highly for preserving delicate foodstuffs during long journeys. We had seized a few such examples as Dales booty, but I had not before possessed a sample of that dark gray-brown close-grained wood. Mereth wrote that it was prized for making bottles which could keep water sweet for many days, as well as containers which would indefinitely keep fresh the best journeycakes—those baked with fruit or meat bits. No Dalesman knew, she added, where to find the trees from which the wood could be cut, but precious objects made of worked lamantine wood were rarely found in the Waste. My trader's quest, guided by the old map, would be considered dangerous, but not so extraordinary as to arouse undue notice.

By the Third Day of the First Whelping Moon, I was ready to depart upon my first stage of travel—the thirty or more leagues from Lormt to Es City. One of Lormt's younger scholars—still old enough to be my sire—agreed to accompany me as far as Es City. It was necessary to leave behind at Lormt all of my baronial trappings, including my signet ring. I felt perilously vulnerable with just the single belt dagger which the Lormt folk insisted was the customary defensive weapon for a traveling merchant. The notion of spending a moon or more—depending upon the weather—aboard a ship manned by Alizon's deadly Sulcar foes with only one inadequate blade at my belt was maddening. I reminded myself that I was ostensibly a trader's apprentice, and as such, I must comply with their practices.

Gathering up my heavy outer cloak, I entered Mereth's bedchamber to collect Elsenar's jewel. She was sitting up in the bed, and nodded approvingly as she surveyed me. She wrote on her slate for me to read, "Our joint efforts have succeeded. You truly present the semblance of an apprentice trader. Take with you now Elsenar's legacy, together with my well-wishings for a fair journey." She held out to me the glittering jewel, which I secured in the innermost pocket of my tunic. At that point, I did not care to wear the cursed object next to my skin. It was unsettling enough having to travel with it on my person. Would it again afflict my dreams as it had in Alizon? I thrust away the unwelcome thought.

"I thank you doubly, Lady," I said, "for both your trust and your farewell. With the aid of your map, I shall find the ensorcelled ruins and restore this mighty stone to our Foresire." I bowed to her, and my hand moved in habitual salute to the bare cloth of my tunic, where my Line badge should have been sewn.

Mereth almost smiled. "May the Flame guard you, Outlander," she wrote, much to my puzzlement.

I bowed again, and hurried down the stairs toward the horses waiting in the windswept courtyard.

CHAPTER 28

Kasarian—account of his
journey from Lormt to Vennesport (3rd
Day, First Whelping Moon-23rd Day,
Moon of the Dire Wolf)

I had often hunted in the mountains bordering upon Escore, so I had no difficulty adjusting to the gait of Lormt's mountain-bred horses. They were smaller, less sturdy beasts than our prized Torgians, but well-suited for maintaining their footing on the snow-shrouded slopes.

My trail companion was Farris, a taciturn Estcarpian. In order to accustom myself to my assumed character, I asked Farris to address me exclusively by the Dales name we had chosen for me: Kasyar. I had to learn to respond to it as if it were my name; my life might well depend upon such details. There was scant opportunity to converse while we were riding, but once we camped for the night, I attempted to engage Farris in speech. It appeared that he had been drawn to study at Lormt because of his single-minded devotion to an encompassing knowledge of herbs. Once he raised the topic, he became tediously loquacious. My own acquaintance with plants tended more toward the noxious and poisonous varieties, but fortunately, I struck upon one aspect we could profitably discuss—the range of herbs employed for enhancing and spicing bland foods. Gennard's sire had been a master cook who had instructed him in the preparation of many pleasing dishes. I recalled sufficient details from Gennard's remarks to prompt Farris' discourse.

The deep snow and rough terrain frequently thwarted our progress. We did not descend to more level ground for over a chill, tiresome week. Gradually, as our unmarked path approached the north bank of the Es River, we encountered a clearer, more travel-worn trail. After a few day's further advance, that trail broadened into a road of sorts, and late on the Thirteenth Day of the First Whelping Moon, we glimpsed our first sight of the massive gray-green wall encircling Es City.

Crouching upon the high ground at the city's center, Es Castle glowered down at us, dwarfing even the great round towers set at intervals along the city wall. In my worst nightmares, I had never thought that I would one day behold the very fortress wherein Estcarp's gray-clad crones gathered like spiders at the hub of their web of far-flung spells.

The next morning, as we rode through one of the narrow gates, I had to make a constant effort to preserve an outwardly untroubled aspect. It was daunting to penetrate into the heart of the territory of Alizon's prime enemy, alone, without the backing of a properly equipped army. I sternly suppressed my apprehensions that at any moment, we might be confronted by one of the gray-robed Witches who could instantly discern my true identity.

Fortunately, once we passed inside the gate, Farris immediately turned away from the street leading to Es Castle, guiding his horse into the crowded lanes of a commercial quarter near the outer wall. He led the way into the busy courtyard of an inn whose sign bore a bright, if somewhat ill-drawn, painted image of a snow cat. After we dismounted, Farris explained that he planned to survey the city's markets for herbs otherwise unavailable at Lormt, rest here overnight, then begin his journey back to the scholar's citadel. He would first inquire of the innkeeper where I might seek the merchants Mereth had cited as possible sources of assistance to me.

I was deeply relieved to learn that one of the three Estcarpian merchants that Mereth had addressed in her letters was currently present in the city. Bidding Farris farewell, I followed the innkeeper's directions to a nearby warehouse where I presented Mereth's letter. My cordial reception provided clear evidence of the high regard in which Mereth was held by these trading folk. The merchant, who recalled her recent brief stay in Es City on her way to Lormt, expressed an active interest in handling any lamantine wood I might discover during my expedition to the Dales. He did ask why, as an apprentice, I was not accompanied on such a trip by my master, but I related the tale we had agreed upon at Lormt should anyone inquire: how my master had suffered a fall in the mountains as we had descended toward Es City, and had been forced to return to Lormt. Persuaded by the promising nature of the old map, he had entrusted me with the quest of the Dales. The merchant congratulated me upon my unusual opportunity, and dispatched one of his hirelings to engage a horse for the next stage of my journey, the four or so leagues to Etsport. He graciously invited me to stay the night in the guest quarters adjoining the warehouse.

I guarded my tongue carefully in all that I said, but I

did not appear to arouse any suspicion. During the evening meal, the merchant told me that few trading ships dared the winter seas, but if fortune favored me, I might perhaps find in port a Sulcar captain named Brannun, who sailed no matter what the season.

Early the following morning, I set out for Etsport. A well-traveled road ran alongside the Es River, allowing for much faster passage, even despite the drifting snow. With my larger, rested horse, I covered the distance by nightfall.

I took care to skirt the environs of the local stronghold, Etsford Manor, ruled over by the misshapen former ax-wielder Koris of Gorm, now Lord Seneschal of Estcarp. We had heard in Alizon that, after being severely wounded, Koris had retired to this quiet holding. It was rumored that he and his mate, Loyse, whelp to the shipwreck-scavenging Lord of Verlaine, still provided counsel at times to Estcarp's Witches. Not wanting to attract the attention of such dangerous enemies, I rode straight to the dockside at the river's mouth.

I quickly located the trading house recommended to me by the merchant in Es City. His colleagues there willingly took charge of my horse, agreeing to attend to it until they dispatched their next shipment of goods to Es City. They informed me that the Sulcar shipmaster I sought was indeed in port readying his vessel for a voyage to the Dales. One of the apprentices showed me the way to a tavern favored by this Captain Brannun, and pointed out to me a giant fair-haired man quaffing ale at a table near the door. Once I distracted his attention from his ale mug by bellowing his name, I introduced myself.

He wiped the foam from his distinctively bristling Sulcar mustache, and measured me with a most insolent glance. "For a stripling, you raise a fair cry," he said.

"What matter is so pressing that you intrude upon my refreshment?"

In dealing with Sulcars, we Alizonders had long found it advisable to speak directly—it was pointless to employ subtlety with a Sulcar. I reached into my belt wallet and slapped two bars of silver on the rough wooden table in front of him. Before I had left Lormt, Mereth offered to pay for my passage to the Dales, but I had insisted upon using my own gold. Duratan had objected that I could scarcely present metal branded with Alizonian markings, but Ouen, somewhat to my surprise, had sent for a casket containing unmarked silver bars, from which he carefully weighed out a fair substitution for my gold.

Captain Brannun grinned and poked the bars with a sinewy forefinger. "I do believe your business is urgent," he observed. "I take it you desire to arrange for passage on the *Storm Seeker?*"

"If you are sailing immediately for the Dales," I confirmed. "My master requires me to undertake a trading voyage on his behalf while his broken bones mend at Lormt."

Brannun clouted me vigorously on the shoulder. "Fortune smiles upon you, lad!" he exclaimed. "I have been loading goods these past six days and await only the proper winds to set sail for Vennesport. But do not sit there parched as a desert flower. Master Taverner—ale for my passenger! Ale for me! What stores are you shipping? I warn you, I have scant space left in my hold."

"I hope to return with goods," I replied, "but I travel with none. I carry only minimal baggage."

"All the better," Brannun roared cheerfully. "I feared for a moment that you might require hold space that I could not supply. Come, finish that ale and let me show you the *Storm Seeker*—the finest vessel a man could wish beneath his feet." As he rose, he scooped from the bench beside him a huge tawny mound that I had mistaken for a bale of furs. Noticing my glance, Brannun laughed aloud. "I doubt you've seen the live beast that yielded me this cloak," he declared. "'Twas a true lion—aye, one of those rare beasts from the lands far south of the Dales. When I was a young man—likely your age or less—he came upon me during a coasting voyage. We had put in to shore to replenish our fresh water. I was bending over, filling one of our casks at a stream, when this lion leaped upon me out of the brush. I can tell you, it was a glorious struggle! Had I not had my throwing ax at my belt, I might have suffered a substantial injury. As it was, I gained this splendid skin together with the design for my fighting helm, all at one stroke." Flinging some Karstenian silver bits on the table to settle our account, he swept me toward the door.

I had never before boarded a sea-going vessel. All of my limited sailing experience had been on river craft. Brannun displayed surprising agility for a man of his size as he leaped from the dock to the deck of a typically ungainly, but sturdy, broad-beamed Sulcar ship. Like those of all such vessels, its prow was carved in the grotesque form of a scaled serpent.

Brannun sniffed the breeze, and squinted at the low clouds. "The wind's not yet brisk enough for us to set sail—possibly it will have freshened sufficiently by the morrow. Come aboard! You have a choice of quarters—the cabin beside the wine or the one by the spider silk—unless you'd care to camp on deck?"

I assured him that I preferred a space below decks. I had decided that it might be prudent for me to stay below as much of the time as possible, limiting my exposure to the Sulcars and thus reducing my chance of accidentally betraying my true identity. I confessed to Brannun that this was my first sea voyage, and expressed my concern that we might encounter storms. I thought for a moment he was about to choke.

"Storms—storms!" he sputtered. "Sail in winter, sail amid storms! Why do you think I named my ship *Storm Seeker?*" He waved his arms wildly. "Because it revels in storms—the higher the waves, the faster it runs before the wind." He shook his head, incredulous at my ignorance. "You *may* stay less wet below decks," he conceded reluctantly, then his eyes brightened. "Of course, during the truly major storms, all hands aboard must work the ship together. Your master will count you far more worthy for the experience, I've no doubt."

On the Eighteenth Day of the First Whelping Moon, we sailed from Etsport. Three days later, the first storm descended upon us. I began to learn more about ships than I ever cared to know, both above and below decks. Brannun's crewmen were a boisterous lot—typical Sulcars—but able seamen and, as we Alizonders had learned to our sore cost, formidable fighters. I was expected to lend a hand at any time I was on deck, so I stayed below whenever possible.

Even below decks, I could not entirely seclude myself. Once the initial storm had passed, Brannun marched into my cabin, his arms laden with tally sticks and documents which he dropped upon my plank-rimmed bed. "See what you make of these cargo accounts," he ordered. "Your master would not want you to idle away the time when you have such an opportunity to enlarge your store of trading knowledge."

I should have liked to have told him that I kept a steward to attend to such menial work, but in order to preserve my imposture, I strove to bring some order out of the poorly inscribed chaos. When Brannun blustered back in some hours later, I pointed out to him that his tally sticks proclaimed his cargo short four bales of woven goods when compared with his nearly unreadable loading lists.

"You Dales traders," Brannun declared, "always fretting over exact tallies." He rattled my teeth with another buffet to my shoulder, and bellowed, "Come dine with me in my cabin! We can discuss the proper forms for keeping accounts."

It was during that meal that I nearly betrayed myself. While we were eating some moderately acceptable fish stew, I saw a large rat poke its head from behind a timber rib arching along the wall. Quite by habit, before I even thought, my hand drew and threw my belt knife, impaling the wretched beast.

Brannun drew a sharp breath, and eyed me narrowly. "Where did you learn to throw a knife like that, young apprentice?" he growled.

I cursed my muscles for acting on their own without my conscious direction. As abjectly as I could, I proffered my woeful supposed past experience. "For some years, I was kept as a slave in a castle in Alizon," I explained. "It was miserably overrun by vermin. They kept no such fine beasts as your cats, so we slaves were forced to dispose of any rat we saw in that fashion. I crave your pardon for drawing my blade without your permission."

Brannun guffawed, and struck me such a clout across the narrow table that he nearly jolted me from the seating bench, which like the table, was secured to the deck with wooden pins. "Permission?" he roared. "I would I could toss a knife that swift and sure. I required some

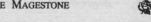

years to master my throwing ax—until I saw your toss just now, I rather fancied my speed. You must show my lads how you do it! I can see that your earlier practice had refined your skill so that you react to sudden motion glimpsed from the corner of the eye. Pray take care that you do not skewer our ship's cat, or one of the smaller hands. We shall be obliged to address you as Kasyar-of-the-Fast-Knife!"

After that near calamity, I attempted to guard my movements as well as my tongue. Such constant wariness, together with the long hours of confinement in my cabin, wore upon my temper. Curiously, one source of restful ease was the ship's cat, whose acquaintance I made the morning following the rat incident.

I had gone on deck to stretch my legs when Brannun bustled past; the man was always on his way somewhere aloft or below, forward or astern. Spying me, he stopped, and exclaimed, "Yonder comes our cat—Sea Foam, we call her—a prime ratter. Give her a few weeks, and you'll have far fewer moving targets aboard to tempt your knife."

I turned to see a large, cream-colored cat regarding me with bright amber eyes. Not knowing exactly how one customarily approached such beasts, I knelt and extended my hand for it to sniff, as I would have done to a strange hound. It cocked its head at me, then stepped nimbly across the slanting deck to rub against my boots.

"She likes the lad!" Brannun boomed approvingly. "Sea Foam's always been a keen judge of character—doubtless recognizes a fellow master ratter."

For the remainder of the voyage, Sea Foam often visited me in my cabin, sometimes curling up on my bed, sometimes even sitting in my lap and purring like a real hound—a most singular animal.

In addition to four more severe storms, we encountered some adverse winds that slowed our progress, but as the Moon of the Dire Wolf neared its close, the bleak horizon bar of bare water was replaced by the welcome uneven bulk of solid land. We had spent thirty-four days at sea, by my best judgment, for during the worst of the storms, it had been difficult to determine when day ended and night began.

I had formed a hearty respect for Captain Brannun and his crew—and an equally hearty conviction that I preferred land travel to sea voyaging. The thought of motionless land or even a runaway horse beneath me had become increasingly attractive. I was ready to present my lamantine wood-questing tale to the traders of Vennesport.

CHAPTER 29

Kasarian—account of his journey across
the Dales from Vennesport to the ruins
beyond Ferndale (26th Day, Moon of the
Dire Wolf—24th Day, Moon of Chordosh)

It took three days for me to deliver all of Mereth's remaining letters: two to kinsmen and two others to traders of her acquaintance. Initially, each of the recipients looked somewhat askance at me, but after reading her letters, they wholeheartedly extended themselves to organize the mounts and supplies I would need for my trip to the lands bordering the ill-reputed Waste. Each of the Dalesmen also inquired anxiously about Mereth. Only one of the traders was of her advanced age; the other three were a generation or more younger than she. They seemed to view her as an honored elder, and appeared genuinely concerned about how she had been received after her long journey across the sea. I assured them that she had been graciously welcomed at Lormt, where her extensive knowledge of kinship lists was highly praised. I did not mention her injuries. It was better that they thought her happily absorbed in scholarly pursuits . . . which she was, after a fashion.

As Mereth had cleverly foreseen, both the ostensible trade goal of my quest, and more especially the area I proposed to search actively discouraged any serious offers by the Dalesfolk to accompany me. One of Mereth's kinsmen, a whelp of her dam's Line, made a halfhearted suggestion that he could try to engage a guide for me, but I asserted that Mereth's personally-drawn maps were more than adequate to direct me to the vicinity where my master's special map could be consulted. I hinted that my master preferred my mission to be solitary, and in a flash of inspiration, I confided that because of my unfortunate circumstances of birth in Alizon, I thought it advisable to avoid populated areas as much as possible. Once he had heard my explanation, her kinsman, looking both abashed and relieved, pressed upon me two hampers filled with all manner of gear to equip me for every calamity likely to befall an isolated rider. He urged me to exchange my riding and pack horses for mountain ponies once I reached Paltendale, and gave me a letter to request assistance from a wool trader of his acquaintance there. I attempted to pay him with some of my unmarked silver bars, but he obstinately refused to accept them, saying that Mereth's letter clearly commanded what he called "family courtesy" to be extended to me. Since I was supposed to understand such Dales arrangements, I had to nod knowingly, but I expressed my gratitude for the consideration.

On the Twenty-sixth Day of the Moon of the Dire Wolf, I set out on the road leading from Vennesport to Trevamper. Mereth had drawn for me a Dales map I could show openly, marked with bold lines linking the populated areas, but she had written a private advisory commentary for me to commit to memory so that I could choose less-traveled paths as I forged steadily northwest-ward.

The Moon of the Dire Wolf fast gave way to the Moon of Chordosh as I toiled, often cursing the variable weather. A day might dawn cold and fair, but in the space of an hour, clouds could form and sweep down from the mountain ridges, pelting me with sleet, snow, or rain—sometimes it seemed that all three discomforts jostled for a turn at assailing the horses and me.

Past Trevamper, there was nothing that could be termed a road, and since I had to shun any trails that exhibited signs of frequent use, my progress at times was maddeningly slow. I rode south of Dorndale, then climbed into the hills to the west as I avoided Haverdale. I sought a northerly course away from the Haverdale area, and scaled the steep flanks of the peaks separating Ithordale to the west from Fyndale to the east.

By that time, I estimated that I must have ridden some sixty leagues at the least, and more than half the Moon of Chordosh had passed. To eke out my supplies, I supplemented my diminishing store of journeycakes by hunting for game. The snares I set before I made camp near nightfall yielded occasional rabbits. I supped several times on a clumsy, slow-flying bird that roosted carelessly within my knife's range.

When I reached Paltendale, I scouted carefully before I descended the winding track into the dale. The wool merchant recommended to me back in Vennesport proved to be another garrulous fellow who talked incessantly about sheep. He did accept a silver bar when I told him I did not know how long I might be searching near the borders of the Waste, and I preferred to purchase his mountain ponies outright. After replenishing my supplies, he insisted upon walking with me as far as the edge of Paltendale. He warned me to beware of late spring snow slides from the higher slopes, then turned back, still prating about the countless vicissitudes besetting the scattered local flocks whose wool he planned to buy.

I had never much cared for ponies in comparison with horses. I soon found that my new mount was a contrary beast which stubbornly pursued its own notions of the most desirable path. I almost regretted my lack of proper Alizonian spurs, and frequently did regret this pony's total lack of proper Alizonian training. As we penetrated farther into the remote northwesterly high country, however, with its nameless valleys squeezed amid sheer peaks, I discovered that both animals were utterly reliable in their footing, especially on the treacherously narrow ledges and steep inclines. Considering the terrain, they were nearly as able as our Torgians. I resigned myself to the willful nature of my riding pony, and allowed it to set a prudent pace along any track it chose that led in my desired direction.

Now that I drew nearer to the peaks and valleys that Mereth had described as adjoining Ferndale, I adopted a new nightly practice. Once I had settled the ponies and wrapped myself in my travel blanket and cloak, I would withdraw Elsenar's jewel and hold it in my hand. I had not taken it out at all during the sea voyage, nor previously during the many weary leagues of transit across the Dales. At Lormt, when I had taken the jewel from Mereth, I had wondered whether its odious magic would again oppress me as it had done from just my mere initial sighting of it in Alizon. To my private relief, I had not noticed any worrisome intrusions into my dreams, nor signs of bodily weakness such as I had also briefly experienced in Alizon. I was, however, constantly aware of the stone's physical presence. I could feel its hard shape through my tunic when I lay against it, but I had sensed no suspicious magical effects from it until I left Paltendale.

As I rode into the trackless wilderness, I found my hand kept straying unbidden to my chest. When I camped that first night after parting from the wool merchant, I surprised myself by extracting the pendant from my innermost pocket and slipping the silver chain over my head. The stone seemed unusually chill, perceptible even through my glove, but I told myself it was likely due to the abnormal frost in the air. I slid the jewel inside my tunic against my shirt, and soon fell asleep. I did not dream directly about the jewel, as I had before in Alizon, but I did preserve into my waking the next morning an almost tangible impulse of . . . direction, a faint pulling sensation, as if a barely appreciable breeze was steadily nudging me farther to the north and west.

After that night, I held the jewel each evening before sleeping. I realized with mingled dread and excitement that the tugging sensation was drawing me exactly in the direction indicated on Mereth's final map—the map supposedly locating the site to be searched for lamantine wood. For the last four or five leagues, I no longer bothered to consult Mereth's map to identify landmarks, for the jewel itself guided me straight to an eruption of gray, tumbled stones half buried by drifting snow. According to my tally of days, it was the Twenty-fourth Day of the Moon of Chordosh.

I warily examined the deserted area around the ruins. The snowy surface was trackless, undisturbed save by the wind. I fed and watered the ponies, then tethered them loosely to some nearby evergreen branches so that they could pull free if I did not return. Using a bough broken from the same tree, I swept away the drifted snow until I uncovered the first of a flight of broad stone steps leading underground.

The descending stairwell angled sharply to the left, widening out into a snow-choked landing, then plunging again down a more narrow passageway into darkness. I had brought several torches with me in my supply hamper, but as I turned back to fetch them, I suddenly hesitated. My hand reached to my chest, and before I consciously considered the motion, I found that I had lifted the chain off over my head, so that the jewel could swing freely from my fingers. It sparkled so brilliantly that I thought for an instant it was glowing with more than the natural light. When I advanced toward the shadowed stairway leading farther below, I could not deny the evidence of my eyes: the jewel *was* shedding a cold blue light of its own. I would require no ordinary torch to illumine my way.

The deeper I descended, the brighter the pendant glowed, until it cast eerie shadows along the ancient stone walls of a large, bare chamber that opened outward at the foot of the stairs. As I raised the jewel to survey the space, it began to wax more and more radiant until I had to shield my eyes with my other hand.

Abruptly, I *knew*, as clearly as if an icy blade had pierced my back, that I was no longer alone in the chamber. With a thrill of dread, I dropped my free hand to grasp my dagger hilt, but I was so stricken by the sight before me that I could not draw my weapon.

The eldritch glare from the jewel fell upon the figure of a tall, dark-haired man garbed in pale robes of a curiously antiquated style. Before I could properly focus on him, the jewel flared with such unbearable brightness that I almost dropped it. To my intense dismay, I felt the chain press against my flesh as the pendant slowly but firmly loosed itself from my grasp. I could not completely stifle a cry of disbelief as the blazing stone floated through the empty air toward the robed figure, which had raised a hand in obvious summons.

I was further appalled to realize that I could discern the far wall's masonry lines *through* the very substance of the figure. My opponent was horridly transparent, as if his lineaments were drawn upon a vertical sheet of river ice. As the jewel halted just beyond the figure's outstretched fingers, its painful radiance subsided to a level more acceptable to the eyes. Eyes . . . I was shaken when I gazed upon the figure's ghastly face and saw that his eyes lacked whites, but were solidly dark orbs whose regard held me as a serpent's stare overawes its prey.

All this while, our confrontation had been soundless, save for my rapid breathing. Suddenly, I thought I heard him speak to me in totally unintelligible words, although his tone was reassuring. I did cry not aloud when I realized that what I had mistaken for a normal voice was instead the result of some hideous magic causing sounds to form within my mind! My legs would no longer support me. I sank to my knees, fighting to avoid an unmanly swoon from stark fear.

The calm "voice" intruding in my mind was instantly intelligible. "Has it been so long that the very style of speech has altered?" it observed. Then, as I knelt, the tone sharpened. "No, no—do not kneel to me! I am but a scholar, not your lord demanding fealty. Arise, I say! You have restored to me my jewel; you are of my blood, yet your hair is stained as if in disguise. I would ask you to relate your tale, but as you see, I am not fully present in the body. Indeed, now that the presence of my jewel has broken the bonds that have enthralled me here, my

time is limited. Unless I act soon, I shall vanish irretrievably. If you will allow me, I will touch your mind and
learn from you without consuming the time required for
speech. You are alarmed—do not be. I am your kinsman,
Elsenar, Servant of the Light. We of the Light do not
harm or compel any creature against its will. May I enter
your mind?"

I could not trust myself to speak to this mighty mage,
the scourge of our land more than a thousand years past.
My flesh crawled at the thought of his touch . . . yet I
knew in my bones that I could not prevent him from
dealing with me as he would, no matter his fair words.
Still, I had come this far unscathed. If Elsenar was himself in danger of vanishing altogether, perhaps his Power
was greatly diminished. What damage could he wreak
against me, other than to kill me? I sternly suppressed
my recollection of rumors that Estcarp's Witches had
been known to transform men into animals. I had no
time to indulge such foolish fears. I took a step toward
Elsenar, and nodded my assent.

His strange, penetrating gaze swept over me. He
raised his hands, and his jewel drifted closer to me, puls-
ing a deeper, darker blue that expanded into a great sap-
phire pool of light that engulfed me in its azure depths.

CHAPTER 30

Elsenar—events at Narvok's abandoned
lair, recalled subsequently by Kasarian
due to their mental linkage
(24th—25th Day, Moon of Chordosh)

Time—an unbelievable span of time had elapsed since
my duel with Narvok. It seemed to me only moments
ago that my fateful struggle with the Dark Adept had
aroused the Force which had lain dormant in this place
since the Elder Days. Once it had lashed out, expelling
Narvok through his Gate and rending me in twain, it had
sunk back into unreachable somnolence, stranding this
wisp of me in a bodiless condition, unable to move or
speak. After an immeasurable interval, a woman had intruded into my place of confinement. By the Power of
my jewel, I attracted her attention, and obtained her permission to employ a spell to breed a Child of my Mind
capable of wielding my jewel to release me at some future time. When she, perforce, departed with the jewel, it
was impossible for my ensorcelled remnant to gauge
how long I hung suspended in the darkness.

It was not until my mind sensed the approach of my
jewel that I roused from my torpor. I was still totally im-

mured, but my awareness waxed as the stone drew ever
closer. By the surge of Power, I was alerted when the
jewel's bearer entered the chamber. I hailed my jewel
joyfully—as a vital part of my mind, it invigorated me
by its closeness, enabling me to assume at least partial
visibility. I could not, however, take physical possession
of the stone, for I had no substance, no means to touch
or be touched. Neither could I speak orally to the young
man whose blood called to my blood. But why was his
hair stained dark when he was obviously a son of Aliz
stock?

I summoned my jewel to leave his hand and approach
me. Its energy warmed my mental essence like life-giv-
ing rays of the sun. I drew upon its strength, and bespoke
the young man mentally, in the speech of the Alizon I
had known. At first, he seemed not to understand me,
then he gave a great cry, and fell to his knees.

I realized that he must be frightened by my mindspeech. Disturbed that he should fear me, I urged him to
rise, employing the intimate mindspeech that transcends
all spoken language. I explained to him that my apparent
revival was merely temporary; that I must take immediate action to reunite the shards of my magically cloven
self or else I would soon disperse into nothingness.

In order to achieve the swiftest transfer of information, I requested that he allow me to touch his mind directly, thus permitting me access to his memories. As in
my previous experience with the Lady Veronda of the
Dales, I could not and would not act without the willful
consent of my respondent.

The young man did not reply to me vocally—indeed,
his body trembled as he stepped forward toward me, but
he faced me despite his understandable trepidation, and
firmly nodded his assent.

By the Power of my jewel, I reached into his memories. To my initial surprise, I learned that this Kasarian of Alizon was not the Child of my Mind whom I had expected to rescue me; that child, borne by the Lady Veronda, had been a female named Mereth. Through Kasarian's eyes, I viewed her as he had last beheld her, abed, recovering from grave injuries she had suffered while risking her life to retrieve my jewel. Alarmed, I scanned Kasarian's store of background knowledge. Mereth had been born in the Dales nearly seventy-six years ago, but Kasarian recalled my activities in the land of Alizon as having occurred over a thousand years in the past!

I was deeply disheartened that my expulsion of the treacherous Shorrosh and my destruction of the Gate to the homeworld of the Aliz should still be regarded by Alizon's current inhabitants as a betrayal of such magnitude that they dated their very calendar from that event. Still, I had been aware of the cruel flaws in the nature of the very first transferees from Aliz. I could not be truly surprised—although I was filled with regret—that the descendants of the folk I had originally rescued should have preserved, and even apparently intensified the deplorable qualities that so marred the character of their foresires. On the other hand, I was distinctly gratified that I could detect no taint of the Dark in Kasarian. Indeed, ironically, because of their burning sense of betrayal by Shorrosh and me, the Alizonders had denounced and rejected magic with such single-minded ferocity that their culture ever since, for all its appalling faults, bore no trace of influence by the Dark . . . until . . . until now!

With increasing dismay, I concentrated upon the nascent threat posed by Baron Gurborian's schemes to seek alliance with surviving forces of the Dark yet active in Escore. I viewed the physical duel in which Gurborian had fittingly received his death wound from his own poisoned blade. I saw how Kasarian had recovered my jewel from Gurborian's body, and had then carried Mereth through my private postern to Lormt, where awaited a group of scholars, champions of the Light, anxious to thwart any attack by Escore upon the lands to the south of Alizon.

I surveyed Kasarian's knowledge and opinions of each of his companions at Lormt; theirs was an uneasy relationship forged by the necessity to defend against a common enemy. To my great sorrow, I learned of the war waged by Alizon against the Dales. Kasarian, while not of an age to have taken part in the failed invasion, still considered Alizon to be at enmity with both the Dalesfolk and the descendants of those devoted to the Light who had fled from Escore and now called themselves Estcarpians.

There can be no deception in direct mind touch. I was instantly aware of Kasarian's tumultuous feelings toward me—how he was both fearful of and repelled by my magical Power, yet at the same time, he cherished some hope that I might reward him for freeing me. He recoiled from the possibility that I might return to Alizon and seize total control there, but he also entertained the speculation that I might conceivably aid his Lormt faction in devising a plan to prevent any survivors adhering to Gurborian's faction from allying with Escore's Dark Adepts.

I ranged through the brief span of Kasarian's life experiences, tapping his memories of his father—murdered, I learned, by Gurborian. Kasarian's lineage extended back directly to Krevonel, the son I had never seen, borne by my beloved Kylaina so many centuries ago. Through all the intervening generations, echoes of her singular beauty had been preserved—I glimpsed her again in the color of Kasarian's eyes, and in the grace of his carriage.

I longed to stay in this new time, so far removed from the age I had known, and yet similarly menaced by the deadly blight of the Dark. Even as that desire swelled within me, I knew I dared delay no longer. From the core of my being surged a sense of overpowering necessity to hasten toward that unknown Gate beyond which the remaining fragment of me languished in aching incompleteness.

As Kasarian's mind had lain open before me, so would my thoughts during this linkage become accessible to him upon later reflection. There could be no secrets between us. I knew that I must work quickly, before my strength ebbed. Using my jewel's energy, I dissolved our linkage gently, so that Kasarian would suffer no lasting ill effects.

CHAPTER 31

Kasarian—events at Narvok's abandoned lair (25th Day, Moon of Chordosh) & subsequently at Lormt (1st Day, Moon of the Spotted Viper/2nd Day, Month of the Fringed Violet)

Never before had I experienced such complete mental submersion. The disorientation and sensory deprivation associated with travel through Elsenar's postern had been violently debilitating. When my consciousness was captivated by Elsenar's jewel, however, the impressions I received were curiously pleasant. What seemed to be my initial absorption into an all-enveloping blueness gradually altered as a shimmering cascade of colors rippled around me, mingled with echoing musical tones like none I had ever heard. I was also aware of fragrances sweeter than the scent of our bloodwine bushes in bloom, or even the stupefying perfume of the stranglevine's flower. Yet I knew that I was not seeing with my eyes, hearing with my ears, or smelling with my nose; I could not truly claim awareness of any physical body at all. This bodilessness would have been terrifying except that the serene beauty of that peculiar space totally dispelled all apprehensions. For a timeless interval, I was immersed in soothing warmth.

Quite suddenly, the sounds and scents ceased, and the warmth drained away, to be replaced by a bracing coolness amid an encompassing blueness, as if I had plunged into the deep waters of a mountain pool. My hands tingled from the chill . . . hands! I was abruptly aware of my normal bodily sensations. My vision returned, disclosing the bare stone chamber still illuminated by Elsenar's glowing jewel.

Elsenar's ghostly figure loomed almost within arm's reach. His face was drawn, and his transparent features rippled in and out of focus, like pebbles perceived beneath the surface of a rushing stream.

His voice resounded in my mind. "So many great events have occurred since I was stranded in this place. Once again, the menace of the Dark threatens to erupt from its fastnesses in Escore. If I could, I would hasten to aid the Forces of the Light—but unless I unite with the banished fragment of myself, I shall surely perish. You also are needed to assist in the struggle to preserve Lormt and Alizon. I adjure you to be wise in the use of my postern between Alizon City and Lormt; I have no time or energy to alter its stricture against any not of our blood. My other postern spell which I set so long ago between this place and Lormt can be activated for one final passage. I shall alert Jonja the Wise Woman of your impending arrival. Doubtless by now, the lodge where I conjured that spell has been reduced to dust, but she will know by her arts when and where you have emerged. I shall dispatch you first, and dissolve that postern behind you. I must then seek to restore my separated self. Even if I should succeed, it may not be possible for me to return to Lormt from that unknowably far place, so your companions must not expect my further aid. Now must I take my leave of you, Kasarian, blood of my blood. I see

through you the distant face of my beloved Kylaina.
May you and your companions triumph in your vital endeavor! Stand always with the Light!'

Elsenar's jewel, which had been floating motionless
between us, drifted toward him. He raised his insubstantial hands as if to clasp it. The jewel blazed brighter than
the sun, blinding me. I threw up my hands to shield my
eyes, but before I could complete the gesture, my entire
body was snatched into the howling chaos of postern
transit.

I was simultaneously dazzled and jostled by my emer-
gence, half-stunned, onto the dew-soaked grass of a
mountain meadow. I lay still for some time, slipping into
and out of consciousness. The sun was sinking behind
the tallest peaks when I heard horses approaching. I
managed to raise myself to a sitting position. Duratan
rode ahead, followed by the Wise Woman, who was
leading a riderless third horse. Upon sighting me, they
dismounted, hastening to my side.

The Wise Woman offered me a flask of spiced wine,
but after taking a mouthful, I had to refuse more. My
body was still deplorably weakened by the postern's dis-
ruption. I was not at all certain that I could remain upright in the saddle. Fortunately, Duratan recognized my
infirmity, and put me up in front of him on his horse
where he could steady me.

I did not later recall any of the return ride to Lormt.
When we clattered into the vast courtyard, I roused to
glimpse the face of Lormt's provisioner, still talking as if
he had not yet finished his last speech to me. As I slid
down from the saddle into his arms, darkness claimed
me.

I awoke, they told me, the following day, which the
Lormt folk termed the Second Day of the Month of the

Fringed Violet, the last Moon of their Spring Season. I was taken aback. Morfew assured me that it was indeed the First Day of the Moon of the Spotted Viper, the second of our three Moons of the Spring Season. I had been absent from Lormt for almost three Moons.

Before I could ask how the Lormt folk had fared, the Wise Woman entered my bedchamber, bearing a heavily laden tray. Morfew remarked that he had favorably influenced her choice of food for me. The Wise Woman grimaced at him, exhorted me to eat, and left us alone together. I welcomed the succulent slices of roast boar, which Morfew said that Duratan had provided. I complimented the fare, and inquired whether Duratan employed any local breed of hound in his hunting.

Morfew laughed outright. "Few of us here at Lormt are of an age or possess the agility to hunt," he explained. "We acquire most of our game and the food we cannot grow for ourselves by trading with nearby crofters. This particular beast intruded into one of our walled gardens, where he was dining upon our root crops when Duratan cornered him and ended his depredations with a spear thrust. Not so exciting as a horseback chase with our hounds, perhaps, but the reward is equally tasty."

I could now accept the spiced wine I had previously rejected. As I poured a second measure, I asked, "How fares the Lady Mereth?"

"I rejoice to tell you that her injuries seem to be mending," Morfew answered. "Master Wessell has contrived the most ingenious wheeled chair in which she can be pushed about, making it easier for her to assist us with the document reading. When you feel fully restored, Mereth awaits your report in my chambers, together with Ouen and the others. I must confess that our curiosity has been difficult to contain."

Shortly afterward, having eaten sufficiently, I was gratified to discover that my own clothing had been neatly folded atop the chest at the foot of my bed. As soon as I had dressed, I followed Morfew through Lormt's confusing passages to his study room.

It took me some time to relate my experiences. The Lormt folk were keenly disappointed that Elsenar—and his jewel—could not be relied upon to assist them in averting the threat from Escore.

I did not express my private relief at Elsenar's departure. His presence could not fail to be a critical danger to Alizon, no matter how well-intended his actions might be. The traditions and convictions of a thousand years could not be dismissed or swept away overnight. No Alizonder—most certainly no baron!—could view Elsenar's return with anything less than stark horror. Unless Elsenar bound us all in magical thralldom, Alizon would be convulsed with violent reaction. For the sake of Alizon's continued existence, it was necessary that Elsenar remain a frightful figure safely rooted in our distant past.

I was also personally relieved that Elsenar's awful jewel had departed along with him. No man should be capable of meddling in another's mind. And yet . . . I could almost hope that Elsenar had succeeded in locating and reuniting with his missing half-self, so long as he did *not* come back to trouble us in Alizon.

Ouen raised his hand to forestall the continued pointless discussion about Elsenar's utter withdrawal. "We must develop our own offensive and defensive plans without any reliance upon Elsenar's aid," he asserted. "I had hoped that he might greatly augment our resources, but we must accept Elsenar's warning that he is unlikely to return to Lormt."

"In that regard," said Morfew stoutly, "our situation is no worse than it was before we dispatched Kasarian to the Dales. During all this elapsed time, Jonja's and Duratan's foreseeings have not revealed any overt moves by the Dark mages. We have detected no further alarms from Alizon. Surely Gurborian's faction remains in disarray, attempting to recover from his unexplained disappearance."

"I must return to Krevonel Castle as soon as possible," I declared. "It is vital that I learn how matters stand in Alizon City. Gurborian and Gratch have been eliminated, but others in their faction may have assumed their places, and continued to pursue the fatal linkage with Escore. I may be able to rally the elder barons—beginning with the authentic Volorian—to oppose both the pro-Kolder remnant and whatever persists of the pro-Escorian faction."

Morfew peered at me. "I am concerned about your safety," he said. "Will it be prudent for you to go back now? Even though your prolonged absence has been justified by your supposed survey of your far estates, will not your enemies have remarked upon the violent events at Krevonel Castle preceding your departure?"

I could not suppress a smile. "What violent events at Krevonel Castle?" I inquired. "I assure you that no word will have been uttered by my staff regarding the affairs of that night. There were, you recall, no other surviving witnesses."

Duratan nodded grudgingly. "But won't Gurborian's faction still suspect that you were somehow involved in his and Gratch's disappearance?" he asked.

"To suspect is one thing," I countered. "To prove a

suspicion can be considerably more difficult. Unless Gratch uncharacteristically betrayed his master's confidence, none of Reptur's pack can know what befell Gurborian's missing party. Bodrik will inform me of any whispers that may have circulated. I readily confess my own unanswered question: what fortune have you experienced in your search for documents anent Escore while I have been away from Lormt?"

Duratan's mate waved at a table piled with scrolls, books, and loose scraps of parchment. "We have found many references to the great clashes in Escore before our ancestors fled into Estcarp," she replied, then shook her head in obvious frustration. "So much of it is fragmentary, and some is obscure and unreadable. There seems to be no end to the uncovering of new stores of material which we have yet to examine."

"I never thought to behold such insights into the far past," Morfew exclaimed, rubbing his hands together. "It would be more helpful," he conceded, "if the bits and pieces fitted together more coherently, but we press ahead slowly."

I saluted them. "The information you assemble may provide the key that enables us to triumph," I said. "I pray you to persist in your work, and to share with me any facts that may further my endeavors in Alizon."

"The only way we could communicate with you in Alizon is by postern transit," the Wise Woman objected. "Since the postern is restricted to only those of Elsenar's blood, our sole potential messenger is Mereth, and she will be in no condition to undertake such travel for some time to come." She waved one hand fretfully, and exclaimed, "If we could simply cast a message packet through the portal—but one of Elsenar's kin bearing your Krevonel key is required to make the passage!"

"Just as I am, in your terms, Volorian's nephew," I observed, "so do I also possess similar useful pups in my pack. They would be told merely that they were to deliver a message; a solid mask over the face would blind their eyes from seeing to whom the message roll was handed. Pack loyalty would keep their tongues still—that, and a prudent awareness of their personal vulnerability."

Morfew sighed. "It is a sorrowful practice to rule the young by force and fear," he said.

I could but stare at him in disbelief. "The Law of the Pack is best for all," I contended. "The strong become stronger, and the weak are removed before they can breed more weakness."

"So long as none is harmed by your arrangements," Ouen said firmly. "As you rightly say, it is imperative that we keep our location at Lormt a secret. You have been given sufficient reasons to trust us, Kasarian, but your fellow barons would not likely approve or embrace your alliance with us, their perceived mortal enemies."

"It has ever been the Alizonian way to seek advantage wherever it is to be found," I replied, "and to break agreements when better opportunities arise. Still, I have learned that your ways also have unexpected value. You rely upon an oath without fear of subsequent betrayal. That is a different way from ours, but it seems to have afforded you a certain . . . stability that we lack in Alizon. Considering the degree of danger that presses upon us from the east, I believe it may be necessary for each of us to alter some of our ways if we are to survive."

I was interrupted by a loud thump from Mereth's staff. She had been writing busily during our discussion, and now she held out a sheet of parchment to be read aloud by Duratan's mate.

CHAPTER 32

Mereth—events at Lormt
(2nd Day, Month of the Fringed Violet/
1st Day, Moon of the Spotted Viper)

After Kasarian departed from Lormt, I worried every day. Even though Nolar's dye had wrought a startling effect, transforming Kasarian's silver-white hair to the dark brown of shredbark nut hulls, I could not totally convince myself that he would be accepted by Dalesfolk old enough to remember the horrors of the war. When he came to bid me farewell and claim Elsenar's jewel, I surveyed him with apprehension. His newly darkened hair emphasized the Alizonian pallor of his skin, making his blue-green eyes all the more brilliant by contrast. I thought to myself that the only way to disguise Kasarian successfully would be to hide him out of sight in a large hamper. The garments that Mistress Bethalie had provided for him were entirely suitable for a trader's apprentice. If only Kasarian did not have to move about! He could not mask his swordsman's balance or his uncanny hearing. I had to hope that the combination of my letters to the tradesfolk and our tale of his mixed parentage would plausibly excuse Kasarian's otherwise inexplicable attributes.

When I handed him Elsenar's jewel, he did not clasp its chain around his neck, but instead tucked the pendant within an inner pocket of his tunic. I knew that for a magic-averse Alizonder, the jewel had to be an awful object, whose very touch must be loathsome . . . yet Kasarian was willing to risk his life to carry it across the sea and through the Dales. On an impulse, I wrote for him a travel blessing I had learned during my childhood years of residence with the Dames of Rishdale Abbey.

After Farris returned to Lormt we received only one other report concerning Kasarian's progress. Nearly nine weeks later, early in the Month of the Crooknecked Fern, a scholar from Karsten arrived, bearing a message for me which he had been given in Es City when it became known that he was traveling to Lormt. The Es City merchant desired me to inform "Kasyar's" master that his apprentice had reached Etsport on the Seventeenth Day of the Month of the Snow Bird, and had sailed for the Dales two days later on the *Storm Seeker*. I recalled that during my own voyage, Captain Halbec had mentioned that ship to me. He considered the *Storm Seeker*'s Captain Brannun to be one of his few fellow Sulcars whose ship and crew could safely dare the winter seas.

After that heartening word, silence prevailed for many anxious days. We pursued our search of Lormt's documents from first light until dark, and past dark with the aid of lamps and candles. We discovered fragmentary confirmations for Elsenar's journal accounts, and some evidence to support Kasarian's version of Alizon's early history; but we did not find any clear details or specific strategies that we might use against the Dark Forces from Escore now threatening both Alizon and Estcarp.

At least once a week, we gathered in Morfew's study to observe Jonja and Duratan as they consulted their foretelling devices. Jonja explained to me that her rune-board could indicate, in a general sense, how Kasarian was faring. When she concentrated on Kasarian while touching her rune-board, should her moving fingers be halted upon a gold rune, then we might be assured that he was well; a red rune would disclose the presence of some limited peril; while a black rune would indicate mortal danger or death. Duratan said that his crystals could also display signs of external impediments or positive aids. All of us felt relieved when the first few rune-board readings and crystal castings seemed to show that Kasarian was proceeding without adverse interventions. Our concern intensified several times, however, when Jonja's fingers stopped upon red runes, and Duratan's crystals confirmed the existence of danger. Ouen reminded us that we had to expect Kasarian's ship would encounter storms during any winter voyage to the Dales. Morfew suggested that the *Storm Seeker* would likely require four to six weeks for its passage, depending upon the winds and the number and severity of the storms. We therefore calculated that Kasarian should have arrived at Vennesport late in the Month of the Hawk, or possibly early in the Month of the Crooknecked Fern.

As those intervening weeks crept by, we were lulled by the repeated appearance of gold runes and positive crystal readings. Then suddenly, on the last day of the Month of the Crooknecked Fern, when Jonja ran her fingers across her rune-board, they halted on a black rune. Duratan, grim-faced, cast his crystals, and exclaimed with evident frustration, "Kasarian is in danger—but from what? I see two sources of Power confronting him, but both are of the Light. . . ."

"Elsenar!" Nolar's voice shook with excitement. "Kasarian must have located the ruins, and by means of Elsenar's jewel, the mage has been revived. Would not both mage and jewel show as Forces of the Light?"

Jonja's expression remained bleak. "Until the dominance of the black rune loses its hold," she declared, "I shall stay here with my board."

To our puzzlement, neither indicator changed that night, or the next day, despite repeated consultations, but in the late afternoon of the Second Day of the Month of the Fringed Violet, Jonja gave a strangled cry, and slumped forward in her chair. Alarmed, Nolar took her hand, but after only a few moments, Jonja shuddered and opened her eyes.

"I have received a Sending from Elsenar," Jonja announced. She pressed a hand to her forehead, as if still dazed. "Compared to this, the Witches' Sendings were a mere whisper in my mind; Elsenar's Sending bears the force of a shout! I shall have to brew a remedy for this resulting ache . . . but I have no time for such. We must ready a horse—no, two horses."

Nolar gently pressed a cup of barley water into Jonja's hand. "Refresh yourself first," she suggested, but the Wise Woman spurned the drink, setting it to one side.

"We must make haste!" Jonja urged. "Elsenar intends to return Kasarian to Lormt through the same postern by which he traveled a thousand years ago."

Morfew absentmindedly drank the barley water, then remarked, "But all we know about the site of the forester's lodge where Elsenar worked his postern spell is that it was within a day's ride of Lormt."

"Elsenar assured me that I could determine the place," Jonja replied. "He knew about my talents from Kasarian. I sensed the mage's intention to take immediate action. It may well be that Kasarian has already accomplished the transit. Judging by the speed of the displacement from Alizon City to Lormt, we must assume that this far longer distance would still be bridged magically with great brevity."

Duratan swept his crystals back into his hand and tossed them again onto the table. As they scattered, the shining blue stones crisply outlined a wedge pointing to the southeast. Scooping up the crystals, Duratan rose to his feet. "I shall see to the horses," he said. "Our initial direction is clear."

Also standing, Jonja clutched her rune-board. "I will ride with you," she asserted. "We must hurry. Kasarian may be stunned by his transit. What if he emerges impaired and stumbles into a ravine?"

Preceding her toward the door, Duratan said, "We shall discover his condition only when we find him."

The late Spring twilight was fading when they brought Kasarian back to Lormt. I watched from a doorway opening onto the great courtyard as Duratan's horse approached, bearing a double burden. Duratan was mounted on the loin behind the saddle, his arms extended to support the senseless Alizonder. Master Wessell hurried past me to help carry Kasarian inside. Although the injuries to my legs had healed, I still had some difficulty in walking, and was obliged to rely upon the clever wheeled chair that Master Wessell had constructed for me. I could thus be fairly easily pushed about on the ground floor, but I required someone to lift me bodily up and down stairs. It was for that reason that we had changed our meeting place to Morfew's study from Ouen's upstairs quarters.

Jonja did not allow us to confer with Kasarian until

the next day, providing him time to recover his strength. With barely contained impatience, we gathered in Morfew's study. When the old scholar escorted Kasarian between the towering stacks of scrolls and documents, I thought Kasarian appeared even more gaunt than when he had left Lormt, but he moved with the same singular grace. Taking his seat at Morfew's worktable, Kasarian related to us the details of his astonishing journey.

After our spirited reaction and discussion of what responses we should make, Kasarian surprised me by openly recognizing actual positive advantages in our traditions of oath-keeping and mutual trust. He conceded that in view of the Escorian threat to us all, each of us— Estcarpian, Alizonian, or Dalesman—might be forced to change our traditional thinking.

At that point, I thumped my staff on the floor to attract the company's attention. Nolar read aloud my urgent query: "Can we be certain that we are aware of all of the posterns bespelled in ancient times? We know of only two posterns set by Elsenar—the one from Narvok's lair to Lormt, which has been destroyed, and the one from Lormt to Krevonel Castle, which is restricted to those of Elsenar's blood—but might not he and perhaps other mages from Escore, of the Dark as well as of the Light, have set similar postern spells in the past?"

Morfew frowned. "Pray also do not forget the Gates," he admonished. "The Gate through which our Foresires came to found Alizon was sealed by Elsenar, and the Master Gate which was attempted here at Lormt was abolished, but there have been other Gates. I understand that Simon Tregarth himself came to Estcarp through a Gate that opened near the border with Alizon. The Kolder came through yet another Gate that was blessedly shut behind them, but Kasarian has told us that the remnant Kolder in Alizon desired to conjure a new Gate in order to replenish their numbers. We must consider the likelihood of the hidden presence of Gates as well as posterns."

Kasarian's face had blanched. During Nolar's reading and Morfew's alarming remarks, Kasarian had been sitting motionless, not even twisting his restored signet ring. "While Elsenar meddled in my mind," he said in a bitter tone, "I also became aware of some of his thoughts. At first, I did not recall the details of that . . . unnatural experience, but now that you discuss the matter of Gates and posterns, I remember certain of Elsenar's thoughts concerning such things." He gripped the edge of the table, his eyes flashing with anger. "There *were* other postern spells—but it is like hearing echoes in a cave! I cannot fully grasp his thoughts, but I *know* that Elsenar possessed knowledge of other posterns and possibly other Gates." Kasarian paused, then added slowly, "If other accursed magical openings exist into Alizon from Escore, then the danger is even worse than we earlier imagined. I beg you to seek any word in Lormt's archives that could tell us how such horrors might be detected and sealed off!"

"The danger you rightly perceive," Duratan said grimly, "is not limited to Alizon alone. Consider, my friends, what might befall Estcarp should the present-day Dark mages become aware of any former passageways bespelled in ancient times between Escore and Estcarp? Or, for that matter, if they determine to conjure such a postern now for the purposes of invasion?"

I handed Nolar another written query. She read aloud for me, "Should we not send an immediate warning to the Council of Witches in Es City? Surely this new realization of an added dimension to the threat from Escore must be conveyed to them."

"I fear," Ouen said, his voice sharp with regret, "that any warning from Lormt would be doubly discredited by the Witches. They have ever scorned us for our maleness, and they would be all the more offended, if not outraged, that the original source of our warning is an Alizonder baron."

"We must also remember the Witches' painfully diminished strength," Nolar observed sorrowfully. "Even should they pay heed to us, I fear they could not mount any significant countermeasures. Despite frantic efforts to train new Witches, the Council has not yet restored the awful losses they incurred during the Turning."

Grasping for the slightest of encouragements, Morfew ventured, "Perhaps Estcarp's existing spell-watch along the border with Alizon could be strengthened to some degree."

Jonja's face, too, had paled. "I could attempt to establish a Sending to Es City," she offered. "Just before the Turning, the Council of Witches warned us here at Lormt so that we might take some advance precautions. I received their Sending. They maintain a constant mental watch at Es Castle; I might be able to reach that Watch Witch. I must tell you frankly, however, that I doubt a call from Lormt would be accepted."

"We could send a written message," Nolar began, but Duratan interrupted her. "During the prolonged clashes with Karsten," he said, "I served with the Witches as a Borderer. I believe that I could present our case to better effect if I rode to Es City and faced the Council."

"I shall accompany you," Jonja declared. "In the Witches' sight, I may be considered less than those who devote themselves exclusively to mastering the uses of

Power. Although my talents are limited to treating the ills of the body and spirit, as an undefiled female, I may stand before the Council without apology. When Estcarp's very life is vulnerable to so grave a threat, the Council cannot refuse to listen to us."

Kasarian smiled ruefully. "I would request to ride with you," he said, "but I perceive I would be no more welcome at Es Castle than would be a Witch who craved audience before our Lord Baron. It occurs to me that my original warning might impress the Witches more favorably were it not obtained voluntarily. Pray inform the Council of Witches that I betrayed my tale to you unwittingly while your captive and ill with fever."

Nolar shook her head. "A wise person takes care to speak the truth to Witches," she advised. "They can discern any efforts to deceive them."

I handed her another sheet of parchment so that she might read my plea. "Those of us who remain at Lormt must begin without delay to seek any other scraps of writing that may have been left here by Elsenar. Earlier, we found part of his journal. Surely additional documents of his may yet be discovered—perhaps some which identify the sites of other posterns or Gates."

Ouen pushed back his chair. "Morfew and I will compose a corroborative letter," he said decisively. "Since this day is already far advanced, Duratan and Jonja will desire to depart for Es Castle early on the morrow. Meanwhile, we must indeed act upon Mereth's apt injunction. I shall ask all able scholars to join in our search. Any documents bearing Elsenar's unreadable hand will be fetched at once to Mereth for her transcription. May we be guided by the Light in these vital tasks!"

CHAPTER 33

Kasarian—events at Lormt
(2nd Day, Moon of the Spotted Viper/
3rd Day, Month of the Fringed Violet)

Mereth raised a devastating question: might there be other sorcerous posterns existing from ancient times? Morfew compounded the horror by reminding us of those far more substantial magical openings, the Gates, which led to and from strange, unthinkably distant sites such as the place whence Simon Tregarth sprang, or the hideous home nest of the Kolder. I exhorted the Lormt folk to plunder their archives for any word that might instruct us how to locate and seal such frightful breaches.

As I listened to their subsequent discussion on how to warn Estcarp's Witches, my feelings were violently at odds. The very notion of meeting with those redoubtable crones made my skin crawl . . . yet I had to acknowledge the perverse sense of Gurborian's own argument which I had overheard in Alizon Castle. When detestable magical forces were arrayed against you, was it not far better to have similarly empowered forces acting in your defense? Gurborian had schemed to pit Escore's Dark mages against Estcarp's Witches; surely I must admit the advantages of the reverse case. If Estcarp's Witches could be marshaled—however weakened they might be—to respond on our behalf in countering the Escorian threat, then our faction would at least possess some magical Power to turn aside the horrid assaults we must expect to endure. I was privately much relieved that the Lormt folk renounced my participation in the mission to warn Estcarp's Council of Witches.

As the Lormt folk arose to address their individual tasks, I accosted Duratan's mate. Before I could return to Alizon, I had to make a vital request. "If you would assist me, Lady," I said, "I should be grateful. I cannot appear at Krevonel Castle with my hair in this garish state."

Somewhat to my surprise, Duratan's mate smiled. "It seems almost a pity to bleach it," she remarked. "You make a distinguished appearance with dark hair. . . ." Before I could protest, she hastily added, "I shall ask Master Pruett whether the silver nettle preparation we used to lighten Mereth's hair can reverse the effects wrought by my shred-bark dye. Come along with me and we shall attempt to recover your proper baronial guise."

Several times during the acrid herbal drenching that followed, I half-suspected I might drown. To my considerable relief, however, once I wiped the last of the rinsing water from my eyes, I saw from my reflection in the silver tray that my hair had been restored to its natural Alizonian hue.

After I had dried myself to a presentable state, I hurried back to Morfew's chambers, where I found Mereth and Morfew diligently sorting through heaps of documents.

Morfew glanced up at me when I entered, and nodded in approval. "I must say," he observed, "I prefer your authentic aspect. If you are determined to go back to Krevonel without being attacked on sight, you certainly could not bear that remarkable coloration suited to a Dalesman."

"It is imperative that I return to Alizon," I asserted. "I must strive to counter at their source those forces which seek to destroy our land. Just as your work lies here among Lormt's archives, so mine awaits me at Krevonel." I hesitated, reluctant to raise the subject. "I regret that in my unnatural passage through Elsenar's postern from the Dales, I have lost my trader's wallet containing the silver bars given me by Lord Ouen."

Morfew chuckled. "You need not trouble yourself on that account," he chuckled. "Lormt's stores of silver are more than adequate for our rare disbursements. I expect Master Ouen to insist that you take your own Alizonian gold back with you—no, no, do not object. Your activities in Alizon will demand copious bribes, and we truly have no use for Alizonian gold here at Lormt."

Mereth rapped with her staff. Morfew took her slate and read, "When you dispatch your nephews to bring us messages through the postern from Krevonel Castle, how will you explain to them the sensations they will experience during the transit? Will they not be unduly frightened?"

"That is a matter I have carefully considered," I replied. "Fortunately, I know of a reliable posset which will render the pups so drowsy that they will not notice the eerie effects of their passage. I shall tell them they must traverse a way so secret that blindfolding and complete silence are obligatory. There will be no difficulty, and no harm to the pups."

Morfew gathered up an armful of scrolls. "Master Ouen will be gratified to hear of your intentions in that regard," he declared. "I must carry these documents to him, and observe his progress with the final version of the letter to be sent to the Council of Witches. Should I not see you again before your own departure, Kasarian, I wish you abundant hunting and the best of hounds for your pack."

It was pleasing to hear the familiar Alizonian farewell. "Whatever you pursue, may your blade strike true," I responded, touching my Line badge.

When we were left alone together, I gazed at Mereth. I would never have believed that I could feel such justified respect for an elderly female bred in the Dales . . . yet her very sire was Elsenar, my own distant Foresire. It was therefore understandable—although completely contrary to Alizonian tradition—that her wit and fighting prowess should be so remarkable.

I loosed the buckle of my belt and slipped off one of my sheathed daggers, which I presented to Mereth. "Lady," I said, "your actions at Krevonel likely saved my life, thus by our ways obligating me to a blood debt—but by the peculiar interference of Elsenar's magic, we both spring from his Line. We are like littermates far separated in time, and among such, no blood debts may be incurred. I therefore beg you to accept this parting gift as a token of my profound regard."

Mereth at first appeared surprised, then a faint smile twitched the corners of her mouth. She took the dagger somewhat gingerly, and wrote on her slate, "I never expected to receive a kin gift from an Alizonder. Must I beware of its poisoned blade?"

"This was a favorite throwing knife of my eldest littermate," I explained. "Its blade is clean."

She wiped her slate, wrote again, and proffered it to me. "I thank you doubly, Kinsman, for the value blade and for your personal actions on my behalf. Had you not ably defended me, I should have been cruelly burned, if not stabbed and poisoned. I believe that both of us have been given ample reasons to modify our initial views of one another. By surviving severe danger together, we have learned to cooperate. Now an even greater challenge lies before us. As you embark upon your efforts, take with you this silver ring crafted in the Dales. Its design is simple, and should not attract unwelcome attention if you choose to wear it in Alizon."

I bowed to her, and fitted the ring on my right hand's least finger. "The decoration is handsome, Lady," I said, "like the pattern of ribs on a bloodwine leaf. I shall wear it proudly."

Mereth extended her slate to me for the last time. "As Morfew noted, we may not see one another again. You go forth into your perilous land, while I must bide at Lormt awaiting whatever befalls us here. Take with you therefore also my Farewell Blessing: To the day of your journey, a good dawn and sunset; to the endeavor, good fortune without a break. May the Light strengthen our resolve, and ward us against the Dark."

I touched her ring-gift to my Line badge, and bowed. "I thank you for your Blessing, Lady," I affirmed. "It is for me a second gift, for I have received none such before. I shall send you word of my progress with Volorian and the elder barons. It would likely be wise for you and Morfew to address any return messages to me in Alizonian, should the script chance to be seen by prying eyes."

Mereth nodded her agreement. With a final bow, I took my leave of her. The elder's key was ready to hand in my tunic pocket. I made my way directly to Lormt's cellar.

CHAPTER 34 _____

Mereth—events at Lormt
(3rd & 4th Days,
Month of the Fringed Violet)

No sooner than Morfew had left the two of us alone, to my intense surprise, Kasarian unclasped his belt and presented me with one of his many daggers. He made a gracious speech, acknowledging that I had probably saved his life during the combat with Gurborian and Gratch. By Alizonian custom, he would therefore have owed me what he termed a blood debt, but because both of us bore Elsenar's blood, such an obligation could not be imposed. Instead, he intended the dagger to serve as a token of his regard.

I accepted the sheathed weapon with some considerable bemusement. I had to view it as a kin gift . . . from a most extraordinary source. I inquired on my slate if the blade were poisoned, also after the Alizonian custom. Kasarian assured me the dagger was clean; it had belonged to his eldest brother, who had used it as his favorite throwing knife. I tried not to envision at what or whom it may have been thrown.

It seemed evident to me that Kasarian's gesture was motivated by both courtesy and genuine gratitude. Despite the cruel nature of his Alizonian upbringing, Kasarian appeared to possess—at least to some degree—a sense of honor that any Dalesman could respect. From my own experience, I certainly could not fault his courage and daring.

I knew that we might well never again meet. Kasarian was about to plunge into the hazardous currents that swirled constantly around his scheming fellow barons. From my perspective, at any time, Lormt itself might be assailed by Escore's aroused Dark mages. When Kasarian had earlier left Lormt to carry Elsenar's jewel to the Dales, I had impulsively written for him a travel blessing. I now surveyed Kasarian for what could be the last time I should ever behold him, and without any reservations, wrote for him the solemn Farewell Blessing of the Dales. I appended to it my fervent prayer that we might be strengthened by the Light in our resolve, and safely warded against the Forces of the Dark.

Kasarian raised my personal parting gift, the silver Dales ring, to touch his House badge, then with a final graceful bow, he left me.

I recommenced my reading and sorting of documents until Nolar brought the evening meal. After sharing it, we worked on together for some hours. Gradually, my eyes grew weary, and the candlelight dimmed as I drifted into a light sleep.

I awoke quite abruptly when Duratan and Morfew burst into the room. Both of them were as excited as Dales lads opening gifts on their name-day.

"It is only one page," Morfew exclaimed, waving an age-darkened leaf of parchment, "but it is definitely written in Elsenar's hand. The moment I saw it, I set the others to emptying out the entire chest wherein it was found . . . but I said to Duratan that we must bring this to you immediately!"

Nolar urged Morfew to sit down, and handed him a cup of barley water, which he welcomed.

"Thank you, child," Morfew said, subsiding breathlessly into a chair. "I have not hastened this rapidly," he gasped, "since the time of the Turning when I abandoned my exposed position in the courtyard just before the long wall fell."

I reached for a second candle holder to cast more light on the faded ink marks. Although I could not read the writing, being able to see it helped focus my mind upon the message it conveyed. Elsenar had composed it during that time just after the horrendous collapse of the Master Gate. I wrote for Nolar to read aloud, "Before Elsenar launched his second attempt to conjure a postern to Arvon, he wrote this letter to the surviving Mages of the Light remaining at Lormt. He feared that other Gates might be similarly opened by the Dark mages, and pleaded for a concerted effort to frame a spell . . . I find this difficult to grasp, but Elsenar seems to have thought that some . . . device sustained by a spell could detect the presence of threatening Gates, or possibly guard against their opening at a given spot. His letter is incomplete. Were there no other related pages found near this one?"

Duratan shook his head, dislodging a shower of fine, soot-like particles from his hooded jerkin. "As you see, we have been burrowing. Only two days ago, a scholar chanced to notice a crack in the wall of one of the storage bins in our root cellar. Once we shifted the roots, and broke through the back wall, we gained entrance to a small chamber choked with ancient boxes and chests." He sneezed. "And dust," he added. "Ouen is there now, guiding the removal of each container. Many of the wooden boxes have been weakened by age or ruptured during the Turning."

Morfew rubbed his hands together. "Documents are scattered about in glorious profusion," he reported. "This leaf of Elsenar's was atop one small stack, but the pages beneath it belonged to other collections. If any additional fragments by Elsenar were stored in that chamber, I am certain that Ouen will locate them."

Duratan stood up. "I must return to assist him," he said. "Our presentation to the Council of Witches would be immensely strengthened if we could alert them to the magical strategy that Elsenar conceived for discerning the sites of rogue Gates and posterns."

Morfew yawned. "My bones remind me that I should be searching for my bed," he observed. "On the morrow, Ouen will surely amend our letter to include this vital news. You and Jonja must delay your departure until we have examined every scrap of writing hidden in that root cellar."

"I am certain," Nolar said firmly, "that were Jonja here, she would advise Mereth to rest now, so that she will be able to transcribe any further messages by Elsenar." Exhibiting a briskness reminiscent of Mistress Bethalie, Nolar resolutely expelled Duratan and Morfew from the room, then helped me settle for the night in a nearby quiet cubicle which we had converted into a bedchamber for my use. As she turned toward the door with her candle in hand, Nolar paused. "I shall go brew some cordials to sustain the searchers," she remarked with a smile. "Should they find any more of Elsenar's writings tonight, they may hasten back here to implore your interpretation, so you had best sleep while you can."

Once Nolar had closed the door, I lay against the pillows, layers of warming quilts drawn up to my chin. My thoughts were too active to allow me to sleep.

I was concerned about Kasarian's reception in Alizon. Even if he successfully explained his absence, he must henceforth contend with endangerment from all sides. The Lord Baron would be constantly—and justifiably— suspicious of plots against him; the equally vengeful Reptur forces would be pressing to impute responsibility for Gurborian's disappearance; and all the other surviving members of Gurborian's faction would still likely be dedicated to forging an alliance of convenience with Escore's Dark mages. Even if Kasarian contrived to rally Volorian and some of the elder barons to his side, his position would remain extremely precarious . . . yet I had seen how competent Kasarian was, how quickly he acted and reacted. If anyone could thread his way through the deadly maze of Alizon's incessant struggle for power, it should be Kasarian.

I also could not dismiss from my mind the uncertainties besetting us here at Lormt. We *had* to persuade the Council of Witches to take heed of our warning—but would they grant audience to Duratan and Jonja, and if they allowed Lormt's case to be presented, would they agree to act decisively on our behalf? So much depended upon what further evidence we could provide concerning Elsenar's plans to detect and, we had to hope, also seal or render harmless any Gates or posterns through which the Dark Forces of Escore might attack Estcarp. I had to wonder whether even clear instructions by an ancient mage could be successfully implemented by the Witches. Would their collective Power be sufficient to activate his spells? Would Elsenar have written down instructions for setting such spells? There seemed to be no end to the questions buzzing in my mind like a swarm of ill-tempered bees.

I could almost hear what Doubt would have said in his deep, earnest voice. "When you have more questions than you have answers, and when most of the questions demand time to be resolved, there is no use in wasting energy by fretting. Apply your strength to some task that can be accomplished, and let time furnish the facts you require to deal with the excess questions."

My precious Doubt . . . I had dreamed about him only the previous night, recalling an incident that I had not thought about for years. The two of us had been examining the bolts of cloth stacked in one of our warehouses at Ulmsport. Other traders and messengers kept darting in and out, interrupting our tallying, until Doubt was festooned with three loops of cloth drawn out from separate bolts. After the final intrusion, Doubt spun around in frustration, and a great swirl of cloth unrolled from his shoulder down to the floor.

I could not, of course, laugh aloud, but I was quivering with amusement. He stared at me, affronted. "And what, may I ask," he snapped, "is so uproarious?"

In a scrawl woefully mirth-shaken, I wrote on my slate, "You look like a piece of Elderdale twist-bread!"

Doubt glanced down at his unintended entanglement, and voiced a hearty laugh for both of us. "I had best extract myself then," he exclaimed, "before I complete the knotting process. Although," he added in cloth-muffled tones, "I've always heard that a properly knotted twist is a certain charm to ward off ill fortune."

That dream had bridged the years as if no time had passed, but when I awoke, only the warmth of the memory lingered in my mind. I knew that I could never again feel the touch of Doubt's hand on mine, except in memory, just as I could never again hold my betrothal jewel, the Magestone of Elsenar, gone with him to some magical place far beyond our understanding.

I realized how very much I wished that I had been able to present the Magestone to Doubt as the betrothal gift intended by my mother . . . yet I now clearly recognized that such a jewel of Power was not meant to adorn a mere bride. It was bound up in the very life of the mage who had activated and wielded it. By its awesome Power, it enabled Elsenar to travel vast distances and accomplish great works. Somehow, I felt in my heart that the Magestone had conveyed Elsenar to the place he had to go to be restored to wholeness. I could not say how I knew, but I *knew*. Now both Elsenar and his Magestone were irretrievably isolated from us. For centuries, they had been lapped aside, like two floating leaves diverted out of the stream of time into separate backwaters. Elsenar had been magically frozen in Narvok's lair, as if sealed beneath a sheet of winter ice, while his exquisite jewel had passed from hand to hand, unrecognized for what it truly was until, by our efforts, it had been returned to its master. After that restoration, the pair of them had re-entered time's on-flowing stream, now swept away from us to fulfill their magical destiny.

Doubt, too, had been swept away from me, just as inaccessibly. Amid the gushing flow of events, I was now companioned by the Lormtfolk, who had accepted me as their friend and fellow striver. In a most unbelievable fashion, I even had to admit that I had come to consider Kasarian of Alizon as one of my new companions. That he was my kinsman, I could not deny. He had shown me unfailing courtesy and unexpected gentleness. By all that I had known in my life before I came to Lormt, I would have scorned and feared him as my enemy . . . but because of what we had endured together, I began to think that I might possibly, perhaps, someday if we lived to meet again . . . call him friend.

In these twilight years of my life, I had traveled farther than I had ever expected, and seen sights beyond my most fevered imagining. A sense of belonging seeped into my awareness, easing my weary body. At last, I had found my rightful place. Lormt was the refuge I had sought without realizing that I could not fully belong in the Dales. The prospect before me was daunting; we might at any time be driven to fight for our lives, but I had survived such challenges before. Not only could I draw upon my memories for strength and sustenance, but I could rely upon my steadfast friends to pursue the struggle to preserve all that we held dear.

Just before I fell asleep, I glimpsed in my mind a scene that could never be, yet was somehow achieved in the realm of my fancy: Doubt was standing in a shaft of sunlight, holding out his hand to me. Suspended upon its silver chain around his neck flamed the blue glory of a jewel shaped like the Magestone, but freed from the unbearable burden of its intrinsic Power. I sensed that this was indeed the betrothal gift I would have bestowed upon my dear lord had we been allowed to wed.

Doubt's voice seemed to whisper, "For a time yet, you must apply all your skills to defend Lormt . . . but I shall always wait for you, my beloved."

In this golden dream, I smiled, and reached for my quill and a clean sheet of parchment. There remained much yet for me to write.

AFTERWARD

Mereth—events at Lormt
(5th Day, Month of the Willow Carp/
4th Day, Moon of the Fever Leaf)

Kasarian had gone through Lormt's cellar postern back to Alizon on the Third Day of the Month of the Fringed Violet. Because of the discovery of the ancient, incomplete letter written by Elsenar, Duratan and Jonja delayed their departure for Es City for three more days, leaving on the Eighth Day. Our exhaustive search had disclosed two more tantalizing fragments in Elsenar's hand, but neither contained the details we craved concerning how to detect or block posterns and Gates.

During the subsequent days, we waited anxiously at Lormt for word from either Es City or Kasarian. Nolar moved her pallet to Lormt's cellar to watch in case Kasarian sent his nephew through the postern. Because we could not know when such a transit might occur, Ouen and Morfew asked a group of the less elderly (and more reliably alert) scholars to share the watch duty. Morfew carefully taught all of the watchers a set speech in Alizonian. He would have stayed on the site himself had the chill not so pained his bones.

I was gradually recovering my mobility as the weeks passed, and shared some of the later watches as the Spring gave way toward Summer. Morfew had warned Nolar not to speak to the Alizonder lad when he appeared; it was necessary that he should hear only male voices speaking Alizonian, so that he would not suspect he had left Alizon.

Late on the Second Day of the Month of the Willow Carp, Duratan and Jonja splashed through Lormt's gate during the first Summer rain. They were weary and disheartened. Duratan would have made his report at once, but Jonja demanded that both of them change into dry clothing.

When we gathered in Morfew's study, Duratan could not sit still. He paced back and forth, his frustration plain in every bitter word. He and Jonja had been allowed to address the remaining members of the Council of Witches at Es Castle several times over the five-day period of their stay . . . but to no avail. Duratan was convinced that if Koris had been there, he would have listened to and joined in Lormt's plea for action—but Estcarp's Seneschal was absent from Es City, traveling through the countryside to assess the progress of recovery from the Turning. Jonja reluctantly agreed that we should not depend upon any aid from the Witches. Almost all of the prominent Witches had been killed or injured during the Turning, and those who now attempted to rule Estcarp were racked by division. One faction argued for a cloistered withdrawal from all worldly affairs to bastions such as their Place of Wisdom, where over time, the Sisterhood could be replenished. Even those Witches who desired to continue ruling from Es Castle as before were unwilling to make any commitments for concerted action, especially when the request for assistance came from Lormt, and stemmed originally from a hated Alizonder. Duratan told us sourly that the only useful fruit from the trip was his chance hearing that Simon Tregarth was back in Escore. Simon's two sons, Kyllan and Kemoc, were also presumed to be in Escore at present, but the Witches had no good opinion of them, still keenly resenting their rescue three years ago of their sister Kaththea from the isolated Place of Wisdom, where Estcarp's girls gifted with Power were trained to become Witches.

Duratan abruptly stopped pacing, and exclaimed that we *must* alert Simon Tregarth to the threat posed by Escore's resurgent Dark mages, who might employ magical means to erupt at any time into Estcarp or Alizon. Jonja offered—after a night's rest—to attempt a Sending to the Valley of the Green Silences, Escore's stronghold of forces devoted to the Light. Not being a fully empowered Witch, Jonja could not convey our entire, complex warning, but she believed she could express our urgent need to reach Simon Tregarth. Early the next day, Jonja concentrated upon our desire that the Lady of the Valley would dispatch to us one of her blue-green message-carrying birds to fetch our written forewarning.

Jonja had scarcely completed her effort when, to our surprise, Duratan suddenly cried out, not in pain or fear, but with fierce joy. He sat rapt for a few moments, then shook himself as if rousing from sleep. He explained to us that Kemoc, his former shield comrade, had become aware of Jonja's Sending. On a previous occasion, Kemoc had appeared to Duratan in a dream, but this time, Kemoc achieved a waking linkage with Duratan's mind. He now informed Duratan that Simon was

presently scouting the northwesterly border area between Escore and Alizon in response to troubling rumors
that evil was stirring in that quarter. Alarmed by our distress call from Lormt, Kemoc pledged to leave the Valley of the Green Silences immediately and ride to confer
with us. His journey across the intervening mountains
would likely require five days, but once at Lormt,
Kemoc could establish a mind-link with his elder brother
Kyllan back in the Valley, thus eliminating the delays
and hazards of trying to communicate by bird-borne
messages.

While we waited for Kemoc to arrive, a further significant interruption occurred only two days later, during
the evening of the Fifth Day of the Month of the Willow
Carp. Ouen was most fortunately serving on watch in
Lormt's cellar when the postern from Krevonel Castle
abruptly flared into activity, delivering among us a
groggy, docile Alizonder lad who was clutching Elsenar's key in one hand and a tightly-wrapped message
roll in the other.

At once, Ouen guided the lad to a bench and intoned
Morfew's admonition in Alizonian: "Wait here in silence. This message may require an instant reply."

Leaving the lad under the wary observation of a fellow scholar, Ouen hurried to confer with us in a distant
corner of the cellar. Kasarian identified his messenger as
Deverian, a pup of his eldest littermate's Line. His message was brief, but deeply disturbing. Upon his return to
Krevonel Castle, Kasarian had launched discreet inquiries that had just recently confirmed his worst fears.
The leadership of Gurborian's faction had been seized
by two barons, Balaran from Gurborian's own Line
Sired by Reptur, and Ruchard of the Line Sired by Gohdar. They feigned complete cooperation and agreement

with one another, but each was secretly vying to be the sole leader of the faction. Kasarian had taken advantage of their concealed rivalry by bribing underlings in each camp in the name of the opposing side, so that his own interest would remain unsuspected. He had learned that very soon a meeting was to be held just across the border in Escore with a Dark mage known to the barons as Skurlok. Kasarian was apprehensive that neither baron could successfully confront a Dark mage—that without the positive advantage afforded by Gratch's cunning, Alizon's interests would likely be betrayed. Kasarian promised to obtain more details, but meanwhile urgently desired word from us concerning our "southerly venture," as he delicately termed Lormt's plea for aid from Estcarp's Witches.

Morfew quickly composed a reply, using purposefully obscure language of his own in the event our message might be seen by enemies in Alizon. "I regret," he read aloud to us, "that our southerly venture appears to have come to naught. The parties we appealed to are unwilling to commit themselves on our behalf. Within a few days, however, our agent has arranged for a meeting here with his former shield comrade, the second puissant pup of that formidable sire we mentioned to you earlier. You will rejoice to hear that very sire is even now investigating rumors concerning the activity you have reported; he is tracking the matter from the far side of the border. In view of our impending receipt of important further information from the second pup, pray therefore dispatch your messenger to us again in four days' time so that we can share the news with you. We shall expect him at that time, but will also keep watch should you need to send a message before then."

We hastened back to the postern site, where Morfew

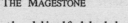

sternly addressed the blindfolded lad garbed in Krevonel's dark blue livery. "Hear me, Deverian of the Line Sired by Krevonel. Bear this message to your Master as carefully as you bore his to us. On your feet, now . . . I shall guide you to the opening of the passageway. Do *not* drop the key!"

Putting a hand on each shoulder, Morfew firmly aligned the lad with the marked paving slab, and gave him a gentle push as the familiar but still eerie postern oval formed soundlessly in mid-air.

When Deverian had disappeared, Ouen remarked, "If the fine weather holds, Kemoc should arrive at Lormt in three more days. We shall assemble all of our documents for his examination."

Duratan was grimly gratified that Simon Tregarth was already aware of a suspicious disturbance near Escore's border with Alizon. There was no question in Duratan's mind that Simon Tregarth and Kemoc would believe our warnings and would take prompt action to counter the threat.

I thumped my staff on the paving and wrote for Nolar to read aloud, "With the aid of this fine new staff that Master Wessell has shaped for me to replace the one I had to leave at Krevonel Castle, I am now well able to move about once again. Should it be necessary for us to send a sudden message to Kasarian, I believe that I can travel through the postern. It would not be prudent, however, for me to wander about in Krevonel Castle by myself. I shall take with me a well-stocked scrip and a pallet so that my period of waiting for Kasarian in the postern chamber may be moderately comfortable. It would be useful to know whether we of Elsenar's blood can activate the postern spell without the presence of Elsenar's key to the chamber in Krevonel Castle."

Duratan smiled. "Lady," he said, "Simon Tregarth himself could not ask for a more spirited ally than you have proved to be. Although our situation is grave, with you and the sons of Tregarth on our side, I begin to see grounds for hope."

"May we remove this discussion to a warmer location?" Morfew asked in a plaintive voice. "Mereth's bones may have mended, but mine are growing stiffer each hour I spend in this cellar. Besides," he added, as we began our long upward progress, "I distinctly heard Master Wessell say something about a cask of well-aged wine he found recently amid all the upheaval. The least we can do is taste a sample to see if it is suitable to serve to young Kemoc when he arrives."

As I followed behind the others, I looked forward to the wine, the fellowship, and the challenge that lay before us. The Dark mage Skurlok would find himself confronted by the iron-hard, unified resolve of forces from Lormt and Escore . . . and even from Alizon. We would be prepared to defend our lands.